P9-BYZ-902

Unwelcome Visitors

The ringing of the phone startled everyone. Laura hurried over to grab the phone.

"The Beauty Box," she said, a bit breathless.

No response came from the other end of the line.

"Hello?" Still no response.

Someone knocked loudly on the front door of the salon. Laura covered the mouthpiece and called, "It's open."

More knocking on the front door harder much louder.

Still not getting an answer, Laura hung up the phone and hurried over to the door.

No one was there. She opened the storm door and checked the porch. Nothing.

Just as she closed the door behind her, the sound of clamoring, hurrying footsteps swelled from the back of the salon.

The phone rang again, but this time it jangled, a high-pitched, irritating sound like that of an old-fashioned dial phone. Laura headed for it again.

Another knock sounded on the door.

Laura picked up the phone, but it only rang louder—louder still, jangling, jangling until she wanted to rip the phone cord from the wall. She dropped the receiver.

More knocking—pounding.

The jangling, clamoring, pounding abruptly stopped, and Matt came stumbling out of the kitchenette.

"We gotta go! They're here!"

Other *Leisure* books by Deborah LeBlanc:

GRAVE INTENT
FAMILY INHERITANCE

A HOUSE DIVIDED

DEBORAH LEBLANC

LEISURE BOOKS NEW YORK CITY

To Dad,
my life mentor and friend.

A LEISURE BOOK®

June 2006

Published by

Dorchester Publishing Co., Inc.
200 Madison Avenue
New York, NY 10016

If you purchased this book without a cover you should be aware that this book is stolen property. It was reported as "unsold and destroyed" to the publisher and neither the author nor the publisher has received any payment for this "stripped book."

Copyright © 2006 by Deborah LeBlanc

All rights reserved. No part of this book may be reproduced or transmitted in any form or by any electronic or mechanical means, including photocopying, recording or by any information storage and retrieval system, without the written permission of the publisher, except where permitted by law.

ISBN 0-8439-5730-1

The name "Leisure Books" and the stylized "L" with design are trademarks of Dorchester Publishing Co., Inc.

Printed in the United States of America.

Visit us on the web at www.dorchesterpub.com.

ACKNOWLEDGMENTS

With heartfelt appreciation and thanks to my editor, Don D'Auria, a quiet, respected giant in a business fraught with clamor; to Brooke Borneman and Tim DeYoung for all their hard work and who make the seemingly impossible happen; to Adolph, who worked miracles at an ice cream shop in Alabama; to my agent and friend, Lynn Seligman, who manages my triple-A personality with such calm and patience; to Kathryn Magendie, author extraordinaire and sister-wolf, who stuck with me 'til the end. (Couldn't have done it without you, Kat!) And last but never least, *"Bien merci, bon Dieu, pour donner moi un autre chance."*

Two halves won't make a whole
If the whole
Is a hole
In a person's heart.

—The Book of Deliberations

PROLOGUE

For two straight days, Morgan Devillier roamed the halls of her two-story home, clutching a bloodstained towel. The blood belonged to her baby. The towel to Crowley General, where they'd scraped the child from her womb. "A miscarriage," the doctor had said, and for a while, Morgan believed him. She suspected shock could do that to a person. Keep their mind locked in space, unable to think.

The whole time she'd rested in that hospital bed, the only thing she focused on was the month and year stenciled in black letters on the calendar that hung near the foot of her bed. One of the nurses had flipped over the page not long after settling her in, all the while jabbering about it being the first of the month. The picture showcased at the top of the calendar didn't capture Morgan's attention. She didn't care about snow-covered mountains. But the month and year, she'd never forget.

February 1968.

Wasn't that supposed to be the month of Valentines and candy? Of love and romance? Not now. Not here. Not for her.

Too many questions came and went without answers for Morgan; the two most important being: *Why her? Why this child?*

It wasn't until two days ago, while waiting for her discharge papers, that God shed some light on her confusion. He'd brought the answer by way of a preacher, who'd stopped by to wish the patients in Ward Sixteen a speedy recover and to say a healing prayer or two. Morgan didn't even remember the man's name, but she kept the small Bible he had offered her.

She didn't open the book until he left the room, and the revelations that soon came to her felt like cool springwater to a woman dying of thirst. She wept with understanding as she read scripture after scripture, feeling the very hand of God soothe her ruptured heart.

The hardest truth to swallow was one Morgan should have suspected for some time—Joseph, her husband, bore the responsibility for the loss of their baby. He was an adulterous drunk, a bigot, a liar, and a blatant hypocrite, who genuflected before the main alter in St. Anthony's Catholic Church every Sunday. A virtual house divided against itself, Joseph was destined to fall. The first brick had already tumbled away, as evidenced by Morgan's empty womb. She should have known, should have suspected adversity of this magnitude would occur, for a person can only spit in God's face so many times before He spits back.

Morgan carried that knowledge home; that and the sense that she too bore some responsibility for this staggering ill fortune. Had she been a more attentive wife, a stronger prayer warrior, Joseph might not have strayed, and God might have shown them mercy. But she hadn't been attentive or prayerful. Instead, she'd whined and complained, screamed and threatened, always trying to get Joseph to notice her, even if only in a negative light.

It was too late for prayer now. God's wrath lay upon them, and Morgan remained convinced that the loss of her child only signaled the beginning. There would be no hope for her four remaining children, for Joseph's sins would follow them forever. The Bible passage she'd been repeating to herself over the last forty-eight hours attested to that fact.

"The iniquity of the fathers would visit their children unto the third and fourth generation."

Morgan refused to let that happen. No longer would she be slothful. She'd already lost one child, she wasn't about to lose the other four to damnation.

Confident now that divine guidance cleared her path, Morgan wanted to rest, even if only for an hour or so. In truth, there wasn't much more she could do until Joseph returned home.

The wide, oak plank floors creaked underfoot as she trudged to a rocker near one of the living room windows. Morgan sat, folded the towel and placed it in her lap, then turned toward the window. Night's heavy veil refused to let her see outside. Instead, it cast back images from within. The bridge lamp behind her with its bell-shaped shade. The console television across the room. A dozen or so tiny flames, dancing in the gas wall heater to her left. Her own face, haggard and drawn. And the image of her seven-year-old son, Clyde, standing beside her.

"Mama?"

Morgan stared at her son's reflection and tipped the chair into motion. She noticed how thin he looked in his blue plaid pajamas . . .

"Mama, did you eat?" Clyde asked quietly. "You want me to get you something?"

. . . How his cowlick fanned out like a small rooster's tail near the back of his head . . .

"I could make you a sandwich if you want."

. . . How his eyes appeared sunken, the dark circles beneath them deep . . .

"You want something to drink? Some KoolAid?"

. . . How his fingers fidgeted with one another . . .

"I put the boys to bed just like always, Mama. I made 'em take baths and everything."

. . . How his left cheek shimmered when the light from the bridge lamp caught the track of his tears . . .

Morgan felt empty, so hollow when her young son leaned over, kissed her cheek, and said good night. She didn't deserve his love, not after failing him so miserably. She'd failed all her sons. They deserved so much better, and she would make certain they got it. At least that thought gave her peace.

Time disappeared while Morgan waited, and memories took its place. She'd been happy once, starry-eyed with hopes and dreams of becoming more than

4

a rice farmer's daughter. At twenty-two, when she met Joseph, she thought she'd found the star gate to her fantasies. They became inseparable almost immediately, and each touch, each kiss lent lightning to the storm of their passion. In a matter of months, that storm cut a tornadic path to a small wedding chapel, where Morgan found herself veiled in white, two months pregnant, and promising to love until death.

Joseph, always the exceptional businessman, viewed that first pregnancy as a challenge and set his sights on building the perfect family. He'd pampered her unabashedly during their first year of marriage, building a huge house, hiring a gardener, buying new cars, jewelry. They were the first family in town to own a color television. But something happened not long after the birth of their first child. Neither of them had truly been prepared for the responsibilities and restrictions that came with raising a baby. That sweet, pink, squirming bundle soon became an eight-pound wedge between them, and with the birth of each subsequent son, that wedge between husband and wife grew to become an unfathomable gulf.

The rattle of the front doorknob startled Morgan, and she steadied a foot against the floor to halt the rocker.

The front door creaked open and she heard Joseph stumble across the threshold, mumbling under his breath. Moments later, he appeared at the end of the foyer and she watched him hunt for a jacket pocket that didn't exist. A circle of keys fell from his hand to the floor, and Joseph leaned over, looking at them as though he'd happened upon an alien insect. When he reached out to grab the keys, the simple motion sent him careening into a half-moon table. Only then did he appear to notice her.

With a grunt, Joseph righted himself and headed her way. Morgan held her breath, unsure of the expression on her husband's face. Contempt? Anger? Pity? Either way, drunk didn't look pretty on a six foot four body.

"'S-matter wiff you?" Joseph asked. Inches away now, he held onto the back of the rocker for support. His clothes smelled of whiskey, cheap perfume, and a brisk-winded night. Spittle ran down the center of his cleft chin. "Ya sick?"

Morgan ignored him and faced the window. Although her eyes burned from lack of sleep, there was no confusing the expression she now saw in Joseph's reflection. Disgust.

He snorted out a laugh. "'Course yer sick. All the goddamn time yer sick." He batted the air with a wind-chapped hand, then turned away and headed for the stairs.

Morgan listened, counting each stomp as Joseph climbed higher. She knew his routine all too well. In a few minutes, he'd be out cold. If his luck held out, he'd make it to their bed this time instead of the bathroom floor.

It didn't take long for the house to grow quiet, and Morgan settled back in the rocker and closed her eyes to the silence. Joseph was home. She had no more thinking to do. Everything sat in God's hands now. He would give her strength to rally through this night triumphant; Morgan was sure of it. She only had to be patient a little longer.

She heard the soft *tick, tick, tick* from the Tambour clock that sat on an end table near the couch—an occasional gust of wind whistling against the window pane—a creak of wood from the chair that held her—and the deepening of her breath as her head slowly bobbed forward.

No sleep!

Morgan's eyes flew open, and she held a hand to her chest to make certain the racing heart behind it didn't escape. Tears stung her eyes. She'd nearly dozed off. How could she? Falling asleep while God waited for you to carry out a plan of salvation had to be the most grievous sin of all. She got to her feet, knowing she had to act now before the temptation to sleep snared her again.

With quiet determination, Morgan clutched the bloodstained towel to her breast and made her way to the wall heater. She turned the control knob to the Off position, then counted five seconds before twisting the valve back on. Without a pilot light or match to bring it into submission, gas hissed freely through the decorative ceramic grill. Morgan drew in a deep breath and moved on to the adjacent room, then the next, and the next.

She made her final stop in the kitchen, where she double-checked to make sure each pilot light on the gas range had been extinguished.

The swelling sibilance followed her up the staircase to the second floor.

Even in stocking feet, Morgan feared the soft patter of her footsteps or the occasional groan of wood in the hallway might wake one of her sons. She crept on tiptoe into the first bedroom on the left.

The firelight from the room's wall heater threw finger-length shadows over little Clyde, who lay sleeping on his stomach as usual, one foot sticking out from under his Hot Wheels comforter. Beside him, in an identical twin bed save for the side railings, lay her youngest son, eighteen-month-old Joseph, Jr. He slept on his back, snuggled in red flannel, footed pajamas. Morgan allowed herself an extra moment to soak in the sight of his tiny pink mouth, which was parted ever so slightly; his perfect button nose; his fingers, curled softly into his palms.

Feeling her resolve ready to dissolve into tears, Morgan lifted her chin and silently mouthed the anthem to her mission. "The iniquity will visit the children unto the third and fourth generation." With that, she went to the heater and completed her task.

In the next room slept five-year-old Peter, with his shock of red hair poking out from the sheet that nearly covered his whole head. Curled up next to him was three-year-old Richard. His right thumb, wrinkled from constant sucking, lay over his bottom lip. After blowing each boy a quiet kiss, Morgan pressed on.

She went through the adjacent rooms quickly—the empty bedroom decorated with Mother Goose wallpaper that had been meant for her newborn, the bathroom across the hall, then the master bedroom, where Joseph snored, sprawled across their bed, fully clothed. Morgan whispered a prayer that God might have mercy on his soul, then she silenced the final heater.

When the last flame flickered to its death and the hiss of gas replaced it, Morgan went into the hall and stretched out on the floor between her sons' bedrooms. After placing the towel she'd been carrying beneath her head, she stared at the ceiling. From the glow of a nearby night-light, she caught sight of a long-legged spider scuttling its way under a strip of crown molding. She wondered if the insect was heading home, to a web, a place whole and complete, mated by threads of purpose. One very different from her own.

After watching the spider a moment longer, Morgan closed her eyes and sighed deeply, knowing she'd earned sleep.

One long, deep breath . . .

One lasting, peaceful thought . . .

Victory, now wafting over her face, never smelled so sweet.

CHAPTER ONE

The blood didn't bother him.

The screaming did. That shrill, mortified cry, almost human in nature, pained him like sugar melting into a rotted tooth.

Grimacing, Keith Lafleur scraped the sole of his right work boot against the lip of the porch, and what remained of the field mouse plopped to the ground. He hadn't meant to kill it, but the damn rodent had startled him by darting out from under one of the hay bales stacked on the porch.

After toeing loose straw over the small fan of blood and mouse innards, Keith checked his watch, then leaned against one of the six columns that supported the roof. Overall, the outside of the house was in better shape than he had expected. It was just ugly as hell. The paint coating the two stories of cypress siding was severely chipped and had faded to a pale pink. One small dormer sat in the center of a fifty-five foot, gabled roof. It looked like a misplaced doghouse. Throw in the twisted wrought iron railings that fronted the upstairs balcony and you had the architectural malaise of New Orleans French Quarter meets Rural Plantation meets Conventional Nightmare.

Keith let out an impatient sigh and watched the hefty flow of traffic moving along the two-lane highway in front of the house. Across the highway sat a neighborhood, its houses an eclectic mix of clapboards and bricks, old and new, so typical of a growing southern Louisiana farm town. In the yard directly ahead, an elderly woman with wispy white hair and a large, prominently hooked nose worked a small garden. Every few seconds, Keith saw her throw a glance his way. He was considering flipping the old broad the finger so she'd take her curiosity elsewhere when a car pulled into the gravel driveway and parked behind his pickup.

"About damn time," Keith muttered, and stepped off the porch.

A woman got out of the car and hurried over to Keith with one hand extended. "Mr. Lafleur?"

Keith nodded, suddenly too smitten to speak. He'd been expecting Ed Bailey, the short, balding acquisitions manager for Costless Drugs, and here he was staring into the eyes of a goddess instead. The woman couldn't have been older than thirty, with short, tousled blond hair and eyes the color of toasted wheat. A taupe suit hugged the curves of her slender body perfectly.

"I'm Patricia Egan, Mr. Bailey's assistant," she said, her words ensconced in a sweet Mississippi drawl.

11

"Unfortunately, something came up at the home office in Jackson, and Mr. Bailey wasn't able to get away. He sent me here with the paperwork instead. I hope you don't mind."

Mind? Hell, if anything Keith figured he should send the man a bottle of Scotch in appreciation. "Not at all," he said, and reluctantly let go of her hand.

"And I do apologize for being late," Patricia said. "My flight got into Lafayette on schedule, but I had one heck of a time finding Crowley, especially this address." A blush painted her cheeks. "I'm afraid I've always been a bit directionally challenged."

Keith didn't know if the helpless Southern belle tone in her voice was an act or the real deal. Either way, it was working its charm all the way down to his groin.

"If you'd like, when we're done here, I can lead you back to the airport." He nodded toward his pickup. "All you'd have to do is follow that truck."

Patricia flashed him a smile, and her eyes took on a mischievous sparkle. "Thank you, but I'm afraid I don't fly out until early tomorrow morning. I'm staying in Lafayette tonight—a hotel right next to the airport."

Keith held back a groan. Could it get more perfect? "Then I'll lead you back to the hotel."

She tilted her head as though sizing him up, the smile never leaving her face. "I'd appreciate that."

Keith barely heard her. His attention had locked on her full, coral-shaded lips. He wondered what they would feel like pressed against his, what they would look like moaning his name. His imagination was about to carry her lips below his belt when another vehicle pulled onto the property. A white pickup truck with LAFLEUR CONSTRUCTION, INC. signs on the doors.

"Shit," Keith muttered under his breath. Of all the rotten timing.

"One of your men?" Patricia asked.

"My lead foreman, Jeff Mabry," Keith said as he watched the man's long-legged stride quickly close the distance between his truck and the goddess.

"Sorry I'm late," Jeff said when he reached them. He held out a hand to Patricia. "Ma'am."

Keith gave a quick round of introductions, then suggested they examine the inside of the house before they lost any more sunlight. Being it was three on an October afternoon, he hadn't actually lied. Dusk normally fell around five. But the truth really didn't have anything to do with lost sunlight. Keith didn't want Jeff touching Patricia, not even in a handshake. She was his prize, his newly found goddess, and he wanted to keep it that way—at least through tonight, anyway.

Agreeing that they should get to the inspection, Patricia pulled a key out of her skirt pocket and led the way to the house.

"Now, Mr. Lafleur, Mr. Bailey did tell you that Costless is on a tight construction schedule and will need the house moved by the end of next week, right?"

"Yes, he did," Keith said, moving past Jeff so he could walk beside her. A breeze carried her scent toward him and he inhaled deeply. She smelled like a magnolia tree in full bloom.

Jeff climbed onto the porch. "Only one week to move this thing? No way that's gonna happen. This house has gotta be what—forty-three, forty-four hundred square feet under roof? It's going to take us a week just to get the permits."

Keith threw him a scowl. "I've already taken care of the permits."

Jeff frowned and looked like he was about to say something else, then thought better of it.

"Here we go," Patricia said, as she stuck the key into the lock. She turned it right, then left, then right again. "I wonder if the lock's rusted."

Keith moved closer, placing a hand over hers. The touch of her skin sent an electrical shock through his body. It took a second or two for words to form in his brain. "Let me try. The door looks like it's off center."

Patricia's cheeks turned the color of overripe peaches, and she slowly moved her hand out from under his.

Hoping his erection wasn't too noticeable, at least to Jeff, Keith grabbed the doorknob, pulled up hard, then turned the key in the lock. It opened on the first try. He pushed the door open and stepped inside.

"Whew," Patricia said, fanning a hand in front of her face. "Mr. Bailey warned me the house was in bad shape, but I didn't expect it to be this bad."

Keith walked past the foyer. Hay was stacked three bales high in the living room and dining room, and he spotted a pile of dried cow dung near an archway. The oak plank floors had more scratches than an abused roller rink, and it was littered with chicken droppings. Most of the wallpaper had been stripped from the walls, and what little remained had faded so badly, Keith couldn't make out the original color. "Looks like someone's been using it for a barn."

"My word!" Patricia cupped a hand over her nose and mouth. "If you don't mind, Mr. Lafleur, I'll wait for you outside. The smell in here is a bit much for me."

"No problem," Keith said, hating to see her leave his side. "We shouldn't be long."

Patricia waved a hand over her head as she made a quick exit. "Take your time."

No sooner had she made it down the steps than Jeff pointed a finger at Keith. "You wanna tell me what's going on here?"

"What the hell are you talking about?" Keith said. "And get your goddamn finger out of my face."

"I saw you all up in that woman's space."

"Yeah, so?"

Jeff's eyes narrowed. "What about Barbara? Remember her? Your wife—my sister?"

"Hey, it's not like I was banging the woman or anything."

"No, but you want to. Don't think I didn't notice that little touchy feely game you were playing with her by the door. I swear, man, if you hurt my sister again—"

"Back off." Keith pushed past him. "I was only looking, and I'm not hurting any-goddamn-body by looking."

Keith stormed off toward what he assumed would be the kitchen, then came to an abrupt halt just inside the entrance. "Whoa!"

Jeff appeared beside him. "What?"

"Gas, man, can't you smell it?"

Jeff gave a tentative sniff. "I don't smell anything."

Keith coughed, his lungs beginning to burn as they filled with fumes. He held a hand over his nose and mouth. "Your sinuses have got to be packed with shit if you can't smell it. We've got to get out of here, out to the truck, call utilities."

Jeff shot him a perplexed look, then went into the kitchen and circled the worn checkerboard tiled floor. "Man, they don't even have a stove in here, and the gas lines are capped with like two inches of dust on them." He pointed to a four foot nook cut out of the counter space near the front of the room. "Check it out for yourself."

Feeling light-headed and a bit nauseous, Keith went over to the nook and examined the gas lines. They were capped, just as Jeff said. Scanning the room for another possible leak source, Keith spotted a wall heater near the walk-in pantry, one identical to the heaters he'd seen in the other rooms. He walked over to it, ran a finger through the layer of dust coating the grill, then leaned in and sniffed. No gas. Keith frowned and sniffed again. Not only was there no gas leaking from the heater, he no longer smelled gas, period.

"Well?" Jeff asked.

"Nothing. It's gone now."

Jeff let out a harrumph that clearly said, "I told you so."

"Shut the hell up," Keith said, irritated and still feeling nauseous.

"I didn't say anything."

"Then get that shit-eating grin off your face." Keith

headed out of the room. "And get your thumb out of your ass and help me check upstairs."

"Why are you bothering with this dump anyway?" Jeff asked, trailing behind him.

" 'Cause it's free, that's why."

"Nothing's ever free. It's gonna cost you a ton just to move this monster from Crowley to Windham. That's forty damn miles. You're talking police escorts, runners, utility crews to manage power and telephone lines, and that's not even touching what it'll cost you to renovate the place. Besides, where are you going to put it?"

"First Street." Keith squinted against a headache forming between his eyes. The clomping of their boots on the hardwood floors sent a hollow echo throughout the house that pained his ears. He felt pressure building behind his eardrums as if he were gaining altitude.

"Where on First?" Jeff asked, coming to a stop at the stairway. "All you've got are two, one hundred foot lots, and they're not even next to each other. This house won't fit on one lot."

"It'll fit if I cut the house in half." Keith signaled for Jeff to keep moving.

"But you'll cut into the load bearing walls if you do that," Jeff said. "It'll collapse."

"Not if we put temporary stud walls up to replace them. Will you just get the hell upstairs already?"

Jeff glanced up the flight of narrow stairs. "Man, look at the friggin' spider webs up there."

Keith peered around him. Silvery threads ran in thick, circular crisscrossing swatches from the middle of the stairway all the way up to the darkened landing. "So? Just knock them down on your way up."

"*You* knock them down on the way up," Jeff said, stepping back.

"Quit being a pussy."

"Hey, there could be brown recluses hiding up there. One bite from those bad boys and you wind up with some flesh-eating disease. No thanks. You can call me a pussy, but you can't call me stupid."

"Aw, just get the hell outta the way," Keith said, and headed up the stairs. When he hit the second step, the pressure in his ears intensified. He gritted his teeth, grabbed the banister for balance, and forced himself forward.

Swatting cobwebs out of the way, Keith kept one eye peeled for creepy crawlers and the other on his footing. Halfway up the staircase, the pain in his ears became so severe he thought he might vomit at any moment. He glanced over his shoulder and saw Jeff on his heels. Judging from his wide-eyed expression, the only thing bothering the guy was his fear of spiders.

When Keith finally reached the landing, he was drenched in sweat. He motioned to Jeff with a shaky hand. "Go check out the rooms down that end of the hall. I'll get the ones back here."

"What am I looking for?"

"Offsets, stuff like that. Anything we might have to sure up for the move."

"Yeah, all right, but let's make this quick," Jeff said, heading off at a brisk pace. "I can barely see up here it's so dark."

When Jeff took a left into one of the bedrooms,

Keith leaned against a wall to catch his breath. He thought about Patricia Egan waiting for him outside and tried to will himself into feeling better. No way did he want to miss out on that golden-haired opportunity. But even imagining Patricia's slender legs wrapped around his waist didn't take his mind off the pain. If anything, it made it worse.

With a groan, Keith pushed away from the wall and trudged down the south end of the hall. Jeff had been right. It was darker up here. A heavier dark, like a thunderhead had parked itself right over the house. He did a quick survey of the bathroom and two bedrooms, noting the gray soot that coated most of windows and walls. The soot appeared thicker in the last room, which was trimmed in Mother Goose wallpaper. He ran a finger along the doorjamb of a closet, and it came away black.

As he studied the soot, rubbing it between thumb and finger, Keith felt a whisper of movement across the back of his neck. Jeff's rant about brown recluse spiders flashed in his mind, and Keith slapped a hand over the spot, imagining the worst. When he checked his hand for blood, all he saw was more soot. Much more than had been on his thumb only a moment ago.

Keith backed out of the room, wiping his hand across the seat of his Dockers. Before he made it into the hallway, a tickling sensation ran across his left cheek. He frantically brushed at it, fully expecting to see a fat arachnid flung to the floor.

Nothing fell from his cheek.

Nearly panting now, Keith stumbled out of the room, the pain in his ears unbearable. He saw Jeff walking toward him from the other end of the hall. His mouth was moving, his hands animated, but all Keith heard was a muffled sound, like so many words spoken underwater. He raised his hands to cup them over his ears, hoping it would relieve some of the pressure, and noticed that soot covered both his palms.

Jeff's gestures grew frantic, his muffled words now one continuous hum. He jabbed an insistent finger in the air, pointing at something overhead.

"What?" Keith called, then cried out when the sound of his own voice seemed to split his eardrums.

More pointing, pointing, stabbing at something overhead—above him, above his head.

Ignoring the soot and pressing his palms to his ears, Keith looked up toward the shadowed ceiling, where Jeff indicated. In the same moment his eye caught movement, Keith felt something fat and solid drop onto his forehead.

The sting came so hot and fast it rendered him immobile. The pain in his ears vanished. In fact, Keith felt nothing at all—save for the wire-thin legs that fluttered against his right eye.

CHAPTER TWO

Laura Toups walked out of the beauty salon, paying little mind to the chill clinging to the February twilight. She hugged the rectangular sign she carried pressed to her chest, and her smile broadened. Although they'd already been open a week and had a decent flow of business, the piece of wood seemed to make everything more real. It was an attestation that dreams really did come true. She wondered what her father would have to say about the shop if he were alive. *Still not good enough, Dad?*

"Don't you be puttin' that thing up without me!" a shout rang out from inside the shop. Within seconds, Tawana Batiste bounded onto the porch, holding a flashlight in one hand and a bottle of Asti Spumante in the other. A small camera swung from a strap looped over her right shoulder. "You didn't put it up yet, right?"

"Of course not," Laura said with a laugh. She felt

giddy, like a schoolgirl about to try on her first prom dress, and judging from Tawana's wide grin and huge bright eyes, she felt the same.

"Good." Tawana turned on the flashlight and aimed it at Laura's face. "You got the hammer? What about a nail? You got a nail?"

"Stop with the light." Laura squinted against the beam. "I took care of the—"

"Hold up then, I'll go get a hammer," Tawana said, already turning away. "We gonna need one nail or two? Two. I'll get two just in case. Two'll make it stronger, you know what I'm sayin'? That way the wind ain't gonna blow it down or—"

"I took care of the nails already," Laura said. "See?" She pointed to the spot they'd chosen earlier that day, between the door and the west end of the building.

Tawana hit the two nails jutting out of the cypress siding with the flashlight beam. She waggled her head and clucked her tongue. "Oh, girl, look how you good! They all straight and everything."

"You want to do the bubbly before or after we hang it?"

"For sure, after," Tawana said. "I don't want my eyes lookin' all glassy in the pictures." She set the bottle of Asti down near the steps, tucked the flashlight under an arm, then reached for her camera. "Now, go park your skinny butt over there by them nails and do like you're hangin' the sign. Then you can take a picture of me doin' the same thing."

"Don't you want to wait for Moweez?" Laura asked.

"She's in the kitchenette, drawing."

"So go get her."

"You know Moweez ain't gonna understand what's goin' on here. She's happy where she's at right now. Let's leave her be."

Laura carried the sign over to its place of honor, feeling a bit guilty about leaving Moweez out of their little ceremony. The twenty-five-year-old was Tawana's first cousin and as different from her only kin as crawfish was to pork. Tawana had a large framed body with skin the color of mahogany. Her fashion sense said, "Yeah, I'm big, but damn I'm sexy," and she wore her hair in short, tight finger-waves. Moweez, on the other hand, reminded Laura of a young willow tree, slight and pliable. Her complexion was flawless, its color a shade lighter than toffee, and her hair hung in thick black braids to the small of her back. Although she turned heads wherever she went, Moweez remained naive to the extent of her beauty. Her mental abilities matched that of a ten-year-old when it came to comprehension, but when she spoke, her sentences were usually short and the words not always in the right order, which made her seem even younger.

"Okay, you gonna have to work it, girl," Tawana said, holding the camera up to her right eye. "Don't just stand there like an egret. Pose or something. Show me some attitude."

Laura slipped the metal hoop attached to the back of the sign over the nails, then pursed her lips and struck a pose. The camera flashed. "Ladies and gentlemen—the Beauty Box!"

The camera flashed again, and Tawana let out a

loud whoop. "Go Beauty, go Beauty, it's ya birt'day!" Two more flashes, then Tawana pranced over to Laura and handed over the camera. "Here, now do me. And make sure you get some of my good stuff."

"You got it." Laura stepped back so she could get a full body shot, then aimed the camera. Tawana, dressed in a pair of black spandex pants and a tight leopard print blouse, shot Laura a wide, toothy smile, leaned over a little so her butt and over-ample cleavage got adequate attention, then pointed at the sign. Laughing, Laura snapped a picture, then shot more as Tawana went through a series of poses. The hand-on-hip/other-hand-on-back-of-head shot; the leaning-over-so-most-of-my-boobs-show/kissy-face shot; and the finger-snapping-head-popping/look-how-hot-I-look-dancin' shot.

When they finished taking pictures, Laura's sides hurt. She couldn't remember the last time she'd laughed that much. Grabbing the bottle of Asti, she said, "We forgot the glasses."

"Not a problem," Tawana said, "We'll pop the lip and sip."

"Huh?"

Tawana snorted out a laugh. "Girl, I swear, you so white." She motioned to the two wicker fan-back chairs stationed in one corner of the porch. "Come on, we'll park it over here and celebrate right out the bottle."

"Works for me." Laura removed the foil cover from the top of the bottle, then held both thumbs against the cork. "Ready?"

"Oh, hell yeah."

A loud *schhpop!* sent the cork flying into the night.

"Aw, man, it didn't give us no spritz!" Tawana said with an exaggerated pout. She pulled up one of the chairs and sat. "Champagne's supposed to spritz. You know, gush out all over the place when you pop the lip. Maybe we got hold to a bad bottle."

Laura arched a brow. "Let's see." She took a long swig from the bottle, then smacked her lips. "Nope, don't think so."

"Hey, business partners are supposed to share," Tawana said, flapping a hand at her. "Bring that over here before you drink it all like a hussy."

An airy belch slipped past Laura's lips as she handed Tawana the bottle.

"Look at that, a hussy and a pig!" Tawana teased.

Grinning, Laura sat, leaned her head back on the chair, and watched her friend guzzle champagne. So much had fallen together so quickly and perfectly in the last two weeks, she still wanted to pinch herself to make sure she wasn't dreaming. Had someone told her four months ago that she'd be working in her own beauty salon today, she would have laughed, thinking the person had their psychic antennas crossed. With her savings, and a lot of doing without for a year or two, she might have been able to scrape up enough money to buy the equipment and supplies. But all the supplies in the world would have been useless without a shop. Four months ago, there wasn't one piece of rental property to be found. Every rental home, apartment, and office building in Windham had been snatched up by people displaced after Hurricanes Katrina and Rita. It was either fate or some cosmic genie that sent her driving through the center of town the day Lafleur's Construction moved two halves of an old pink house onto First Street.

"What's gettin' you all foggy-eyed?" Tawana handed Laura the Asti.

"Thinking about how we got this place."

Tawana slouched back in her chair. "It's all you, girl. If you hadn't grabbed Lafleur when you did, somebody else would be working and living here. We'd still be over at the Maxi-Plaza, you doin' the nappy heads nobody else wanted and me getting the raunchy manicures."

"Yeah, but I couldn't have made it happen if you hadn't thrown in with me."

"That's all Nana's doing. If it hadn't been for her leavin' me that little bit of money . . ." Tawana glanced over at the Beauty Box sign. "You know, I bet she's struttin' around heaven right now, braggin' all over the place. 'Look what my grandbaby did! See that little white and green house lookin' thing down there? That's her! That's where she at.'" Tawana shook her head, laughing. "Can't you just hear that old woman?"

"Oh, she'd be saying that all right," Laura agreed. "But I'd bet she's bragging on a lot more than you being a partner in this shop."

Tawana looked away, her eyes suddenly sparkling with tears. "Stop that jawin' before I start blubberin'."

"It's true, Wana. How many thirty-year-old single women do you know who would take in a mentally challenged cousin?"

Tawana snifled. "Mo's family. You don't throw away family."

"A lot of people would've, though—that's my point. They'd have dumped Mo off at some state institution. You didn't. Not only that, look at all you did just last year. Giving up your apartment and moving in with Nana when she got sick, taking care of her, taking care of Moweez. All that and working full time at the Plaza. Hell, girl, Nana's got a lot to be proud of when it comes to you."

Sitting up taller, Tawana cleared her throat. "Yeah, yeah, okay, I'm Mother friggin' Teresa," she said with a half-smile. "Now pass that damn bottle back over here if you're not gonna drink."

Laura took a sip from the bottle, then handed it over just as a brisk wind swept across the porch. She shivered and pulled her work smock tightly around her. "Feels like another front's coming through." Another strong breeze swooped up behind the first as though to confirm her statement. Dead mimosa leaves danced across the porch steps. Laura shivered again and stood. "Hey, let's take this inside, huh? I'm getting cold."

"Mm-hmm," Tawana mumbled in mid-swallow. "That's because there's no meat on them bones." She got to her feet, stretched her arms out wide and snapped her fingers. "Now you see this? This is prime, grade-A, honey-glazed stock, guaranteed to keep things sweaty all year round."

Laura chuckled, her teeth chattering.

"Okay, girl, come on. Let's get you inside before you turn into a Popsicle."

Once in the salon, Laura propped the camera on

the reception desk, then rubbed her hands briskly together to warm them. "Don't you love how everything still smells so new in here?"

"Yeah," Tawana said, returning the flashlight to a cabinet over one of the workstations. "Not funky like at the Plaza. Chinese food and pizza smells comin' in from the food court, mixin' all up with the shampoo and peroxide and acrylic crap we use for nails—all in that narrow-ass shop. Nasty stuff, girl, just nasty."

"Sure was." Laura scanned the room, pleased with what she saw. They'd decided to go with a homey look since the building was old and sported a front porch and wrought iron railings along their apartment's balcony. A rattan couch with bright, comfy cushions and two matching chairs had been set up in the corner as a waiting area near the entrance. Hairstyling magazines were neatly fanned across a glass-topped coffee table in front of the couch, and a few feet away stood the faux antique desk she'd bought from Vidrine's Used Furniture. Tawana had placed her manicure table parallel to the desk so she could catch gossip coming from any direction—the waiting area, the two workstations across the room, even the washbasin and sit-down dryer behind her on the right. They'd hoped to keep the original oak plank floors, but they were so badly damaged, Lafleur claimed he'd have to up the rent to cover the cost of repairing them. They had to settle for beige tile instead. Beyond the work area was an archway that led to a small kitchenette with an adjoining half-bath and the stairwell that went up to their apartment.

"Hey," Tawana said, waggling the champagne bottle. "You wanted any more of this?"

"Nah, I'm still too cold."

Upending the bottle, Tawana dropped it into a trash can. "Good, 'cause there's no more."

"Now who's the hussy?"

Tawana grinned. "Yeah, but I'm a classy hussy." She patted the double stomach roll pushing against her blouse. "All that talk about pizza and Chinese food got me hungry. Let's go upstairs and see what's in the fridge. I think there's left over—"

A muffled thump sounded from overhead. Another quickly followed. Then another.

"Sounds like Moweez is jump roping up there," Laura said.

Tawana stared at her, eyes suddenly worried. "I don't think so. I left Mo down here." She spun about on her heels and headed for the kitchenette. Laura followed close behind, not caring for the queasy feeling building in her stomach.

They found Moweez sitting at the lunch table, hunched over a sketch pad, drawing with colored pencils. She didn't look up when they entered the room.

"Mo, did you just come runnin' down them stairs?" Tawana asked, glancing at the stairwell in the far corner of the room.

Not looking up, Moweez shook her head. "The come-together."

"What're you talkin' about, girl?" Tawana asked. "What come together?"

Moweez raised her left hand and rapidly drew a circle in the air with a finger. "The come-together."

"What's a come together?" Laura whispered to Tawana.

"Like a bridge. Anything that connects one thing to somethin' else."

Laura frowned. "Maybe she's talking about the stairs? They connect the bottom floor to the top."

"If it had somethin' to do with the stairs, we'd have heard them noises comin' from back here."

Laura glanced up at the ceiling. "I don't hear anything anymore. You?"

Tawana cocked her head, listening.

"Maybe something just fell off the bookshelf in the living room."

"Three times?" Tawana shook her head. "Uh-uh."

"Well, do you hear anything now?"

"Nothing."

"Then I'm going up there to check it out," Laura said, and went over to a utility drawer to look for a possible weapon.

"Girl, you crazy? Suppose there's somebody up there, robbin' us and shit?"

"They would've had to come through the front door, which means we'd have seen them," Laura said, rummaging through the drawer's contents—three plastic forks, a spoon, two straws, a paring knife, and a handful of colored rubber bands. "I locked the back door earlier, and it's got a keyed dead bolt." She chose the paring knife, then went over to inspect the window near the sink. "Window's still locked, too."

Tawana parked a hand on her hip. "If you're thinkin' nobody's up there, what's the knife for?"

"Just in case."

"So what you gonna do if there is somebody up there? Peel 'em?"

"You got a better plan?"

Tawana stared at Laura for a moment, then stuck out her chest and stormed off toward the stairs. "Hell yeah, I got a better plan."

"Where're you going?"

"Doin' my plan," Tawana said loudly, stomping up the stairs. "If there's somebody up there, they gonna have to deal with Tawana Batiste. I'm bigger and louder than you, and besides I'm pissed 'cause they stole my Asti buzz."

"Hold up, I'm coming with you," Laura said, circling the table. Moweez had yet to look up from her drawing.

"No, stay with Mo," Tawana called down. "If I'm not back in five minutes, call somebody."

Laura heard the door that led into their apartment bang open, then listened as Tawana continued to stomp through the rooms upstairs.

"You okay up there?" Laura shouted.

"Yeah. Nothing in the living room or kitchen," Tawana's muffled voice called back.

Laura began to pace. "What about now?"

"Nothing." Tawana's voice was barely audible now.

"The come-together broken," Moweez said, finally glancing up from her artwork. She closed her sketch pad and turned to Laura. "The mama all broken."

Laura halted in mid-stride, a shiver running up the length of her spine. "Whose mama, honey?"

Moweez drew another circle in the air with a finger. "All dead. All broken." She cocked her head abruptly as if startled by a sound and brought a finger to her lips. "Shhh."

With her heart thudding, Laura held her breath,

listening. She heard Tawana thumping around upstairs, then a faint hissing sound, like that of a snake ready to attack or air leaking from a busted hose. It took her a little while to realize the sound was coming from Moweez. Her lips were slightly parted, her teeth clamped together, and her face had gone slack and expressionless.

"Mo?"

More hissing, louder this time.

"What she doin'?"

Laura gasped when she heard Tawana's voice behind her and slapped a hand over her heart. "You scared the crap out of me!"

"Well, y'all was scarin' the hell out of me, makin' all them weird noises down here."

"What weird noises?"

"That hissin' thing." Tawana motioned to Moweez. "What she doin' that for, anyway? I could hear her all the way in your bedroom, back of the apartment."

"I don't know why. She was talking about that come together again, then acted like she heard something and told me to hush. Next thing I knew, she's making that noise. But this is as loud as she's been. No way you could have heard that from upstairs."

"I'm tellin' you what I heard, girl." Frowning, Tawana placed a hand on Moweez's shoulder. The moment she touched her, the girl grew quiet and looked up at her cousin. "What's up with you?" Tawana asked her.

Moweez yawned in response and rubbed her eyes.

"You tired?"

Moweez nodded. "Tired."

"She gets a little *off* sometimes when she's tired," Tawana said to Laura, then took Moweez by the arm and urged her to her feet. "I'll bring her on up to bed."

"Everything okay upstairs?" Laura asked.

"Now you think I would be standin' here if it wasn't?"

"Smart-ass."

Tawana grinned. "No, nobody hidin' in the closets or under the bed or behind the shower curtain. Nothing looked different. Well, 'cept for this." She handed Laura a metal object.

"What is it?"

"No clue. I found it in me and Mo's room in front of the dresser. Maybe Mo picked it up from somewhere."

"Looks like some kind of valve lever, like the kind on the back of a toilet that lets you turn the water off and on."

"Yeah, you right. It does kinda look like that."

Laura held the object out to Mo, who stood beside Tawana, her head leaning against her cousin's shoulder. "Is this yours, Mo?"

Moweez slapped a hand over her eyes as though afraid to look at it. "Tired!" she cried, then took off for the stairs, mumbling, "All broken . . . all broken."

"Whew, definitely time to put that girl to bed," Tawana said, heading after Moweez. "You comin'?"

"Yeah," Laura said. "I'll lock up and get the lights. Be up in a second."

When the two disappeared up the staircase, Laura put the valve lever on the table, rubbed the chill from her arms, then went to the front of the shop and locked up. After killing the lights, she hurried back to the kitchenette and double-checked the locks on the door and window. When she was sure all was secure, she gathered Moweez's sketch pad and pencils from the table and headed for the stairs. Thinking Moweez might have left a clue to the meaning of her "come together" in her pictures, Laura stalled at the light switch and flipped open the pad.

The picture seemed to leap from the page. The colors were blended and shaded, shadowed and highlighted with notable precision. This wasn't the work of someone mentally challenged, but of someone with remarkable talent. Laura shivered, not from the chill in the air but from a cold intuition that she was seeing a snapshot of something soon to come—the salon as one might see it if they stood across First Street: the wide porch with the three white columns that stretched beyond their apartment to support the roof; the wrought iron railings that fronted the balcony on the second floor; freshly painted, white cedar siding; green shutters; the newly installed wooden sign that read, THE BEAUTY BOX. And birds, dead birds, hundreds of them littering the front lawn. In the left-hand corner of the page sat an hourglass, at least two inches in height, and from the thin flow of sand drawn trickling to the bottom, it had been set in motion.

Laura put a hand to her queasy stomach. She had a funny feeling that something else had been set into motion tonight. Something that would change them all.

CHAPTER THREE

The incessant beeping pulled Laura from sleep, and she reluctantly opened one eye. At first she thought another police car was racing past the shop, just as they'd done most of the night, then realized it was only her alarm clock, insisting she get out of bed.

Last night, she'd been awakened three times by the scream of sirens, an odd occurrence in this town. The biggest crimes in Windham she could remember were the occasional shoplifters at the Dollar General and a few teens dealing pot in Miller's Park. Whatever the hoopla was about last night, she was sure the shop would be buzzing with the news this morning.

After slapping the alarm clock into silence, Laura yawned and stretched, and was about to hop out of bed when she heard someone sniffle. Startled, she sat bolt upright in bed. Moweez stood in the corner of the room near the bureau, wearing a pink flannel nightgown. Her long braids were frayed, as though she'd tossed and turned on them most of the night.

Thinking of the picture she'd seen in Moweez's sketch pad the night before, Laura's heart picked up an extra beat. "Is something wrong? Where's Wana?"

Moweez rocked on her heels. "Wana sleeping." She pointed to Laura's bedroom door, then inched towards it. "Come with Mo. Come see."

"Is something wrong?"

She motioned for Laura to get out of bed. "Come. The mama's broken."

"I don't understand, Mo. Who's—"

"The daddy's all gone, too. All broken." Moweez hurried over to the bed, grabbed Laura by the hand and pulled until she practically fell out of bed. "Come. Come see." She tugged, urging Laura toward the bedroom door.

"Wait," Laura said, trying to pull away. "I'm not dressed." Having slept only in a T-shirt, she grabbled for the pair of navy blue jogging pants at the foot of the bed and managed to hook them with a finger before Moweez yanked her out of the room.

"Mo, wait a minute!" She pulled out of her grasp, and Moweez shifted nervously from foot to foot while Laura slipped into the jogging pants. No sooner did the elastic band snap against her waist than Moweez grabbed her hand again.

Laura had never seen her so anxious before, and it began to dawn on her that something might actually be wrong. "Mo, hang on—let's wake up Wana, okay?"

Moweez yanked harder, urging Laura toward the stairs. "Come see!"

Laura stumbled along after her. Halfway down the stairs Moweez stopped and cocked her head as though listening intently.

"What?" Laura asked.

Instead of answering, Moweez hurried down the remaining steps, muttering, "The come-together, all come-together." After crossing the entranceway that led into the salon, Moweez let go of Laura's hand and ran through the shop. She came to a halt at the front door and waited for Laura to catch up to her.

Moweez pointed to one of the locks that secured the door. "Open."

"It's too early to open the shop. I'm—"

Moweez slapped the door with the flat of her hand. "Open!"

Laura jumped, startled by her aggression. "Mo—"

"Open!"

Frowning, Laura quickly opened the security latch, then unlocked the dead bolt and tab lock on the knob. As soon as the last lock clicked free, Moweez hurried out onto the porch before Laura could stop her.

"Mo, wait!" Fearing she'd run out into the street, Laura took off after her and wound up running into Moweez's back when the girl came to abrupt halt. They both stumbled to the edge of the porch, and only then did Laura see what had stunned Moweez motionless.

Dead birds—black ones, maybe a hundred lying across the front lawn—just like in the drawing she'd seen last night.

"See?" Moweez whispered loudly. "Just like Moweez say. Come-together broken."

Laura stepped alongside her and sucked in a breath, taking in more of the sight. So many dead birds, beaks opened as if they'd expired in mid-caw, small legs pointed skyward, four toes curled in, shiny black feathers ruffling in the wind. She looked back at Moweez, who was rocking back and forth on her heels. "You drew a picture just like this, didn't you, Mo?"

She nodded, drawing a circle in the air with a finger. "Just like Moweez say."

"Mo, where you at?" Tawana's voice, hoarse with sleep, called from inside the shop.

"Out here," Laura said.

The glass storm door banged open, and Tawana charged out, dressed in fire-red pajamas, blue fuzzy slippers, and a white sleep cap that wrapped around her head like an Ace bandage. "What in the name of Jesus's uncle y'all doin' out here at seven-thirty—" She gasped and stumbled over to the porch steps, blinking rapidly. "Where—where'd all them dead birds come from?"

"I don't know," Laura said.

Folding one hand into the other, Tawana tucked both beneath her large breasts, then crept closer to the edge of the porch. "Merciful Jesus." Her head bobbed from left to right as she scanned the yard. "They got to be a hundred out here."

Laura made her way down the two steps to get a better look. A few morning commuters slowed in front of the shop, evidently wanting a better view as well.

"Girl, don't go out there!" Tawana said. "What if they all dead from that bird flu?"

"I'm not going to touch anything."

"Be sure you don't. And you neither, Mo. Y'all don't touch nothin'. I'm gonna go call Percy Schexneider and tell him to get his butt over here."

"What's the police chief going to do about a bunch of dead birds?" Laura asked.

"Who else I'm supposed to call, the Zoo of Acadiana?" Tawana said with a snap of her head.

"Wildlife and Fisheries in Opelousas. Check the phone book."

"A fishery?"

"*Wildlife* and Fisheries. It's a state department . . ."

Tawana tsked loudly. "I ain't messin' with no slow-ass state department. They wouldn't show up here 'til some time next Christmas." She headed for the shop. "I'm callin' Percy."

Shaking her head at Tawana's stubborn streak, Laura stepped timidly onto the walkway that led to a sidewalk, which paralleled First Street. She couldn't walk far because of her bare feet and the birds that covered the ground, but far enough to realize there were no dead birds in the neighboring yard to her left or her right. In fact, the only other place she saw birds was in front of the Tin Cup Café, the two-story twin to her beauty salon. Nestler's Sewing Cottage sat between her shop and the café, and the two buildings overshadowed the little clapboard like hundred-year oaks over a single thorn bush. With the same paint job and wrought iron railings, the only differences between her building and the café were the signs and who lived and worked inside. The café had been in operation for about a month, but she'd been so busy getting the salon ready she hadn't had time to meet the owner, much less sample the food.

The front door of the café suddenly swung open and a man stepped outside. A small, involuntary gasp escaped Laura when he walked past the shadows of the porch and she caught him in full view. He looked to be in his late thirties with light brown hair and broad shoulders. The shoulders were hard to miss because he wore only jeans. Snug fitting jeans that either snapped or buttoned just below a muscle-lined stomach. He leaned against one of the porch columns, examining his yard and looking as bewildered as she was. From where Laura stood, his yard appeared to be covered with charcoal briquettes.

Laura doubled back onto her own porch before he saw her in the faded jogging pants and T. Why were the birds only in his yard and hers? Surely they wouldn't have fallen from the sky that way, targeting only two lawns. This had to be some kind of sick joke. She wondered if there might be a tie-in between the birds and the sirens she heard last night. But then again, what about Moweez's drawing?

Laura glanced over at Moweez, who still rocked on her heels and stared out into the yard. She didn't appear to be shocked or distressed over the birds, just curious. How had she known about them?

"Mo?"

Moweez looked at Laura briefly and smiled.

"Honey, what made you draw that picture last night? Did you see something?"

She nodded. "Come-together broken."

"What's a come together? Show Laura what you mean."

Moweez stopped rocking and walked over to the

edge of the porch. She leaned over, one hand search-ing through a bare azalea bush, then came away with a short, crooked stick. With the stick in hand, Moweez tiptoed down the two steps to the walkway, then squatted near the first dead bird within reach. She nudged it with a stick as though to wake it. "Come-together," she said, sadly.

"Girl, what the hell you doin' out there?" Tawana said, her voice booming from the doorway. She stomped outside. "Get your butt back on this porch!" She turned to Laura. "How come you didn't stop her? Them birds could have some kind of disease!"

Looking like a whipped puppy, Moweez scampered onto the porch, then ran into the shop.

An elderly man in a pickup slowed in front of the shop, his mouth agape. "What happened?" he yelled from the cab.

Tawana aimed a finger at him. "Don't you be wor-ryin' about what happened over here. What's the matter with you? Actin' like you ain't never seen a dead bird before. Now go on about your business!" For a moment, the old man seemed more afraid of Tawana than he'd been shocked by the birds. The truck tires squealed as he sped away.

"Mo was just trying to explain something to me," Laura said. "And she wasn't touching anything, so chill out."

"Explainin' what?"

"What she means by a come-together."

"I told you last night what that meant."

"Yeah, but did you see what she drew last night?"

"What?"

"A picture of the shop—with a bunch of dead black birds in front of it."

Tawana's head snapped back in surprise. "Get the fuck out."

"Go see for yourself. It's in her sketch pad. She was in my room this morning, waiting for me to get up, then she practically dragged me down here to see this. When I asked her how she knew about the birds, she said something about a come together. I couldn't figure out how the explanation you gave me last night tied in, so I asked her to show me what she meant. That's what she was doing when you came out."

Tawana blew out a breath and put a hand on her forehead. She looked back at the salon, as though searching for Moweez. "So what did she mean?"

"I still don't know."

Tawana stood silent for a while, then dropped her hand and turned to Laura. "Okay, straight up—the picture thing is freaky as hell, but we ain't got time to worry about that right now. It's almost eight. The shop opens in two hours, and we got a shitload of birds to pick up before customers start gettin' here."

"*We've* got to pick them up?"

"I talked to Verneese, the dispatcher over at the police station, and she told me Percy wasn't in, but that he already knew about the birds and had called that fisheries place."

"How'd Percy know about the birds?"

"Probably somebody drivin' past here called it in. Anyway, those damn state people can't get out here 'til this afternoon. Verneese said if we wanted the birds out of the yard before we open, we've gotta take care of it ourselves. Stick 'em in trash bags until those fishery people get here. Can you believe that shit?"

It was Laura's turn to blow out a breath. "Figures. All right, I'll go change clothes and get some gloves. You grab the trash bags from the kitchenette."

It took an hour and a half for them to clean the yard. It wouldn't have taken quite as long if Tawana hadn't stopped every ten minutes to yell at a passerby. Donning latex gloves Laura normally wore to color hair, they'd each carried a trash bag and worked as fast as they could. Every once in a while, Laura stole glimpses at the guy from the café, who gathered birds into his own trash bags. He'd worked alone—and without a shirt.

Strangely enough, they'd found very few birds between the salon and the sewing cottage and none in the backyard. When they'd finished, Laura used up most of the hot water in the shower, scrubbing her skin until it burned. Even with gloves, she'd still felt the weighty lifelessness of those little heads flopping against her hand when she picked up the birds. That sensation seemed to travel through her glove and soak through her pores. Even now, as she draped a towel around the shoulders of her first customer, she still felt it.

"Use those little pink rollers this time," Maude Romero said as Laura led her to the wash station. "I need the curls tight if my tiara's going to stay put."

"Your tiara?" Tawana said from the manicure table. She held a miniature blow dryer over Sadie Babineaux's plum-colored nails.

"Yes, for the ball. Krewe of Bon Ton."

"Don't the Mardi Gras balls start Saturday?" Laura asked.

"That's right," Sadie said, giving Tawana her left hand. "This Saturday coming. February seventh, to be exact. I know because that's the day before my birthday."

"No kidding?" Tawana said. "How old you gonna be, Miss Sadie?"

"Sixty-one."

Maude snorted as she sat and rested her head against the washbowl. She held the towel in place beneath her thick double chin with two fingers. "If you're going to be sixty-one, Sadie Marie, then I'm going to be thirty-two come my birthday in December."

"Well, I'm still younger than you." Sadie smoothed her paisley skirt with her free hand.

"By ten months."

"Ten months is ten months. I'm still younger."

"If the ball's Saturday, why are you worried about your tiara now?" Laura asked, jumping in before the discussion overheated. She aimed a spray of luke-warm water over Maude's thinning white hair.

"Because I've got to practice wearing it," Maude said. "I'd die of embarrassment if it fell off or tipped sideways in front of King Phillip during the procession."

"You'll be lucky if Phillip isn't the one who tips sideways," Sadie said. "That old fart can barely walk."

"He's not that old," Maude said.

"Eighty's old." Sadie waggled her head. "Now if you ask me, they should have made Thomas Sterner the Krewe king this year. He's younger, holds a prestigious position in the community, and he's better looking than Phillip."

"Prestigious position?" Maude cackled. "He's Windham's postman for heaven's sake. And he might be younger, but he's got nose and ear hair sticking out every which way."

"Oh, now that's nasty." Tawana wrinkled her nose. "A man who can't trim his nose and ears sure don't need no crown on his head."

Sadie blushed. "The man is a bit hairy."

The salon filled with laughter, and for a moment, Laura could almost pretend the bird incident never happened. She rinsed the last of the cream rinse from Maude's hair, then sat her up.

"Now, if y'all wanna talk about good lookin'," Tawana said, "y'all should check out that hunky piece of meat over at the café."

"Are you talking about Matt Daigle over at the Tin Cup?" Maude asked.

Sadie tsked. "You know of any other café around here?"

"There's the Dairy Freezo on Burman Road," Maude said.

"That's not a café." Sadie wrinkled her nose. "It's a roach drive-thru."

"It is not!" Maude insisted. "They make good hamburgers . . . but it looks like they might have to close down for a while, anyway, after what happened last night."

"What happened?" The question came in unison from Laura, Tawana, and Sadie.

Maude, practically glowing from all the attention, took her time answering. She pulled the towel in tighter around her neck and waited until she'd settled into one of the hydraulic chairs at a workstation before giving up the goods.

"Well, you know Sherry Miller, that redhead who works over at the Piggly Wiggly?"

Everyone nodded.

"Her seventeen-year-old daughter, Tracy, got stabbed while she was working there last night."

"No way!" Tawana said, letting the blow-dryer fall away.

"So that's what all the sirens were about last night," Laura said.

Tawana arched a brow. "You heard sirens? I didn't hear nothing."

Laura nodded as she combed out Maude's hair. "Three or four times during the night."

"Is the girl all right?" Sadie asked.

"Last I heard, they'd moved her over to Lafayette General and put her in an intensive care unit. They don't know if she's going to make it."

"Hold up a minute." Tawana wagged a fingernail file. "How did the girl get stabbed in the Dairy-Freezo? They don't have any sit down tables over there. It's only a drive-thru."

Maude shrugged. "Maybe she let somebody in, somebody she knew."

Sadie shook her head. "I'll tell you this whole world's just going to rot when you can't even trust people you know. Who would have ever thought anything like this would happen in Windham?"

"I know," Maude said. "It feels strange, worrying that a killer might be running loose in this town."

"Something else that's strange," Sadie said. "Those dead birds this morning."

"You heard about that?" Laura asked.

"Everybody in town's heard about it."

"That don't surprise me," Tawana said. "This town churns out more gossip than a butter factory full of women."

"Well, you can't blame them," Maude said. "A whole flock of birds lying dead in only two yards—that's a pretty big chunk of news."

"Did y'all get any news yet as to what might have caused it?" Sadie asked.

"Not yet," Laura said. "Someone with the Department of Wildlife and Fisheries is supposed to come out here this afternoon."

Tawana huffed. "Yeah, if we're lucky."

Maude shivered, and her double chin jiggled. "I sure hope it's got nothing to do with that bird flu going around."

"That's what I'm sayin'," Tawana said.

Sadie rolled her eyes. "There's no bird flu going around. That's in southeast Asia."

"Then how do you explain all those dead birds?" Maude asked.

"I don't know," Sadie said. "But even if it is the bird flu, which it isn't, how do you explain them dropping dead just in front of the beauty salon and café?"

Everyone fell silent, and Laura thought about Moweez's sketch. Whatever had inspired the girl to draw the birds and salon might have also inspired a clue, something in the picture she might have missed. What about that hourglass?

Maude glanced up at Laura. "Have you talked to Matt this morning to see if he knows anything?"

"Matt?"

"The guy who owns the Tin—"

"That hunky piece of meat two doors down," Tawana tossed in. "He was out there doin' the same as us this morning, pickin' up birds. Only he was doin' it with no shirt on and had his cute little butt wrapped up in some fine-lookin' jeans. Girl, you can't even tell me you didn't notice."

Laura grinned. "Oh, I noticed. I didn't know his name, though."

"Matt Daigle," Maude said. "He used to have the Tin Cup on the south side of town, closer to the sugar mill. I guess business got slow after they closed the mill, so he decided to move here. He's been open about a month."

"Married?" Tawana asked.

Laura laughed. "You would ask."

"Girl, you know I like my meat dark roasted." Tawana waved a nail buffer. "I'm askin' 'cause it's about time *you* get some nourishment on your bones."

Laura felt her cheeks grow hot.

"He's divorced." Maude handed Laura a pink roller. "But his son lives with him. I think the boy's seven or eight."

"Good-looking, responsible daddy, hardworking, that's a hard combination to find in any man these days. You should go over there, Laura, introduce yourself." Sadie's eyes shone mischievously. "The café's open for breakfast and lunch, so take your pick."

"Okay, y'all stop with the matchmaking already." Laura grinned. "I'm sure, since we're not that far apart, we'll meet up sooner or later."

"I don't know." Maude peered up at her. "If I were you, I wouldn't wait too long. There're quite a few single women in Windham already eating over there pretty regularly. Wait too long and you might lose your shot."

Laura shook her head, laughing. "Miss Maude, you've been trying to get me hooked up for three years, ever since I started doing your hair at the Plaza."

"You're right." Maude chuckled. "You know, I'm so glad y'all moved over here. Now we don't have to fight that traffic getting to the mall in Lafayette."

"Oh, you know what just came to me?" Sadie sparked to attention as though she'd just received an epiphany.

"What?" Tawana asked.

"Something my mama use to say."

Maude groaned. "Lord, Sadie Marie, don't start with your mama stories."

"No, it's got to do with those dead birds," Sadie said.

"What about 'em," Tawana asked.

"Why do you want to bring that up now when we're talking about ways for Matt and Laura to meet?" Maude asked.

Laura glanced over at Tawana and rolled her eyes.

Sadie swatted a hand at Maude. "My mama used to

49

say if you happened across a dead bird, it was a sign you'd have bad luck for three months."

"Say what?" Tawana's eyes grew wide.

Laura flinched, wishing Sadie hadn't mentioned her mama's old wives' tale. No one was more superstitious than Tawana.

"Sadie Marie, you stop that," Maude said. "Look how you're scaring poor Tawana."

"Well, it's true. Mama used to say the luck might be so bad, somebody in your family could die. I just can't imagine what it means if you happen across a whole yard of dead birds."

Laura bit back another groan when she saw Tawana's mouth drop open.

"Sadie Marie!" Maude nearly sprang from her chair. "You stop talking that nonsense right now."

Tawana dropped the bottle of clear-coat she'd been using to finish Sadie's nails and took off for the kitchenette, yelling, "Mo?"

"Who's she calling?" Sadie asked.

"Her cousin, Moweez," Laura said, wondering if she should go after Tawana. She looked petrified.

"Her cousin lives here, too?" Maude asked.

"Yes."

Tawana marched back into the shop, leading Moweez over to the reception desk by the shoulders. Moweez had her sketch pad and colored pencils clutched to her chest.

"Now you sit here where I can see you." Tawana sat her down, then glanced about nervously, as though expecting some kind of attack.

"Aren't you going to introduce us?" Maude asked.

"Oh—this is my cousin, Moweez."

Sadie smiled. "Nice to meet you. That's certainly an unusual name for such a beautiful young lady."

Moweez frowned and hunched over the desk. She opened her sketch pad to a clean sheet and rummaged through her box of pencils. After choosing a green one, she stared down at the blank page.

"Shy, huh?" Maude said to Tawana.

"She just don't talk much," Tawana said, heading back to Sadie. "And her name is really Angelica Batiste. She got the name Mo when she was little. When her asthma would kick up, she'd wheeze really bad, and she'd go runnin' to find our grandma and say, 'Mo' wheeze, Nana, mo' wheeze.' She did it so much, the name stuck."

Maude grinned. "Isn't it funny how people get their nicknames?" she asked, addressing Laura's reflection in the workstation mirror.

Laura didn't answer. She was too busy watching Moweez, who was drawing now, leaning so close to the sketch pad that her nose almost touched the paper. It made Laura nervous. First the birds, now what? Laura had a feeling this was one question she might not want answered.

CHAPTER FOUR

"Lerna Mae, bring me over another one of them yams, will ya, hon?" Percy Schexneider called over the din in the café. Then he shoveled more chicken fricassee into his mouth.

"I'll 'hon' him," Lerna Mae Fontenot muttered to Matt behind the lunch counter. She marched to the swinging impact doors that led into the kitchen. Matt quickly followed, not caring for the "play ball!" expression on Lerna Mae's face.

Sure enough, she went straight for an oven mitt, shoved it over her right hand, then scooped up a sweet potato.

Matt grabbed the yam from her and dropped it gently on the counter. "No yam throwing in the café." If he'd learned anything about Lerna Mae in the five years she'd worked for him as a short-order cook and dishwasher, it was not to be fooled by the gray hair and short, pudgy frame. Her walk might have slowed over sixty-one years, but there was nothing sluggish about her temper.

"That greedy half-wit already ate three," Lerna Mae said, a little too loudly. "If he keeps eating them like that, we're not going to have enough yams for the other customers. And if he calls me hon one more time, I'm going to throw more than a sweet potato at that ugly bald head."

He patted the air with a hand. "Take your voice down a notch, will you? I'll bring it to Percy."

Lerna Mae stripped off the mitt and slapped it on the counter. "Okay, but don't come crying to me, Matt Daigle, when you run out of yams." She stormed out of the kitchen like an irate bulldog.

Shaking his head and grinning, Matt quickly peeled the potato, placed it on a small salad plate, and reminded himself as he carried it out of the kitchen that most of the customers loved that feisty old broad.

The café was packed, just as it had been almost every day since he'd opened a month ago. Not only did he see new faces coming in for breakfast and lunch each day, quite a few of his regulars from the old diner, like Percy, had followed him here. Fortunately, Lerna Mae had been willing to follow him as well, as did Sam, the nineteen-year-old waiter busboy who'd worked for Matt since he was sixteen. Without them, he'd have a tough time handling the business.

Matt had been apprehensive at first about making the move to First Street, as he'd never rented half of a house before, especially one nearly forty years old. But the renovations had proved sound, and the space more than adequate. He'd had the bottom floor decorated with the same country motif he'd used in his old location, and it had plenty of room for four booths complete with bench seating, and five tables that sat four customers each. The lunch counter, something he hadn't had room for in his old location, held another five stools. The kitchen had all new appliances and contained an adjoining half-bath and the stairwell that went up to his apartment.

The apartment was in fact the only part of the building with which Matt had issues. The first time he'd walked upstairs, he'd been struck with a sense of déjà vu so intense it raised the hair on the back of his neck. He'd stood in the hallway between his bedroom and his son, turning, feeling, looking, like a satellite dish searching for a signal. Since then, there were occasions when he'd go upstairs with nothing more on his mind than the events of the day, when suddenly he'd find himself anxious, fretting that he'd forgotten something of monumental importance, something that if not tended to might be detrimental to—*what? Whom?* He didn't have a clue, which always left him frustrated. That irrational frustration was a small price to pay, however, for a more secure future for his son.

"This has got to be the best doggone chicken fricassee I've ever eaten," Percy said when Matt placed the sweet potato in front of him. "Ain't that right, Verneese?"

Verneese Credeur, the local police department's day dispatcher, held up a finger, chewing quickly. Her bottle-black hair was pulled up in a short ponytail, and her police uniform had a gravy stain over the left breast pocket. At forty-one, she wasn't much older than Matt, but her face, which held the wear of a chain-smoker and one carrying too many troubles in life, made her look well past fifty. Verneese swallowed loudly. "Better than my mama's."

"I'm glad you like it," Matt said. "Need anything else, Percy?"

"Aw, take a load off for a minute, boy. Pull up a chair." Percy leaned back and rubbed his paunch absently. Although he sat beneath one of the three ceiling fans in the room, sweat dotted his bald head.

Matt did a quick survey of the room. No lines at the counter, most of the customers were seated, Lerna Mae at the register, and Sam was busing the first empty table. "I guess I can spare a couple minutes." He pulled up a chair next to Percy.

"You hear the latest?" Percy asked.

"About the birds?"

"No, man, about this year's Courir," Percy said. "I'm going to be le capitaine."

The Courir de Mardi Gras was an annual tradition in Windham. On Mardi Gras Day, hundreds of men rode on horseback through the countryside collecting ingredients for that evening's communal gumbo. Most wore pointy, conical hats or capuchons and homemade costumes made from gold, green, and purple material. Everyone wore masks, except the capitaine, who wore only a cape over his street clothes. He carried a white flag and was responsible for keeping the revelers in order, which was no easy task. By noon most of the Mardi Gras celebrants were rowdy and drunk, dancing atop their saddles, even attempting handstands. Accompanied by flatbed trailers carrying musicians or others who didn't have horses, the riders would stop at each farmhouse and wait for the capitaine to get approval from the owner to enter the property. If the owner agreed, the capitaine waved his white flag and the revelers charged the house. There they'd sing and dance and beg for gumbo ingredients. Often, the owner would throw a live chicken into the air, and the revelers would chase it like football players trying to recover a fumble. When they finished the run, they held a huge parade through the center of town with lots of music, food, and dancing. Everything stopped at midnight, though, when Ash Wednesday began.

Matt gave Percy a nudge on the arm. "I hadn't heard. What'd you do, threaten to bust old man Thibodeaux for making his rice wine if he didn't make you capitaine?"

Percy let out a giant belly laugh, giving anyone who cared to look a view of the yams in his mouth. When he finally settled down to a snorting chuckle, Percy said, "And lose my monthly supply of hooch? Not a chance. Thib's in the hospital right now, getting his gallbladder taken out, so he's not going to be in any shape to make the run on Tuesday. He asked me to do it. You riding in the Courir this year? Want to ride up front with me? I'll make you a co-capitaine."

"Can't. I'm opening the café on Mardi Gras."

"You're opening on Mardi Gras?" Verneese shook her head. "Now that's not right. You own the place, just stick a closed sign on the door and come out and party with the rest of us?"

Matt grinned. "Hungry riders mean lots of plate lunches."

"Well, you'd better see about pulling in some extra help," Percy said. "You'll probably need it. So far, we've got twelve hundred riders signed up. Even if a third of them stop in here off and on throughout the day, you'll have more than you'll be able to handle."

Matt let out a low whistle. "You're not kidding."

"Only a year or two ago, I knew nearly everybody in this town by name," Verneese said. "But not anymore. Too many new people. This town's growing way too fast."

"Most of 'em still trying to find roots after Katrina and Rita," Percy said, then sucked down the last of his sweet tea. "Hey, you check out your new neighbors yet?" he asked Matt.

"At the beauty shop?"

"Yeah."

"I saw them picking up dead birds this morning, but we haven't officially met."

Percy sat back, laced his fat fingers together, and plopped them down on his belly. "I been knowing Laura Toups' family for years. She's a decent girl. Don't know why she'd want to go into business with a colored woman, though."

"Percy Francis Schexneider!" Verneese slapped a hand on the table. "How can you say something so prejudiced when a third of the people who voted you into office were black?"

"Hey, all I'm sayin'—"

"All you're sayin', nothing," Verneese said in a loud whisper. "I know Tawana Batiste, and she's good people. That woman took care of her old grandma 'til the day she died, then took in her retarded cousin after that to boot!"

"Keep your dang voice down," Percy said, glancing nervously about. "No need to get your feathers in a ruffle."

"Then take back what you said," Verneese demanded.

"I think you need to remember who you're talkin' to, young lady," Percy said.

Matt leaned into him. "I think you need to do what Verneese said."

Percy frowned. "What the hell's your problem?"

"I don't care for that kind of talk in my café."

Percy looked from Matt to Verneese, his face turning red. "All right, all right, I take it back." He slumped in his chair and twirled a piece of napkin between a thumb and finger. "So when's Lerna Mae gonna bring my dessert?"

Matt winked at Verneese, then signaled for Sam to bring Percy a slice of apple pie. "So how's the beauty shop getting along, anyhow?"

Percy continued to pout, not answering, and only grumbled a thank you when Sam brought him his pie.

"From what I can tell, they're getting busier every day," Verneese said. "You should go over there sometime and introduce yourself. That Laura's quite a looker, you know."

Matt cocked his head. "You trying to hook me up, Verneese?"

"Honey, if I were a few years younger and had a little less wear and tear, I'd be hookin' you up with me."

Matt laughed. It had been a long time since he'd bothered with a relationship. After his divorce two years ago, he'd focused on his business and his eight-year-old son, Seth. Both filled his life completely, and aside from the occasional date, he'd not been interested in pursuing any kind of romance. But he had to admit, the woman at the shop did more than grab his attention. He'd watched her bagging dead birds this morning, and even in an old pair of jeans and sweatshirt, he found her beautiful. Her shoulder-length hair the color of chestnuts, her body slim and well proportioned, something he couldn't help but notice when at one point she'd place a hand on the small of her back and arched, stretching in the morning sun.

"Hey, either of y'all see Lafleur lately?" Percy asked, as though their earlier conversation had never happened.

"Keith Lafleur?" Verneese asked.

"I haven't seen him since I signed the lease on this building," Matt said.

Verneese pulled out a pack of Marlboros from her shirt pocket. "Can I smoke in here?"

"Sorry, I didn't put in a smoking section," Matt said.

Verneese gave an offhanded shrug and repocketed the smokes. "I heard Lafleur got into some trouble with the LHBA and has been laying low."

"What's LHBA?" Matt asked.

"Louisiana Home Builders Association. Lafleur's been a member for years."

"What kind of trouble?" Percy asked.

"Don't know." Verneese pulled the straw out of her soda glass and started chewing on it. "Something about a contract or a lien—I'm not sure. You'd think he'd show up this morning, though, after all the commotion with those birds."

"Still no word from Wildlife and Fisheries?" Percy asked Matt.

"Nothing. I've got the birds in trash bags in the shed out back. If they don't show up soon, they're going to start smelling, and—"

A shrill scream suddenly ripped through the café, and Matt jumped up from his seat.

Another scream, and pounding on the bathroom door. "Help! I can't get out!"

Matt took off for the bathroom, which was located near the west end of the building, not far from the kitchen. He saw Lerna Mae poke her head out of the swinging doors.

"Help! I can't get out! There's no light in here!"

Matt reached the door and grabbed the knob. "Ma'am, the door locks from the inside."

"Get me out!" More pounding on the door.

Matt felt her shrieks vibrate down his spine to his tailbone. He turned the knob and pulled, but the door wouldn't budge.

"You're going to have to unlock the door from the inside," Matt called to the woman.

"I did! But the door won't—" She let out a scream so loud and piercing, it made Matt clench his teeth.

When it finally lost volume, he heard her breathing hard and fast.

"Ma'am?"

"Some—something just bit me!" She started to cry hysterically.

Percy stepped up to the door and nudged Matt aside. "Let me try." He wiped his hands on his khaki pants, then took hold of the doorknob. He twisted and pulled until his face turned purple from straining.

"Oh, God, gas!" the woman screamed. "I smell gas in here! Hurry, please, get me out!"

Matt glanced over at Percy, perplexed. "The place is all electric. How can there be gas in there?"

A loud retching sound echoed from behind the door, and a few customers closest to the bathroom groaned and got up from their seats. They hurried over to the lunch counter, where they threw down some money, then nearly ran out of the café.

"Y'all get away from that door," Lerna Mae said, appearing next to Matt with a long butcher knife.

Matt and Percy backed away, while Lerna Mae worked the blade of the knife between the door and its jamb. In a matter of minutes, the door popped open.

A blond woman, who looked to be in her late thirties, collapsed face down across the threshold of the bathroom. Matt motioned for Percy to help him lift her, and together they got her to her feet and into a chair that Lerna Mae had waiting.

Matt squatted beside the woman. A zigzagging strip of vomit ran the length of her tan blouse. Her eyes were open but unfocused.

"She sure was bit," Percy said. He lifted her left

hand and pointed to the red knot growing just above her wrist. "Looks like a spider bite."

Matt heard a symphony of chairs legs scraping against the wood floor, and he looked back to see more customers hurrying out of the café. He winced, wishing Percy hadn't said "spider bite" so loudly. Not exactly an appetizing notion in a café.

Turning back to Percy, Matt said, "We need to call an ambulance."

"It'll take them a half hour to get here from Lafayette if they don't have a unit nearby," Percy said. "I can have her at the hospital in five minutes in my cruiser. I'll run my lights and sirens if I have—"

Another scream cut Percy off, this one coming from the dining area instead of the bathroom.

Matt swiveled around on the balls of his feet and saw a woman standing near one of the booths with one hand over her mouth and the other pointing toward the front door. Her eyes were wide, fixed with fear. He turned, almost afraid to look—then wished he hadn't.

A young woman with a tangle of long black braids stood in the entrance of the café, gasping for air.

Chapter Five

The mirror didn't lie. Neither did the red, swollen skin around the bandages. He looked like a pustulant freak that had escaped a sideshow carnival.

Keith touched the bandage on his forehead and flinched. He was afraid to remove the gauze, afraid to see if the skin had blackened any more around the wound. He knew by the yellow wet patch spreading from the center of the gauze that it was still oozing. After multiple doctor visits and conflicting diagnoses that ranged anywhere from a brown recluse spider bite to cutaneous anthrax, he was no better off than he was a month ago. If anything, he was getting much worse. Festering boils had formed on both of his cheeks, and the drawing salve he had been given to use on them smelled like tar, which made him so nauseous he had to discontinue its use. He sweat profusely, no matter the time of day or temperature, and his eyes burned constantly. The pressure he'd felt in his ears the day he had been bitten still occurred from time to time, but fortunately not with the same intensity. All the symptoms combined, however, did not compare with the necrosis. Watching your flesh rot right before your very eyes did something to a man, and that something was not good. Too many jumbled thoughts, too little memory. Keith felt like he was losing his mind.

Yesterday, Dr. Robins had insisted he be hospitalized, but he'd refused. He didn't want anything to do with a hospital. He hated their smells, their food, the beeps and squeaks and buzzers that kept patients awake all night. No, if he was going to be miserable, he'd be miserable in his own home.

Keith heard a soft tap on the bathroom door.

"Keith, honey, are you okay?"

The sound of his wife's voice made Keith grind his teeth. Its timbre reminded him of a dentist's drill, high and whiney.

"Keith, there's—"

"Leave me the fuck alone!" he shouted, wishing he had the strength to kick the door for emphasis or to punch through it with a fist and have his knuckles connect with Barbara's face.

"I wanted . . . you don't . . . Jeff's here and . . ." Barbara's voice trailed off to a sniffle, and he heard her tiptoe away.

Seething, Keith peered at his grotesque reflection in the bathroom mirror. It was all her fault, such a whimpering, pathetic excuse for a wife. No wonder everything was falling apart on him. She needed to be more supportive, encourage and praise him once in a while instead of sucking on every dollar he earned. Years ago, when they'd first married, he thought changing the company name from her father's to his would help. It hadn't. She'd still nagged him incessantly, especially about giving her brother, Jeff, a job. And she spent money like they had a tree sprouting twenty-dollar bills in the backyard. Jewelry, expensive hair salons, closets and closets of clothes. If she was worth looking at with all that bauble clutter, like Patricia, it would be worth it. But Barbara Mabry Lafleur would never be Patricia Egan. Not even in her wildest dreams, much less his.

Thinking about Patricia angered Keith all the more. A month ago he'd had a real shot with the goddess, but not anymore, not looking like this. No woman would want to touch him now.

He curled a pool of saliva on his tongue and spat at the mirror. Screw Barbara, screw Patricia, screw everybody. He'd show them. He'd show them all.

Keith yanked the bathroom door open and went in search of Jeff, knowing the little bastard hadn't come to bring him a get well gift. The only reason his brother-in-law ever came over was to eat or dump bad news on him.

The swish of his wind pants and the slap of his bare feet on the linoleum must have signaled his pending arrival, because Barbara already had her phony smile in place when he reached the living room. Jeff stood next to her, wearing jeans, a brown plaid shirt, and a scowl.

"What do you want?" Keith asked.

"We need to talk," Jeff said, a steely edge to his voice.

Keith narrowed his eyes, studying Barbara. If she went whining to her brother about him again, she'd need a crowbar to get his foot out of her ass.

Barbara patted Jeff's arm. "I'll go get you two some tea."

"I don't want any goddamn tea," Keith said.

Barbara's smile collapsed. "I thought . . . since you're sweating so much—"

"I don't want any goddamn tea!"

"Hey!" Jeff stepped between his sister and Keith. "Don't talk to her that way."

Keith rolled his hands into fists.

"Barb, go on to the kitchen, okay?" Jeff said, never taking his eyes off Keith. "I'll have some tea with you a little later."

With her head lowered, Barbara gave her brother a little smile, then hurried away, keeping a wide berth between her and Keith.

When she was no longer within earshot, Jeff said, "What the hell's wrong with you, man, talking to my sister like she's a worthless employee?"

"My wife is my business," Keith said through clenched teeth. "Now what the fuck did you come over here for?"

Jeff gave him a long, hard stare, his jaw muscles flexing.

Keith refused to be the first to look away. "I said, what the fuck did you—"

"The building inspector shut down the Landreau job," Jeff said flatly. "The house didn't pass the open wall inspection."

"And why the hell not?"

"Not enough bracing in the attic."

Keith threw a hand up. "Then add some goddamn bracing. Hell, even a moron can figure that out." He shook his head in disgust and walked over to his recliner.

"How am I supposed to add bracing when I can't even get a friggin' paint stirrer on credit at the lumberyard?"

"What are you talking about? I've got plenty of credit at Milo's." Keith settled into the chair and picked up the Ron Guidry autographed baseball that sat on the end table beside him. He worked his fingers around it, as he did almost every night, kneading, flexing, stretching.

"Not anymore. They're saying they haven't received a payment from you in over a month."

"Stanford Milo's a shit-faced liar!"

"Yeah?" Jeff folded his arms over his chest. "When was the last time you sent them a check?"

"Last week—ten days ago, fifteen at the most."

Jeff's frown deepened.

"What the hell you staring at me like that for?"

"You used to know the exact date you'd written a check *and* the check number."

Keith felt a trickle of sweat run down his bare chest. He wiped it away, then rubbed his palm clean on the chair's upholstery.

"Did you hear what I said?"

"Yeah, I heard you, goddammit!"

Jeff aimed a finger at him. "Look, if you don't start taking care of this business, you're going to lose it."

Keith narrowed his eyes. "Are you threatening me?"

"That isn't a threat, Keith, it's a fact, and it doesn't have anything to do with me. Your name's on the truck, the suppliers want to see you, so do the home owners. The work crews I can handle, but the rest of it you can't keep running away from."

"You don't—"

"I'm not finished." Jeff's stance widened. "Ever since you moved that house here from Crowley, you've let everything else go to shit. You don't even come out to the jobs anymore. I mean, look at you, you're falling apart."

Keith stood slowly, anger blurring his vision. "You done?"

A hint of fear flickered in Jeff's eyes, then he lifted his chin. "No, I'm not done. You need to quit treating Barbara like a dog. My sister's been nothing but good to you. Her and my whole family. We don't deserve your shit. You need to get some serious help."

Keith squeezed the baseball so tight his fingers burned. He walked up to Jeff until they stood nearly nose to nose. "Let me tell you something, Jeffrey Douglas Mabry. If it hadn't been for me taking over this company, your family would be on welfare right now. I'm sick of all of you taking and taking and taking, and do I ever hear a word of gratitude from any one of you? Hell no!" He leaned forward, forcing Jeff to step back. "And in case you haven't fucking noticed, I've been sick, or are you blind as well as greedy and stupid?" He jabbed a finger at the boil on his left cheek. "You want some of this? You want to see what it feels like to carry this around all day, to try sleeping with it at night?"

Jeff took another step back, a look of disgust crossing his face.

"Yeah, I didn't think so," Keith said, his voice picking up volume. "So you need to get the fuck out of here, Mabry. Get the fuck back to Milo's and tell him he made a mistake, get the fucking inspector to clear the open wall, just fucking handle the shit that needs to be handled!"

Jeff's nostrils flared and his eyes sparkled with fury. He opened his mouth, closed it, then did an about face and stormed out the front door.

Keith gave a little nod of satisfaction and tossed the baseball into the recliner. When he heard Jeff's pickup roar out of the driveway, he walked over to a glass gun cabinet, opened it, and pulled out a Bersa Thunder .380. The weight of the nickel-plated pistol felt good in his hand, the grip sure. He slid open a drawer just beneath the display and removed a single stack magazine, all seven 9mm rounds in place. Slapping the magazine into the pistol, Keith turned to head for the bay window and felt something hard and round, almost marble-sized, beneath his left foot. He groaned and leaned against the gun cabinet to examine the bottom of his foot. Just as he feared— another boil.

Like a wild animal suddenly waking to find itself trapped in a holding pen, Keith let out a howl of rage so long and loud the neighborhood dogs started barking.

It didn't take long for Barbara to appear, running pell-mell into the living room. "What in the name of—" Her eyes froze on the gun in his hand.

For the first time in weeks, Keith felt a laugh building in his belly. The look of perplexity and fear on her face was priceless. At last, he'd found something to shut her up.

"W-what's the gun for?" Barbara asked, visibly shaken.

He slowly tapped the barrel of the pistol across his left palm, making sure it was aimed directly at her.

"Please—put it away. Keith—put—"

"Didn't I tell you to leave me alone?" He kept his voice low and even.

Her fingers trembled as she fidgeted with the cameo pendant that dangled from a thin gold chain around her neck. "But—but I thought you were hurt. I wanted to help."

Keith chuckled and slowly shook his head. "You think I'm stupid, don't you?" He cupped a hand over the pistol's slide, then pulled, cocking it.

Barbara held out a hand, tears streaming down her face. "No, I never . . ."

He casually pointed the pistol at her, and she whimpered.

"Keith—"

"No, no," he said, waving the gun slightly. "No use denying anything. I know what you and that sniveling brother of yours are up to."

"I don't know what you're talking about."

The snot leaking from her nose infuriated him. He

drew the pistol's sight up to his right eye, targeting Barbara's chest.

"Keith!" She put a hand over her mouth and stepped back.

"That building inspector, how much did you have Jeff pay him to dump that inspection?"

She shook her head, sobbing.

"What about the lumberyard? What'd you do, give Stanford Milo a blowjob so he'd cut me off?"

"No!" Barbara stumbled forward, then, evidently realizing she was heading in the wrong direction, whirled about so quickly she fell to the floor.

Keith walked casually toward his wife, nodding. She inched backward like a crab. "Oh, yeah, I'd bet anything that's what you did." He aimed the pistol at her face. "Tell me! Tell me that's what you did!"

"No, I swear!"

"Tell me!"

Crying hysterically, Barbara's arms and legs scrambled for purchase as she tried to pull herself backward faster.

The sound of a lawn mower engine sputtering to life captured Keith's attention. *Who in the hell cut grass in February?* he thought, and hurried over to the bay window. The last thing he needed was someone eavesdropping.

Only a neighbor mulching leaves in his front yard.

Keith watched him for a moment, envious of the carefree manner in which he gathered leaves. Why couldn't his life be that simple? Nothing to worry about but keeping a tidy lawn. He frowned, remembering Barbara.

It didn't surprise Keith when he turned back and saw only an empty room. She was probably running out to find Jeff right now. No matter. He gently tapped the barrel of the pistol against his right thigh. They'd both get their due soon enough.

CHAPTER SIX

Matt rose slowly to his feet, not wanting to scare the girl away. Something about her reminded him of a fawn standing on wobbly legs, cautiously examining the new surroundings to which she'd been born. Despite her horrible wheezing and desperate gulps for air, she looked ready to bolt at any moment.

"Who the hell is that?" Percy asked, still standing beside the woman they'd just rescued from the bathroom.

"I saw her in front of the beauty salon this morning." Matt took a cautious step toward her.

"That's Tawana Batiste's cousin," Verneese said. She got up from the table where they'd been eating lunch. "The one I told you about. I don't know her name, though."

"Do you need help?" Matt asked the girl, then felt stupid. A blind man could see she needed help. "Do you need someone to take you to a doctor?"

"This one sure does," Percy said, indicating the

woman slumped in the chair beside him. "That bite's not looking good and neither is she." He took hold of one of her arms and signaled for Verneese. "Help me get her into the squad car."

"What about Tawana's cousin?" Verneese asked.

"I'll see about her," Matt said.

While Percy and Verneese helped the woman in the chair to her feet, Matt made his way to the girl, who was gasping even louder than before.

Her eyes, a striking swirl of green and dark brown, followed his every move, and as he neared her, they widened, seemingly more curious than frightened.

"C-co—ether?" she said, getting out more wheeze than words. She crept backward.

Not understanding her, Matt held up a hand. "I just want to help you. My name's Matt."

"—att," she said with an abrupt nod, then struggled to suck in another breath.

"I think you need a doctor."

"Look out," Percy said, coming up behind him. He and Verneese had the woman hanging between them with her arms over their shoulders.

Matt stepped aside and the girl reached out, as though she feared he'd disappear.

"—att." Her wheezing sharpened as Percy and Verneese stepped towards her. She snatched her hand back, then spun around and pushed through the door.

"Wait," Matt called after her, catching the door on the backswing. He held it open for Percy and Verneese. The girl didn't wait. She stumbled down the steps and staggered across the lawn toward the beauty shop.

"Go see about her, Matt," Verneese said as they hobbled off the porch. "I don't think she's going to make it all the way over there by herself."

He didn't think so, either. Sticking his head into the café, Matt apologized to the two remaining customers for the chaos, told them lunch was on him, then called for Lerna Mae to watch over the café until he got back. When he turned back around, he noticed Percy and Verneese had already loaded the woman into the cruiser and were in the middle of a heated argument. There was no sign of the girl.

"How'm I suppose to know if she had a purse?" Verneese yelled as she climbed into the cruiser.

Matt scanned the yard. "Did y'all see where she went?"

"Sonofa—get a paper bag or something back there, Verneese, that woman's hurling!" Percy bellowed.

Before Matt could get an answer from either of them, Verneese slammed her door shut and the light bar on top of the cruiser came to life, blinding him with twirling red and blue lights. His eyes were barely back into focus when the car sped out of the parking lot.

Puzzled and a bit worried over the girl's whereabouts, Matt headed for the beauty shop. He didn't think it possible for her to have made it over there so fast in her condition, but where else could she have gone?

Along the way, Matt peered down the grass alley

that ran between the café and Nestlers's Sewing Cottage. At the end of the alley stood a huge oak tree, its branches naked and drooping from winter and age. He saw a squirrel scamper up its trunk, but no sign of the girl. Fearing she might have taken to the street, Matt jogged over to the sidewalk that ran parallel to First Street and peered down both sides of the road. No girl, just a steady flow of after-lunch traffic. A horn bleeped at him from the westbound lane, and Matt sent a return wave to Mr. Sterner, who rumbled past in a rusty Taurus.

The only other place he could think to look besides the salon was the alley that ran between it and Nestler's.

No sign of her there, either.

Matt cornered the side of the salon, then jogged up the steps, listening to the laughter and chatter of women inside.

Feeling a little awkward, he opened the door and stuck his head into the shop. "Excuse me."

Every head turned in his direction. He spotted two of his regular customers: Sadie Babineaux, getting her hair curled by the attractive woman he'd seen on the front lawn this morning, and Maude Romero, who was having her nails polished by a large, stylish black woman. He didn't recognize the two teenage girls sitting on the rattan couch, and he didn't see the girl who'd left the café.

"Matt!" Maude fluttered a freshly manicured hand at him. "We were just talking about you this morning, you handsome devil."

"Oh, come on in here, sugar, we won't bite," Sadie

said, the top of her head rowed with pink curlers. "Will we, Laura?" She glanced up at the woman doing her hair and gave her a mischievous grin. "This is Laura Toups, Matt, and that's Tawana Batiste over there doing Maude's nails. They own the beauty shop."

Matt recognized Tawana's name from the tiff Verneese had had with Percy during lunch. He also remembered Verneese saying the girl was Tawana's cousin.

"Pleasure to meet you, ladies." He stepped inside. "Good to see you again, Miss Sadie, Miss Maude. Sorry to bother y'all, but I'm looking for a girl who left the café a little while ago. She was heading this way. She was pretty sick, so I thought I'd come by and make sure she'd made it here okay."

"Sick?" Maude frowned. "Sadie and I've been here since ten. We haven't seen any sick girl come into the shop."

"What did she look like?" Laura asked.

Although her question was brief, it was enough for Matt to pick up the soft timbre of her voice. "She looked around twenty-two, twenty-three years old, wearing jeans, a plain blue sweatshirt, and she had a lot of long braids that were sort of mussed up."

"Hold on a minute." Tawana got to her feet, her brow furrowed. "You talkin' about Moweez?"

"She never told me her name."

"Mo?" Tawana called, looking toward the open entryway at the back of the shop. She rounded the manicure table.

"Isn't she in the bathroom?" Laura asked.

"Last I saw." Tawana headed toward the back.

Laura absently handed Sadie a curler, then followed Tawana. "It couldn't have been Mo. We'd have seen her leave."

"But what about the back door?" Sadie scooted off the hydraulic chair and quickly fell into step behind Laura. "Couldn't she have gotten out that way?"

Maude, evidently not wishing to be left behind, popped up out of her chair and took off after Sadie. "Yeah, what about the back?"

Matt followed the parade, glancing back at the two teens, who stood with craned necks for a better view.

They crossed an entryway that led into a kitchenette. A metal dinette table sat in the middle of the room with four accompanying chairs. Scattered across the top of the table were colored pencils, a spiral-bound sketch pad, salt and pepper shakers in the shape of roosters, an open bottle of ketchup, and a can of Vidal Sassoon hairspray. Against the back wall was the door Matt assumed to be the one in question. To the left of the door stood a stacked washer dryer combo, a narrow laundry table, and a mini fridge. A long countertop with a sink hugged the west wall, and a few feet past it was the entrance to a stairwell. The opposite side of the room held only a wooden coatrack and a door with a silver stick-on sign that read RESTROOM. Tawana knocked on it.

"You in there, Mo?"

Maude and Sadie huddled closer to Tawana, listening.

Laura looked at Matt. "You said she was sick—what was wrong with her?"

With her standing so close, Matt saw worry darken her amber eyes, making them even more beautiful. Forcing his attention back to Tawana, he stuck a hand in one of his jeans' pockets. "Looked like a bad case of asthma."

"Moweez has a history of asthma," Laura said, her voice filled with concern. "But it's been a long time since she's had an attack."

Tawana knocked again, harder this time. "Mo!" She pressed an ear to the door. Sadie did the same.

"I heard something!" Sadie's face brightened. "A whistle—a faint whistle."

"Okay, y'all back up." Tawana spread her arms out wide. "None of y'all need to be seein' Mo's yahoo if she's still on the commode." She waited until everyone had gathered near the table before opening the door, and then only wide enough for her to slip through.

Tawana's gasp was the only acknowledgment they needed to know Moweez had been found. "Laura, get her inhaler! Top dresser drawer!"

Without pause, Laura bounded for the stairwell.

"Is she okay?" Sadie asked, wringing her hands. The pink curlers on top of her head no longer sat in neat rows. They hung askew, threatening to fall out.

"I need a washrag," Tawana called. "Look in the dryer."

Looking relieved at having something to do, Sadie took off for the dryer.

Maude pulled a chair out from under the table and sat, her face flushed. She grabbed the sketch pad from the table and fanned herself with it. "You know my uncle had asthma. Had to carry a puffer with him everywhere he went."

Matt nodded, only half-listening. He heard water running in the bathroom, then the familiar sound of wheezing.

"Got one!" Sadie said, and hurried back to the bathroom, waving a white washcloth. She stuck the cloth through the opening of the door while looking the other way.

Seconds later, Laura came running down the stairs, an asthma inhaler in each hand. Before she reached the bathroom, the door swung open, and Tawana walked out, an arm around the girl Matt had seen at the café. She looked worse than she had earlier. Her face had the appearance of a mannequin's, waxen and pale, except for her lips, which were almost as blue as her sweatshirt. Her head hung low, chin nearly touching her chest. Her braids swayed like coiled curtains on either side of her face. Had it not been for the voluntary movement of her feet, Matt would have thought the girl unconscious.

"Oh, you poor dear, look at you!" Maude cried, getting to her feet. "Come, sit." She turned the chair around so it faced Moweez.

"Do you want me to call an ambulance," Matt asked as Tawana settled her cousin into the chair.

Without answering and with an intensity that would have matched any operating surgeon's, Tawana took one of the inhalers from Laura and put it between the girl's lips. She depressed it once, and the girl sucked in a short breath.

"I think Matt's right," Sadie said, hovering over

Tawana. "Don't you think we should call an ambulance?"

"We could call for you," a young voice said from behind them. The two teens who'd been sitting on the couch now stood side by side in the entryway of the kitchenette.

"No ambulance," Tawana said firmly. "She'll be fine, won't you, Mo?" She depressed the inhaler again, and this time the girl's intake sounded much stronger.

Everyone stood silent for some time, watching Moweez's shoulders shudder as she drew in one agonizing breath after another. From somewhere in the front of the salon, a phone rang, and Laura started.

"I could get that for you if you want, Miss Laura," one of the teens said.

Laura gave her a grateful smile. "Thanks, Alisha. Just get a name and number. Tell them I'll call back later."

Both girls took off for the phone, leaving the rest of them watching Moweez as though she were a piece of abstract art.

Tawana was on her knees next to her cousin, petting one of her hands. "Better?"

Moweez gave the slightest nod, then yawned expansively.

Everyone let out a collective sigh, and Sadie clapped softly.

Tawana got to her feet and muttered, "Thank you, Jesus."

"Oh, you're right about that," Maude said. "And thank Matt because—"

"That's right," Sadie said. "If he hadn't come in here when he did, we might not have found her in time."

At the sound of his name, Moweez sat up straighter in her chair, and looked about. When she spotted Matt, she smiled. "—att."

"She knows you?" Laura asked.

"I told her my name at the café. I guess she remembered."

Tawana put a hand on her hip. "Yeah, but I still can't figure how Mo got over—"

"Miss Laura?" The teens were back at the entryway, fidgeting and bright-eyed. Alisha looked ready to burst with news. "Patricia Guillory called."

"Thanks for getting that," Laura said. "I'm sorry you two have had to wait so long, but I'll phone your mom—"

"She canceled her appointment," Alisha blurted. "Said there was too much drama over here, and she was going to Lafayette to get her hair done."

"What?" Tawana said so loudly the teens jumped. "What's she talkin' about, drama?"

Alisha chewed her bottom lip and glanced at her friend. "She—uh—well, she said something about her niece getting bit by a snake at the Tin Cup, then the police went over there, and then—well, then all those dead birds. She said there was probably a disease or something around here."

"Oh, no she didn't!" Tawana's nostrils flared.

"A snake?" Sadie said, putting a hand to her cheek. "In—in the café?"

"No, no," Matt said. "That's not what bit—"

"Was it poisonous?" Maude asked. "A water moccasin or—"

"There was no snake." Matt quickly gave them a rundown of what happened, starting with the woman in the bathroom and ending with his arrival at the salon.

As soon as he finished, Moweez let out a loud yawn, then held out a hand to Tawana. "Tired," she said, her eyelids drooping to half-mast.

"That poor woman." Maude shook her head. "She must have been scared to death in that bathroom."

"Any idea what bit her?" Sadie asked.

"Looked like a spider bite," Matt said.

"Tired!" Moweez's eyes were closed, and she waggled her fingers until Tawana took her hand.

"You see what I was tellin' you this mornin'?" Tawana said to Laura. "All the busybodies in this town worry about is fresh gossip, even if it ain't the truth." She helped Moweez to her feet. "I've got a mind to stick a few of them dead birds up Patricia's—"

"Wana," Laura warned, throwing a glance at the teens who were snickering.

Matt hid a grin.

"Yeah, yeah, okay." Tawana led Moweez to the stairs. "But that blabbermouth better stop talkin' trash about us or it's gonna get ugly 'tween me and her." She looked over at Maude. "Miss Maude, I'm gonna bring Mo upstairs for a nap, but I'll be right back down to finish your manicure—no charge." With that, she led Moweez up the stairs.

Laura nodded. "Same with your hair, Miss Sadie, and you too, girls, since you've been so patient."

"Oh, no," Maude said, absently tucking the sketch pad under an arm. She ticked a finger at her. "I don't want to hear another word about us not paying. None of this has been a bother at all."

"That's right," Sadie added. "Not another word. Now y'all go ahead and take care of whatever you need to, and we'll be waiting out front." She headed out of the kitchenette, motioning for Maude and the teens to follow.

"Be right there," Maude said. "I've got to make a stop in the little girl's room first." She grinned sheepishly at Matt. "All the excitement, you know."

Once everyone had cleared out, Laura said to Matt, "I'm sorry if Moweez caused problems for you at the café."

"She didn't cause me any problems. If anything, we probably caused problems for her. I think all the commotion at the café scared her and probably made her asthma attack worse."

"I still can't figure out how she got past us without anyone noticing. And why the café? Usually Mo won't go anywhere without one of us."

"What about that door?" Matt nodded past her. "Couldn't she have gotten out that way?

Laura shook her head, setting her thick ponytail into motion. She walked over to the backdoor and reached for the knob. "It has a keyed dead bolt that I keep locked almost all the time."

"Maybe she got hold of the key."

"Even if she had, she wouldn't have used it. Mo won't even touch a regular knob lock."

"Why's that?"

"I don't know. I never . . ." The backdoor opened a crack when she tested the knob. Laura stood motionless for a moment, then looked back at him, her eyes worried. "I—I checked this myself last night. It was locked. And I didn't unlock it this morning."

"What about Tawana? She could've—"

"Oh, Lord!" A shout rang out from inside the bathroom, and before Matt or Laura had time to react, the door flew open and Maude stumbled out. The look of horror on her face sent a rush of adrenaline straight to Matt's heart. "Hurry!" Maude cried. "It's everywhere!"

Matt and Laura took off for the bathroom at the same time. He wanted to hold her back, to keep Laura safe until he had time to investigate, but she wound up beating him to the doorway.

"Aw, geez," Laura said, then leaned over and hiked up her linen pants at the knees.

Matt was never so glad to see water gushing over a toilet bowl in his life. He gently took hold of Laura's arm just as she lifted a foot to step into the rising tide.

"I'll get it." He squeezed past her before she could object. The water hadn't reached the threshold yet, but it wasn't far away. Two more steps into the bathroom and water crested over his sneakers. Matt went for the control valve behind the bowl and shut it off. "Got a mop or towels?"

"Mop's upstairs," Laura said, already turning away, "but I've got plenty towels in the dryer down here."

"Oh, I'm so embarrassed and so sorry," Maude said. "After I flushed and saw the water going up and up, I jiggled the handle, but it wouldn't shut off."

"No need to be embarrassed," Matt said. "It's happened to all of us at one time or another."

"I can clean that up," Laura said, returning with four towels.

"No need for both of us to have wet feet." He grinned.

She returned his smile and handed him the towels. "Thanks."

Matt formed a fort around the water with the plush towels, then slowly worked them toward the toilet. He heard Laura escorting Maude to the front of the salon, all the while assuring the woman she had nothing to apologize for. He liked the gentle way Laura spoke to Maude, comforted her. Most of the women he knew her age, which he guessed to be around thirty, were impatient with anyone who'd collected a few years. They either rushed around them or ignored them altogether.

"Need any help? More towels?"

Matt glanced back, surprised to see Laura back so soon. Pleasantly surprised. "I think I've just about got it all." He gathered up one of the soaked towels. His intent was to do a fast lift, then dump the towel into the lavatory so he could wring it out, but he only got as far as the lift. That's when he spotted the sketchpad Maude had carried around earlier lying on the lavatory counter. He didn't want to get it wet.

Evidently spotting the pad at the same time, Laura scooped it up. "I forgot Maude even had this," she said with a nervous laugh.

Matt dumped the towel into the sink. "Are you an

artist?" He turned on the faucet, quickly rinsed his hands, then shut if off.

"I can't even draw a straight line. Moweez is the artist."

"Really?" Even in the little time he'd spent with Moweez, Matt had suspected she was mentally challenged, but had no idea to what degree. "Do you think she'd mind if I peeked at her work?" He wiped his hands dry on his jeans.

"I—uh . . ." Laura pursed her lips.

"It's okay if you'd rather I didn't."

"No—no, here." She handed the pad to him. "I'm sure Mo won't mind." Laura folded her arms across her chest. She appeared anxious, as though she expected something to jump out when he flipped it open.

"You sure?"

"Hey, for a man willing to clean up a toilet disaster, it's the least I can do," Laura said a little too cheerfully.

Feeling a bit awkward now, Matt flipped open the pad, then felt his mouth drop open.

Every exceptionally drawn detail seemed to capture his eye all at once—the beauty shop with its barren azalea bushes, wicker chairs on the porch, and little wooden sign; Nestler's Sewing Cottage beside it, captured to perfection, even down to the speckles of greenish-black fungus on the clapboard's fascia board; and the Tin Cup, with Percy's squad car parked in front. Stranger still were the faint, thin silver lines superimposed over most of the scene. They swooped and dashed, line upon line, circle upon circle, like a giant spider web connecting the salon to the café. Just above the web, in the upper left-hand corner, was a half-empty hourglass, a trickle of sand drawn trailing down its narrow middle.

As much as he appreciated the significant display of talent, the sketch left Matt feeling apprehensive, even a bit fearful, but of what he wasn't sure. It was as if he were peering into a window, spying on something or someone he shouldn't.

He glanced up at Laura, turning the pad so the drawing faced her. "Have you seen this drawing?"

She let out a small gasp, then cupped a hand over her mouth. He read disbelief in her eyes as they scanned the scene again and again. With a slow shake of her head, Laura inched closer, seemingly mesmerized. She took her hand from her mouth, gingerly touched the hourglass with the tip of a trembling finger, then trailed that finger lightly across the drawing to one of the café's second-story windows. "D-do you know him?" she asked without looking up.

Puzzled by her question, Matt turned the sketch pad back around and peered closely at the indicated spot. He gaped, not believing he'd missed such a critical detail—that face—that small, frightened face nearly hidden behind the eyelet curtains.

"Do you?" she asked again.

Matt nodded reluctantly, fearing his answer would give substance to this impossibility. "He's my son."

CHAPTER SEVEN

Thunder rumbled in the distance, promising rain. Seconds later, a crisp breeze pushed past the living room curtains and carried in the earthy scent of dormant sugarcane fields and memories of winters long gone.

Leaning back in his chair, Matt closed his eyes and brought to mind the old farmhouse porch, where he used to sit with his daddy in the evenings, drinking hot cocoa and listening to the whine of a thousand insects in the dark. Completing that circle of peace were the sounds coming from inside the house, the clatter of supper dishes being washed and put away, and Mama humming a George Jones tune.

If life had only stayed that simple.

Opening his eyes, Matt let out a sigh and checked his watch. Nearly midnight. Except for dinner with his son, the afternoon and evening had gone by in one hazy blob. He hadn't been able to get his mind off Moweez's drawings.

After he'd told Laura that the face drawn in the upstairs window looked exactly like his Seth's, she'd shown him another one of Moweez's drawings. The one with the dead black birds. Same exquisite style, same attention to detail. But when he'd flipped back and forth, comparing one sketch to the other, he'd gotten a sense he was viewing some sort of storyboard yet to be finished.

How had Moweez known about the birds? Coincidence? One dead bird, maybe. But not over a hundred. And how did she manage to sketch Seth's face so perfectly when she'd never met him? How did she know Percy's squad car would be parked in front of the café earlier today? And the emptying hourglass—what did it signify? Time was running out? If so, for what? Or worse, for whom?

Laura had told him she'd questioned Moweez about the first sketch, but said the girl's answer hadn't made any sense. They made plans to talk to her together around three that afternoon, after the café closed for the day and he had Seth settled in from school, but the plan never materialized. Moweez refused to get out of bed, claiming, "tired," every time Laura asked, so they'd had little choice but to hold their questions until tomorrow.

Matt rubbed his face with his hands. His cluttered brain had had enough for today. He sat up just as Seth shuffled into the living room.

"Hey, champ, what're you doing up so late?"

Droopy-eyed, Seth yawned and scratched the top of his head. The waistband of his Spiderman pajamas slipped dangerously low on his hips. "I can't sleep 'cause they're talking too loud."

"Who?" Matt patted an arm on the overstuffed chair, signaling him closer.

Seth stumbled over to him and flopped against the chair. "Them boys."

Matt looped an arm around his son's shoulder and kissed him on the head. "I think you were dreaming, buddy."

"Uh-uh, I wasn't dreaming."

"No?" Matt grinned. "Then what were they talking about?"

Seth shrugged and yawned again. He snuggled closer to Matt and mumbled, "Can I have some milk?"

"Sure. Want me to get it?"

Seth nodded but didn't pull away.

Matt waited, his chin nestled in Seth's tousled brown hair. To feel his son safe and warm filled him with immeasurable peace. He treasured these moments. They were becoming fewer as Seth grew older.

Figuring the milk had already been forgotten, Matt asked quietly, "Want me to go tuck you back into bed?"

Stirring against him, Seth shook his head. "I'm a big guy now. You don't tuck in big guys."

"Oh, that's right. Sorry."

Tugging his pajama bottoms up with one hand, Seth righted himself and headed out of the living room. "Night, Dad."

"Night." Matt watched him trudge out of sight before getting up to close the living room window.

He had just slid the window latch into place when he heard Seth shuffling back into the room.

"Dad?"

"Yeah?"

"Um . . . can you come tuck me in?"

Grinning, Matt walked Seth to his bedroom.

A night-light glowed near the foot of his twin bed, illuminating evidence that a little boy did indeed sleep here. The Spiderman comforter, the coloring books and miniature race cars strewn across the dresser, the stick horse lying across a Hot Wheels track on the floor, and sneakers barely longer than Matt's hand sitting on top of a beanbag chair. All boy, all little boy. The only thing that didn't seem to fit in the room was the blue eyelet curtains hanging in the window. Matt never cared for them, but they'd been Lerna Mae's idea, and since Seth didn't seem to care one way or the other, Matt hadn't had the heart to tell her no.

He waited until Seth slipped under the sheets, then he tucked the comforter around him and sat on the edge of the bed.

"Can you close the closet door before you leave?" Seth asked.

"Yep. Any particular reason?"

Seth turned on his side and pulled his pillow in close. "Maybe I won't hear those boys so loud if the door's closed."

Matt glanced over his shoulder toward the open closet. "They talk in there?"

"Uh-huh."

"Any idea why?"

Seth yawned, then closed his eyes. " 'Cause they don't want their mama to hear what they're saying."

"Are they saying bad things?"

Seth frowned, burrowing deeper into his pillow. "I don't think so."

Matt smoothed a few strands of hair away from his forehead. "Do you hear them now?"

"Uh-uh. Do you?"

Biting back a grin, Matt leaned over and kissed him on the cheek. "Uh-uh."

He sat for a while, watching Seth's breathing grow steady and deep, and wondered, not for the first time, how any mother could leave such a son. His ex-wife had walked out on them three years ago, leaving only a note to tell him she was headed for Europe to "find" herself. The divorce papers came soon after. It wasn't long before Matt discovered she hadn't traveled to Europe alone. A twenty-seven-year-old yoga instructor had accompanied her. In three years, she never once called to check on their son. In three years, Matt never once tried to find her.

He got up from the bed and went over to the closet. He peered inside and with a quiet chuckle whispered to the tangle of hanging clothes, sports balls, and dirty socks, "Y'all quit making so much noise in there." Then he closed the closet door and left the room, leaving the bedroom door slightly ajar.

Yawning himself now, Matt went into the living room and picked up an empty Coke can from the coffee table. He double-checked the windows to make sure they were locked, then headed for the light switch. He was about to flip it off when he heard sounds coming from the kitchen. A soft patter of footsteps, then rustling noises, like groceries being removed from a plastic sack.

"Seth?" Matt walked toward the kitchen. "If you don't get some sleep, son, you're going to be one worn out puppy at school tomorrow."

But Seth wasn't in the kitchen. No one was.

Puzzled, Matt scanned the room, listening. No more footsteps or rustling sounds. Nothing seemed out of place—dishes still in the drain board, a fruit bowl with one overripe banana in it on the counter, the open box of Ding-Dongs he'd left on the kitchen table a couple of hours ago. He reached over and tagged the light switch on the wall beside him. The kitchen went black. He stood in the gloom a moment longer but still heard nothing.

"Probably a damn mouse," he muttered, and made a mental note to set a couple of traps in the morning.

After switching off the lights in the living room, Matt went to his bedroom, set the alarm clock for five A.M., then stripped down to his boxers. Even in winter, he felt restricted and overheated in pajamas. He climbed into bed, pulled the covers up to his chin, then stuck a foot out from under the blanket.

When he closed his eyes, Laura's face immediately came to mind. Matt studied it at leisure, forcing away thoughts of Moweez and her drawings. He couldn't deny his attraction to Laura Toups. Not only to her natural, physical beauty, but to her intelligence and wit. He liked that she had her own mind, choosing to go about life the way she wanted despite what other people might think. That was no more evident than in her relationship with Tawana and Moweez. All of these qualities combined sparked a need in Matt to learn more about her. And he hadn't felt that kind of spark in a very long time.

The weight of sleep began to pull on his body and he allowed it to take him. In some barely conscious part of his brain, he heard the swish of tires as a car or truck rolled down First Street—the ice maker in the kitchen, dropping ice into its bucket—the thrum of the central heating unit as it kicked on—creaking as the apartment settled in for the night. More creaking . . . creaking . . . footsteps?

Matt's eyes flew open and he sat up in bed. The creaking continued, like someone slowly pacing the length of the hallway. But the footfalls, if they were footfalls, sounded too heavy to be Seth's. Frowning, he got out of bed, threw on his jeans, and crept into the hall to investigate.

The light he normally left on in the bathroom at night illuminated the hall, but he saw nothing down the corridor except the oak plank floors. Seth's bedroom door was still ajar, and he went over to peek inside.

Seth lay on his stomach now, one foot sticking out from under the comforter. The stick horse still rested across the Hot Wheels track, and the closet door was still shut. It wasn't until Matt backed out of the room that he realized the creaking sounds had stopped.

He stood in the hall, listening for noises in other areas of the apartment. All he heard was a faint whistle of wind. The storm was drawing closer. Maybe that's what had the apartment creaking more than usual. As logical as that explanation sounded to

Matt's brain, it didn't keep anxiety from building in his chest. He stuck his head into Seth's bedroom once more. Nothing had changed.

Matt reluctantly padded back into his bedroom. He started to remove his jeans again, then changed his mind. He'd feel too naked, too exposed with this apprehension still bubbling inside him. So he sat on the bed, his back against the headboard, and watched the erratic strobes of distant lightning through the bedroom window. A gust of wind pressed against the pane, and its howl sent a shiver through him. Such a mournful, lonely sound, a cry for the lost and forsaken. Without warning, its voice slipped behind the walls that surrounded Matt's heart and squeezed. He closed his eyes against the ache.

"—att!—att!"

Matt sat bolt upright with a gasp, his heart slamming against his chest. It sounded like Moweez had shouted in his ear. He groped for the lamp on the nightstand, found it and switched it on. The glaring light only confirmed what he already knew. Moweez wasn't anywhere in the room. Of course she wasn't. How could she? Somehow he must have drifted off to sleep, dreamed it—either that or his subconscious had recalled her voice all too vividly. Matt got out of bed, too much adrenaline pumping through him now for sleep to be possible.

The wood floor felt colder beneath his feet than it had earlier, and the chill quickly spread through his body and speckled his skin with gooseflesh. Hoping the heater hadn't gone on the fritz, Matt went over to the dresser and pulled a T-shirt out of the top drawer.

He slipped it on, then went to check the thermostat in the hall.

It read seventy-two degrees. It felt like fifty-two.

Matt tapped on the thermostat cover with a knuckle, then squinted at the gauge. The needle hadn't moved. Still seventy-two. He pushed the small plastic lever beneath the cover to seventy-five, then listened for the hum of the heater. He heard a click. Another click. Then a faint, steady hiss, like air leaking from a tire.

Cocking his head, he tried to get a bead on the sound's origin.

The ceiling? No—his bedroom?

Matt closed his eyes, concentrating. He backed up a few steps. It did sound louder the closer he got to his room. What the hell was that?

"Dad."

Matt started and opened his eyes, expecting to see Seth standing beside him. He wasn't.

"Dad!" Seth sounded frustrated now, like he needed something done but couldn't manage it himself.

Matt headed for his room.

The first thing he saw when he pushed the bedroom door open was an empty bed.

"He won't wake up. None of them will wake up."

"What?" Matt turned to see Seth standing near the window, peering out. Something in the rigidity of his son's stance gave him pause. He approached him slowly. "Seth?"

"What am I supposed to do?"

The question sounded contemplative, as though Seth were thinking out loud. Was he sleepwalking?

"I tried and I tried but it won't turn off," Seth said, his voice threatening tears. Suddenly, he sidestepped to the right, staying close to the wall, then curled the fingers of his right hand around something he evidently saw attached to the wall and began to turn his hand counterclockwise. He grew more agitated with each turn.

Matt instinctively reached out to touch him, then pulled his hand back. Seth had never sleepwalked before, so he wasn't sure about what to do. Would he harm him by waking him? Hadn't he read somewhere or seen on a talk show that you should never wake a sleepwalker?

Seth gasped and pulled his curled fingers towards his chest, like he was afraid to drop something. "It broke," he said, his voice filled with disbelief. He glanced over his shoulder right at Matt, but his eyes, terrified, seemed to look right through him. "Dad!"

The look on his son's face made Matt's heart lurch. He bit his tongue to keep from calling out and waking him. He wanted more than anything to grab Seth, yank him away from the horrible dream, but fear for his safety kept Matt frozen in place. He kept reminding himself it was only a dream, and that Seth was safe as long as he was here, watching over him.

Seth turned away. "He won't wake up, and it broke," he said quietly. "What am I supposed to do now?" He sidestepped back to the window, his hand still curled to his chest. When he reached the window, he stood on tiptoe to peer out, then let out another gasp. "A witch!" He quickly ducked behind the eyelet curtain.

Matt stepped behind him and looked out the window. He saw the roof of the sewing cottage, the darkened windows of the apartment above the Beauty Box, part of First Street bathed in soft yellow light from a street lamp, and something that nearly stopped his heart.

In the bottom right-hand corner of the window, Matt caught Seth's reflection as he peaked out from behind the curtain. That image looked exactly like the one he'd seen in Moweez's drawing.

"Big nose, crooked nose," Seth said breathlessly, then turned away from the window and calmly walked over to his bed.

Matt watched him, still too dumbstruck to move.

"I won't let her see me," Seth mumbled. "The witch won't see me." He climbed into bed and curled himself into a tight ball, his hands mated fist to fist in front of his face. After a moment or two, his little body began to relax, and his breathing took on the rhythm of deep sleep.

Feeling like his world had suddenly lost all sense of normalcy and reason, Matt went over to his son and did the one thing he knew for sure was normal. He covered him. Seth mumbled and rolled over on his back, spreading his arms out wide. Something fell out of his right hand and clattered to the floor. Matt saw it glinting near the head of the bed and leaned over to pick it up. No sooner did his fingertips touch it than his vision blurred and a wave of vertigo dropped him to his hands and knees.

Disoriented and bewildered, Matt groaned and slowly lifted his head. A metal valve lever glinted back up at him.

CHAPTER EIGHT

Laura had a difficult time keeping her mind on work. Too many worries vied for her attention. It was barely noon, and three people had already called to cancel their afternoon appointments. Tawana, who'd been on edge ever since Laura had shown her Moweez's latest sketch last night, had been testy and irritable all morning. Not that she blamed her. Aside from the drawing, which Tawana refused to talk about, they were both worried about Moweez. Her breathing was much better than it had been last night, but the girl still refused to get out of bed.

"You all done, Shakita," Tawana said to the young black woman sitting at her manicure table.

"Oh, girl, look how they look good." Shakita held her hands out, admiring her four-inch, purple and gold striped fingernails. "I'm gonna be stylin' at that zydeco dance tonight."

"Yeah, well, you just better be careful not to poke

somebody's eye out with those nasty things," Tawana said.

"Why you say they nasty?"

Tawana got to her feet and went over to the register. " 'Cause I know what gets caught up in them nails after you go to the bathroom and have to clean yourself."

Laura grimaced, expecting a catfight to start.

"Uh-uh, not me," Shakita said. "I'm always careful when I go. Gotta keep them nails lookin' good for my man, Tyree. He likes 'em long and colorful like this. Says they make him wanna do . . ." She glanced over at Laura, who was sweeping up hair from around her workstation, and winked. "You know—do the nasty."

Tawana scowled. "Girl, gimme my eight dollars and go on about your business. Nobody wants to hear about you playin' the nasty."

Shakita handed her a ten-dollar bill. "What you so grouchy for?"

"I ain't grouchy."

Blowing out a raspberry, Shakita took her change from Tawana and left the shop.

"That damn hussy didn't even leave me a tip," Tawana grumbled.

Laura dumped the hair she'd gathered in a dust-pan into the trash. "You blame her after what you said about her fingernails?"

"I just told her the truth."

"And she told you the truth."

"About what?"

"You being grouchy." Laura offered her a little smile.

Tawana tsked and headed for the kitchenette. "We got any bologna in this damn place?"

Laura followed her. "I think there's some in the fridge upstairs." She put the dustpan and broom in the utility closet, then pulled a chair away from the table and sat. "You want to talk about it?"

"About the bologna?" Tawana opened the fridge and took out a diet soda. She wiggled it at Laura. "You want one?"

"No, and you know I didn't mean the bologna."

Tawana closed the fridge, popped the tab on the soda can, then downed half the drink in a couple of gulps.

"Well?"

"What's to talk about? Mo won't get out of bed." Tawana went to the table and sat across from her. She hunched her shoulders and stared at the soda can, tapping the side of it absently with a blunt fingernail.

"There's something else bothering you, though. I can feel it."

Tawana shot her a look. "What you mean, you can feel it? You psychic now?"

"No, I'm not psychic now," Laura snapped back. "But I've known you long enough to know when there's a burr stuck up your butt. So what is it? Mo's drawings?"

Tawana leaned back in the chair and folded her arms under her large breasts. "Don't you think I got bigger problems to worry about than some dumb-ass picture? We was doin' so good, but now customers are startin' to bail on us. How we gonna pay the bills if this keeps up? And how'm I gonna pay for a doctor if Mo needs to go to one, huh? We don't even have insurance. What we gonna do if everything we worked so hard for just gets flushed down a goddamn toilet? Where we gonna go?" She dropped her head and sniffled.

Laura frowned. It wasn't like Tawana to take the pessimistic side of an issue. She got up, moved to a chair closer to Tawana, and put a reassuring hand on her friend's arm. "Hey," she said, then waited until Tawana looked at her. When she did, Laura saw a tear sliding down her right cheek. "Look, we're a team now, remember? Family. Me and you. Me, you, and Moweez. We'll figure out something if Mo needs to see a doctor. And nothing's going to get flushed down any toilet. You'll see. Once the rumors die down, those customers will come back and—"

"But what if they ain't rumors?" Tawana blurted, swiping tears away. "What if there *is* something bad here?"

"What are you talking about?"

Tawana turned away and stared at the soda can.

A chill crept across the back of Laura's neck. She didn't like the feel of this silence. It had bad news written all over it. "Wana?"

"Should've told you last night," Tawana said, still staring at the can, "After you showed me Mo's other drawing."

"Told me what?"

Tawana propped her elbows on the table and weaved her fingers together, as though preparing to pray. She turned slowly toward her. The deadpan look in her eyes sent another chill through Laura, this one rappelling down her spine. "Mo's done this before," Tawana said quietly.

"You mean draw?"

She didn't answer.

"But that's nothing new," Laura said, perplexed. "Mo's always drawing."

Tawana sighed heavily and pushed away from the table. "I'm gonna have to show you, 'cause it's too hard to explain." She got to her feet. "It's upstairs in my room."

"Want me to go with you?"

"No, I'll bring it down." Tawana glanced toward the stairwell like a clubfooted climber about to take on Everest. "You stay, in case we get a walk-in."

When Tawana disappeared up the stairs, Laura left the table in search of something to do with her hands, anything mundane to keep her nerves from frazzling. She'd never seen Tawana look so defeated, so resigned before. And if it had anything to do with Moweez's drawings . . .

Refusing to consider anything past that thought, Laura went to the dryer and opened it. She'd deal with whatever she had to when it got dropped in her lap. Until then, there were towels to fold. She gathered an armful from the dryer and set them on the narrow laundry table. After pulling a towel from the jumbled pile, she folded it and let her mind wander over to Matt. He'd been so patient yesterday— dealing with Moweez's asthma attack in the café, the overflowing toilet, coming back to the salon later only to have Mo refuse to get out of bed and talk to them. He hadn't even looked perturbed over that. Most of the men Laura knew or had known, including her father, wouldn't have come to the salon to see about Mo in the first place, much less clean up toilet water. She wasn't used to that kind of chivalry. The men she'd dated had made vain attempts at it from time to time, but usually after the third or fourth date their egos came bursting out of whatever little box they'd stuffed them in and ruined everything.

Hearing footsteps descend the stairs, Laura's pulse quickened. She hurriedly folded the last towel and stuck it on an overhead shelf with the rest of them.

"Took me a while to find it," Tawana said when Laura turned to her. Holding a King Edwards cigar box, she sat down at the table, then placed the box on her lap. "Couldn't remember where I put it after we moved."

Laura joined her at the table, pulling her chair up close. "Mo doing okay?"

"Still sleeping."

Laura nodded, then motioned to the cigar box. "So what's this?"

"Some of Nana's stuff," Tawana said, her voice sad and low. "After she died, I took a couple things from her room that reminded me of her." She gingerly opened the lid to the box, and pain flickered across her face, the loss of her grandmother still too fresh.

"You sure you want to do this?" Laura asked.

Ignoring the question, Tawana removed a small pocketknife from the box and showed it to her. "See this? Nana use to clean her fingernails with it." She smiled softly. "She never would let me do her nails. Said I pinched her."

Laura watched Tawana place the pocketknife gently on the table. She didn't understand what any

105

of this had to do with Moweez's drawings, but she remained silent, allowing Tawana time to wade through her memories.

"These were Nana's glasses." Tawana held up a pair of black cat-eye glasses that had electrical tape wrapped around one arm. "She always said she didn't want to be buried with them 'cause they made her look ugly. Wouldn't spend the money to have 'em fixed, either." She put the glasses beside the pocketknife, then removed a miniature plastic statue of the Blessed Virgin. Tawana chuckled. "Nana used to put this on the dash of my car whenever I had to drive her somewhere. Guess she didn't think I was too good of a driver."

Laura smiled. "Smart lady."

Tawana chuckled again, a short, heavy-hearted sound. "Yeah, she was."

After placing the Virgin beside the other objects on the table, Tawana removed four sheets of tri-folded paper from the cigar box. Three were cream colored, one white and official looking. She put the white one on the table without opening it. "Bill of sale for Nana's little shotgun house," she said without looking up. Then she unfolded one of the cream colored sheets and handed it to Laura. "This—this was the first one."

Laura took it from her, recognizing Moweez's artwork right away. The picture was of a thin, elderly black woman lying on a hospital bed. Her eyes were closed, her face overrun with wrinkles, and the brilliant white of her hair appeared to glow on the page. Although Laura had only met her twice, there was no mistaking Nana. The room surrounding her had been drawn out of focus so the only things clearly visible were Nana, the hospital bed, the miniature Blessed Virgin statue standing on a nightstand beside the bed, and an hourglass, three quarters full and dangling in midair over the head of the bed. Laura's mouth went dry.

"Mo drew that a week before Nana took sick," Tawana said. She handed her a second sheet of paper. "She drew this one a couple of days before the doctors put Nana on the tubes."

Nana, dressed in a hospital gown and curled in a fetal position on top of a bed in a stark white room. Plastic tubes of varying thicknesses and lengths snaked around her shriveled body. Some were attached to her arms, others to her mouth and nose. This time the hourglass hovered in the top right-hand corner of the drawing, half empty.

Laura looked up at Tawana, the paper rustling in her trembling hands. "Moweez knew."

Tawana nodded and handed her the last sheet. "I found this one the day before Nana died."

Laura sensed the contents of the drawing even before she looked at it.

Nana lay in a pink shaded casket lined with rose-colored satin. She wore a simple brown shift that looked far too big for her, and the plush pillow she rested upon seemed to swallow most of her gaunt face. Her gnarled hands lay in repose, one atop the other, over her stomach. The hourglass sat on the closed bottom lid of the casket, empty.

"Mo knew what the casket would look like, even

down to the doodads I had them put on the corners."
Tawana pointed to the Last Supper replicas attached
to the front corners of the casket. Then she sat back
and clutched the cigar box, her face drained.

"How did she know?" Laura asked, hardly hearing
her own question. She couldn't believe what she was
seeing. She placed the drawings on the table in
chronological order. "How?"

Tawana shook her head. "I wish I knew. Nana used
to say Mo had the 'gift' like Uncle J, her daddy."

"The gift?"

"Yeah, Uncle J . . . saw stuff."

"Like a psychic?"

"Sorta like that. Nana always said the reason Mo's
head didn't work too good was because she had the
gift stronger than Uncle J, and it took over her
brain." Tawana leaned over and picked up Nana's
eyeglasses from the table. "I always thought Nana was
just saying that to make an excuse for Moweez being
slow. I never figured it was true 'til I saw those drawings of Nana." She put the glasses over her eyes, and
the lenses made them appear doubled in size.

"Wana, how—how come you never showed these to
me before?"

Tawana shrugged and took off the glasses. She
folded the arms and returned them to the cigar box.
"Guess I just never thought about it."

"Even after I told you about the drawing with the
dead birds?"

Tawana looked down at the cigar box.

"And what about last night, after I showed you both
drawings? Why didn't you tell me then? You saw the—"

" 'Cause I was scared!" Tawana threw the cigar box on the table and jumped to her feet. Her chair keeled over onto its back. "And I didn't want you to be!"

"Wana—"

"Laura, I seen the hourglasses in both them drawings, and I knew then, I just knew, Mo was doing it again." Tawana began to pace from the dryer to the table, wringing her hands.

Laura's stomach rolled into a knot as she looked from the sketches to Tawana, then back to the sketches. She didn't know what to think or believe. She'd never heard of anyone predicting the future through sketches before. And if she were basing this just off the drawings of Nana, she might be able to create a plausible argument against it. Tawana had been under a lot of stress while Nana was sick. Maybe she'd been mistaken. Maybe Moweez drew the pictures *after* each event. But this wasn't just about Nana. Laura had witnessed the impact of Moweez's sketches for herself. She'd seen the drawing of the dead birds *before* the actual event occurred. And what about the second sketch? What was Moweez trying to tell them?

Tawana's pacing grew more frantic, like she was ready to jump out of her skin. "You know what them new drawings mean, right? You know what Mo's sayin', right?"

"I don't—"

"The Beauty Box, girl! The Beauty Box and that goddamn hourglass. We gonna lose the Box. That's what she's tellin' us. We gonna lose the Box!"

Laura got to her feet and grabbed Tawana by the

shoulders before the woman had a nervous break-down. "We're not going to lose the Box. You hear me?"

"How can you say that after I showed you the pic-tures of Nana? You seen it for yourself! The drawin's, they—"

"Yeah, I saw them, but think about it, Wana—the new ones don't show the Box destroyed. It's still standing."

Tawana blinked, as though considering that thought, then she shook her head adamantly. "No, look. . . ." She marched over to the drawings of Nana and stabbed the hourglass in each sketch with a fin-ger. "This first one's almost full, just like in the bird picture. This second one is half-full, like the picture with all those thread things. In Nana's third picture, the damn hourglass is empty, and she's dead. It goes from half to empty, Laura. What's gonna be dead when the hourglass shows up in Mo's next picture? The Box! I'm tellin' you, it's the Box!"

Or worse, Laura thought, following Tawana's logic. It could be Matt's son.

CHAPTER NINE

She didn't need the introduction to know they were father and son. They had the same coffee-brown hair, the same cleft chin, the same intensity in their caramel-colored eyes.

After a short exchange of names and hellos, Seth pointed to one of the hydraulic chairs in the salon. "Miss Laura, can I sit on one of those?"

"Help yourself." She hoped her smile didn't look as strained as it felt. It was disconcerting, meeting him, knowing his face was etched in colored pencil on a purported psychic drawing in the next room.

Seth ran up to the first chair and hopped on it. He examined the arms and sides of the chair as though searching for the controls.

"I hope you don't mind me bringing him along," Matt said. "Lerna Mae, the lady who does my short-order cooking, usually watches Seth if I have errands to run after the café closes. She couldn't today."

"I don't mind at all," Laura said. And she didn't mind. But she was concerned. She didn't think the information she'd planned on sharing with Matt would be suitable for a little boy's ears. Especially this little boy.

"How do you make it go up?" Seth asked, still searching for a go button.

Laura went over to the chair and stepped on the wide metal triangle attached to its base. She pumped it twice with her foot, and the chair popped up a few inches. "How's that?"

The light in his eyes and his openmouthed, gap-toothed grin was answer enough. She laughed and made the chair go higher. He squealed with delight.

"If you're not careful, he'll have you working that chair like it's a yo-yo until midnight." Matt gave her a tired smile. "How's Moweez?"

"Tawana's with her now, seeing if she'll come down. She's been in bed most of the day." Laura depressed the bar, and with a hiss of hydraulics the chair eased back down to floor level.

"I like the going up part better," Seth said. "Can we do it again?"

Laura winked at him and was about to get the chair moving again when Matt gave her a subtle signal that they should find someplace else to talk.

"Maybe a little later, champ," he said to Seth. "Right now, I want to talk to Miss Laura."

"Aw, Dad."

Wanting to soften the disappointment, Laura went over to one of the workstation supply cabinets and took out a large package of hair clips. "Hey, you like puzzles?" she asked Seth.

"Sometimes."

"Then come check this out." She brought the clips over to the coffee table, opened the package, then pushed hairstyling magazines out of the way. She dumped the four-inch long alligator clips onto the table. "These make the coolest towers and bridges."

"But that's not a puzzle." Seth scooted off the hydraulic chair.

"Not a picture puzzle. It's a figure-it-out puzzle."

"A what?" Seth went over to the table, picked up one of the blue clips and examined it.

"A figure-it-out puzzle. That means you get to figure out what you want to make with it instead of that already being decided for you." She quickly clamped four clips together to form a square, then showed him how to build upward from there. Before long, Seth had his tongue pinched between his teeth and was adding clips of his own.

"You know, you're pretty good at this," Laura said.

Seth nodded. "I'm gonna build a castle." He tilted his head first one way, then the other, as though examining what might be the best position for the next clip.

Seeing he was well occupied, Laura motioned for Matt to follow her. "Your dad and I will be right over there in the next room if you need anything, okay?"

Seth nodded again, seemingly oblivious to anything but alligator clips.

As they crossed into the kitchenette, Matt asked, "Do you have any kids?"

Laura shook her head.

"You're a natural with them."

She smiled. "I had two rambunctious younger brothers."

His return smile only lasted a moment. "Has Moweez said anything to you yet?"

"Nothing."

As though her answer exhausted him even more, Matt leaned against a wall and briefly rubbed his eyes with a thumb and finger. He appeared to be more anxious today about Moweez providing answers than he had yesterday. She debated on whether it would be a good idea to show him the drawings of Nana. If they couldn't get answers from Moweez now, those drawings would generate more questions for him, just as they had for her. And a lot more stress. Either that or he'd strongly suggest she see a shrink. Still, if the tables were turned, wouldn't she want to know?

Having little doubt to the answer of that question, Laura went over to the table, where Tawana had left the drawings of Nana. "I want to show you something," she said, and began to unfold the sketches. As she laid them out in chronological order, Matt came over to her. She felt him stiffen when he saw the one of Nana lying in her coffin.

"Tawana showed me these today," she said.

As she told him about Nana and the time line between Moweez's drawings and her grandmother's illness and death, Matt leaned over with his palms on the table, studying each one carefully.

"It could all be coincidence," she said when she'd finished relaying the story.

"But you don't think it is, do you?"

"I really don't know what to think."

"What about Tawana?"

"Well, she—she thinks we're going to lose the shop. Mostly because of the similarities with the hourglass, how the sand level changes from picture to picture."

"Do you have the two drawings from this week?" he asked solemnly.

Laura went over to the drawer where she'd stored the sketch pad and pulled it out. As soon as she handed it to him, Matt flipped the pad open and placed it beside the other drawings on the table. Seeing them side by side, matching hourglass to hourglass, made her dizzy. Reality felt tenuous, as though at any moment it would careen off its axis and leave far too much room for the impossible, the improbable, the imperceptible to slip in and take root.

Matt pointed to the hourglass in one of Nana's sketches. "The only symbolism Moweez uses in these is the hourglass. But here . . ." He traced one of the silvery lines that ran across the last sketch. "She adds this web, this abstract design. Everything else is drawn true to life, just like in the ones with her grandmother. Any idea why? Or what this web means?"

"No. I didn't—"

"Hey, podnuh, what you working on?"

Laura and Matt turned at the sound of Percy Schexneider's voice.

"What's he doing here?" Laura asked, then went to the entranceway of the shop to find out. Percy was examining Seth's puzzle project, which now looked like a crumbling Tower of Pisa. "We're in the back, Chief," she called.

Percy glanced her way, signaled that he'd heard, then tousled Seth's hair before leaving him.

"Matt with you?" Percy asked.

Laura stepped aside as Percy entered the kitchenette so he could see Matt, who was leaning with his back against the table. She noticed he'd already collected the sketches and turned them face down.

Matt nodded a greeting. "Percy."

"Good, glad y'all together," Percy said. "Wanted to let you know I talked to Butch Reynolds with the Wildlife and Fisheries Department. He's the lead man assigned to the case."

"Do they have any ideas on what happened to those birds?" Laura asked.

"No, and they probably won't for another month or so."

"Why so long?" Matt asked.

Percy hooked his thumbs in his utility belt. "What can I say, it's a state department. But Bruce did say he's seen something similar to this before."

"In Windham?" Matt asked.

"No, Lake Charles, out by the refineries. He says a few years back Paramount Refinery had one of their relief valves malfunction. Caused some kind of nasty emissions that killed a flock of killdees."

"No people?" Laura asked.

Percy shrugged. "He didn't give specifics, and I didn't ask. Didn't seem relevant, you know? We got rid of the only emissions problem Windham ever had when they shut down the sugar mill. And even then, the most dangerous thing about it was the stink. Oh, hey, talkin' about stink, either of you seen Keith Lafleur lately?"

"I haven't," Laura said.

"Me either," Matt said. "I tried calling him this morning about the problem we had at the café with the lights shorting out in the john and the lock sticking, but nobody answered, not even an answering machine. How's that woman you took to the hospital, by the way?"

Percy shot Laura a sideways glance.

"Laura already knows about what happened at the café," Matt said.

"Oh, yeah, okay," Percy said, visibly relaxing. "I just didn't want to add anything you might not have mentioned, know what I mean? There's already enough stupid talk going on in this town."

"You're telling me," Laura muttered.

"The woman's doing fine, I suppose," Percy said. "After they checked her out at the hospital, she went back to Jackson."

"Mississippi?" Matt asked.

"Yeah. That's where she's from. Works for a big drug retailer out there."

"What was she doing here?" Laura asked.

"Traveling through from Crowley, I think." Percy arched a brow at Matt. "You know, not to add more to your sh—uh, problem pile, but that whole incident at the café could be a potential lawsuit. You got insurance for that?"

"Thanks for not adding to the pile." Matt blew out a frustrated breath and raked his fingers through his hair. "I didn't even think about a lawsuit. I've got insurance, but I don't know if it covers that sort of thing. For all I know, it might wind up in Lafleur's lap since he owns the building."

Percy harrumphed. "The way I hear it, Lafleur might not even *have* a lap much longer."

"What do you mean?" Laura asked.

"Got a call from Barbara, Keith's wife. Claims he flipped out and threatened her with a gun."

"What?" Matt said, his voice awash in incredulity.

"Yeah. Said she got so scared, she hightailed it to her mama's. I went over to Lafleur's house to see what was going on, but his truck wasn't in the garage and nobody answered the door. I found his foreman, Jeff Mabry, who happens to be Barbara's brother, by the way, doing roofing work over at the Baptist church on Ambrose Avenue. He's another one claiming Lafleur's lost his sh—uh, his head. Said Keith wasn't paying his bills so the suppliers cut him off, and some of them even have liens on his construction projects now. Must have gotten pretty bad 'cause Jeff up and quit, and that used to be his daddy's company."

Dumbstruck, Laura peered over at Matt. He looked more worried than surprised. She couldn't blame him. Dead birds, spider bites and potential lawsuits, psychic messages drawn in colored pencil on a dime store sketch pad—the last thing they needed to be concerned about was a deranged landlord.

"I'll make another run over to Lafleur's house before I head back to the station, but in case I miss him again, let me know if he shows up here, okay? Just give Verneese a call and she'll radio me in the squad car."

"Yeah, sure," Matt said, his brow deeply furrowed.

Percy nodded. He rocked back on his heels and glanced around the room as though seeing it for the first time. "You know, you've gotta give a dog his due. Considering the shape this building was in when Lafleur brought it here, he did a damn good job fixing it up. I had some serious doubts in the beginning. A lot of people did." He looked from Matt to Laura. "Some still do. That's why there's so much talk stirrin' around town, especially with the older folks. They think when Lafleur dragged this house to Windham, bad luck came along with it." He gave a small shake of his head. "Sure looks like it did, for Lafleur anyway."

Laura cringed. Having lived in Windham all her life, she wasn't a stranger to superstition. It was as common in south Louisiana as the humidity. Normally, she took the notions with a grain of salt, but on occasion, one would gnaw at her until she paid attention—just like this one was doing now.

"Anyway, gotta run," Percy said, and turned to leave. "I'll let y'all know if I hear anything more from Wildlife and Fisheries."

"Appreciate you coming by, Chief," Laura said, and with Matt following right behind, she walked Percy back into the salon.

"No problem. Just wish I'd had better news." Percy grinned and hooked a thumb toward Seth as he walked past him. "Looks like my little podnuh over there's really got something going on."

Seemingly oblivious to the comment, Seth stood poised over his tower, pink and blue alligator clips in hand. His project had grown to nearly a foot in height, and looked ready to topple at any second. Laura found herself holding her breath as the boy aimed one clip at the uppermost peak. The glass storm door shut behind Percy with a loud *clonk*, and Seth flinched, which sent the tower to its demise.

"Oh, no!" Seth cried as the clips clattered across the coffee table. "No! Dad, look, no!" He spun about and ran over to Matt, who immediately crouched and gathered his son in his arms. Seth buried his face in Matt's shoulder. "It broke, Dad! It's all broken!"

"Shh." Matt patted his back and looked up at Laura apologetically. "We'll fix it, champ, don't worry."

Shaking his head, Seth pulled out of Matt's arms. "It won't be the same if we fix it. It'll be dif—" His eyes suddenly locked on something past his father's shoulder, and Laura turned to see what it was.

Moweez was standing at the back of the shop, barefoot and dressed in a faded pair of jeans and an old U.L. sweatshirt. Her hair was disheveled, her long braids tangled. Her eyes were swollen from sleep. She took a tentative step toward them, her gaze moving from Seth to Matt, then back to Seth. She looked confused.

"—att?" Moweez inched closer and held a hand out to Seth. To Laura's surprise, the boy went over to take it.

Matt stood, speechless, watching them, apparently just as amazed as she was.

Just then, Tawana came barreling into the salon

from the kitchenette. "Mo, where the hell you think you—" She pulled up short when she saw Moweez with Seth. She glanced over at Laura, who shrugged.

Still holding his hand, Moweez led Seth to the coffee table. She picked up a clip and handed it to him. Seth smiled, took the clip, then they both dropped to their knees and started untangling his previous masterpiece.

Frowning, Tawana walked over to Laura and Matt. "I'd just gotten Mo to change out of her pj's when we heard somebody yellin' down here. She took off so fast, I thought she was gonna wind up headfirst at the bottom of the stairs." She looked over at Matt. "That's your boy?"

He nodded.

The three of them stood, silently watching as Seth and Moweez worked side by side. He babbled on about what clip went where, and she nodded, following his instructions.

"You'd swear they've known each other for years," Laura said.

"I know," Matt said.

Seth laughed at something Moweez said, and she clapped him on the back as though appreciative he'd enjoyed her joke.

"Maybe they met up somewhere without us knowin', like when Mo showed up at the café," Tawana said, keeping her voice low. "Maybe that's how she knew what your boy looked like."

"I don't think so," Matt said. "Seth would have said something to me."

Tawana lifted a hand, as though surrendering.

"Then I'm lost. All this is just gettin' weirder and weirder. What're we supposed to do now?"

"I say we ask them," Laura said, then headed for the kitchenette. She was tired of dancing around issues that made no sense. She wanted to get to the bottom of this.

Finding the sketch pad on the table where they'd left it, Laura quickly scooped it up, purposely leaving behind the drawings of Nana. They were a bit too graphic for an eight-year-old boy. She flipped the pad open to the drawing that included Seth and went back into the salon.

With Matt and Tawana watching expectantly, Laura made her way around the coffee table to the couch behind it and sat. Seth and Moweez didn't acknowledge her.

"Hey, you two," she said.

When neither of them responded, she turned the sketch pad around so it faced them. "Mo, you drew this, right?"

Moweez tossed a glance her way, as though she were a foreign noise that needed identification. Instead of answering, she inched closer to Seth, who was busy attaching clips end over end.

Laura lowered the pad and tried another approach. "Seth, did you meet Moweez before today?"

Swiping his nose with the back of his hand, Seth looked up. He held a distant look in his eye, as if he were gazing across an empty room while contemplating a serious matter.

"Miss Laura's talking to you, son," Matt said.

Without acknowledging his father or Laura, Seth

leaned over and whispered something to Moweez. She nodded grimly and handed him another clip.

"Seth?" Matt walked over and put a hand on his shoulder.

"Huh?" Seth looked up, startled.

"Didn't you hear, Miss Laura?" Matt asked.

Seth frowned. "Uh-uh."

"She asked you if you'd met Moweez before today."

"Who's that?"

Matt's brow furrowed. "The girl kneeling next to you."

Seth sat back on his haunches and looked over at Moweez. "Oh—that's not her name."

Matt and Laura exchanged a quick, puzzled glance. "What's her name then?" Matt asked.

Seth shrugged. "I forget." He pulled himself back to his knees. "Can I play now?"

"So you've met her before?" Laura asked.

"I—I don't think so," Seth said.

"Then how do you know Moweez isn't her name?" Matt asked.

"'Cause she told me."

Tawana came around to Moweez and leaned over so her face was only inches from her cousin's. "Mo, what you been tellin' him?"

Moweez gave a grunt of frustration and turned away from her.

"Look here, girl, straight up, you gonna have to talk," Tawana said, standing upright. "How you know this boy? How come you don't wanna talk to Laura about them drawin's?" She tapped Moweez's shoulder. "You hearin' me?"

Another grunt.

"She's not going to talk 'cause she's scared," Seth said, snapping two clips together.

"Scared of what?" Laura asked.

"That they're gonna hear her, then come back and get her."

Tawana snapped to attention. "Who?"

Seth shrugged.

"Who's messin' with you, Mo?" Tawana asked, her expression earnest. "Tell me where they at! Tell me—"

The ringing of the phone startled everyone, and all but Moweez turned toward the sound. Laura tossed the sketch pad on to the couch, got up, and hurried over to grab the phone.

"Beauty Box," she said, a bit breathless.

No response came from the other end of the line. In fact, she heard no sound at all.

"Hello?"

Still no response.

"Hel—"

Someone knocked loudly on the front door of the salon. Laura covered the mouthpiece and called, "It's open."

More knocking on the front door—harder—much louder.

"She said it's open, fool!" Tawana shouted.

Still not getting an answer, Laura hung up the phone and hurried over to the door.

No one was there. She opened the storm door and checked both sides of the porch. Nothing.

Just as she closed the door behind her, the sound of clamoring, hurrying footsteps swelled from the back of the salon. Laura spun around to face whatever raced her way. She saw Matt already heading for the kitchenette.

Tawana stood in front of Moweez and Seth, her hands held out in front of her, both balled into tight fists. "Who—who's—"

The phone rang again, interrupting Tawana, but this time it jangled, a high-pitched, irritating sound like that of an old-fashioned phone. Laura headed for it again.

Another knock sounded on the door.

"Lord, the devil's comin' to visit," Tawana said.

Laura picked up the phone, but it only rang louder, then louder still, jangling, jangling, until she wanted to rip the phone cord from the wall. She dropped the receiver.

More knocking—pounding.

Just when Laura thought she would go mad from the din, she saw Moweez get to her feet, grab Seth by the shirt collar, and shove him past Tawana.

"No!" Seth shouted, reaching for Moweez.

"—att, home!" Moweez shouted back. "Home!"

Seth began to cry, turning in place, as if lost. "Dad!"

With Seth's cry still echoing throughout the shop, the jangling, clamoring, pounding abruptly stopped, and Matt came stumbling out of the kitchenette. He looked as lost as Seth.

Seth raced over to him, grabbing his hand. "We gotta go home! They're here! We gotta go home now!"

"Son, wait—"

"—att, home!" Moweez shouted. She pushed her

way past Tawana, her face set with determination. She rounded the coffee table, went to the couch and picked up her sketch pad. Jabbing a finger against the cover, she said insistently, "—att, home now!" She threw the cover open, flipped to the sketch that showed Seth peering from a window, and slapped it with an open palm. "Home! Home!"

Then, before anyone could move, Moweez's eyes rolled back in her head, and she fell forward, her forehead smacking into the corner of the coffee table with a loud *crack!*

CHAPTER TEN

With all the rot collecting beneath his flesh, Keith Lafleur felt like a pressure cooker without a release valve, ready to explode. The boils had festered and multiplied so quickly and to such an extent, he didn't even bother bandaging them anymore. They covered his face, his genitals, much of his back and chest. His hair stayed matted with pus from the boils leaking on his head. Sheets, blankets, and pillows, small comforts he'd always taken for granted, were now luxuries he could no longer afford. Within minutes, they'd become saturated with purulent discharge and wind up sticking to his arms, face, and feet. He'd had to peel the last pillowcase off his right cheek, taking two layers of skin along with it. Since then, he slept sitting up in his recliner with an elbow propped on an arm of the chair and his head resting between his thumb and forefinger. Sleeping through the night had become impossible, and he was lucky if a catnap lasted longer than twenty minutes. The one he'd just woken from had only lasted ten, which was just as well. He had business to tend to.

With a grimace, Keith eased himself out of the recliner. The back of his pajama pants clung to the leaking sores on his calves, but he didn't bother pulling them away. It would just cake up again.

The house was empty now, and he liked it that way. The groan of Naugahyde as he got up from his chair, the whir of the central heater, the muted bark of a dog outside—all sounds he could live with. All better than Barbara's nagging. She hadn't returned home since he'd accused her of playing swallow the pickle with Stanford Milo. He'd found her, though, early this morning, hiding out at her mother's, the sedan parked behind the old broad's house. No matter. Barbara would keep for a little while, as would her mother, then he'd be able to scratch their names off the list.

The list. It was the only thing holding his sanity together now. It gave order to the fragmented thoughts filling his mind. It gave him purpose.

Keith hobbled into the kitchen, the boils under his feet shooting pain all the way up to his knees. He went to the fridge, found a bowl of leftover tuna salad, and used the first two fingers of his right hand to shovel the tuna into his mouth. By the third scoop, he felt nauseous, so he stuck the rest of the tuna back in the fridge for later and wiped his fingers on his pajama pants. His ability to eat had become as limited as sleep. Everything tasted like bile. But he had to force food down from time to time to preserve his strength.

Otherwise, he'd never be able to finish the work ahead of him.

He had to stop twice on his way to the bathroom to give the soles of his feet a break. When he finally made it inside and reached the vanity, his body shimmered with sweat.

The mirror again.

That cold, hard glass of truth.

He was Job reincarnate. The boils—everything he'd worked so hard for stripped away.

But crying out to God was the last thing Keith planned to do. If this torment was a test, screw it. He planned on failing. If this was his escort to death, so be it. He wouldn't be heading for that abyss alone.

Turning the single-handled faucet on, he waited for the water to warm before cupping his hands beneath the flow. He held his breath and splashed water on his face. The first douse was always the worse, like gasoline contaminating an open wound. He hissed through his teeth and waited for the burning to stop. It didn't. He doused his face again. The burning gave way to an itching sensation, and he quickly splashed on more water. It made it worse, like hundreds, thousands, millions of ants crawling beneath his skin.

With a roar of frustration, Keith pressed his hands to his cheeks and rubbed hard, then harder. The blinding pain did nothing to quell the itching, and soon he dug his fingernails into his flesh, scraping, scratching, until the pain shouted louder than the ants.

The image in the mirror peered back at him, a bloodied, swollen mess. Boils that had been ripped open drained their yellow-green poison in thick rivulets down his face. It reeked of soured cabbage and decay. Giving it no more attention than deserved, Keith yanked a hand towel off its rod and patted his face to staunch the flow.

Carrying the towel with him, he went into his bedroom and checked the mirror on the dresser. The list was still there, taped exactly where he'd left it in the center of the glass. He ran a finger across each name he'd scribbled across the page in blue ink. Traitors every one.

Barbara Mabry Lafleur—sins of selfishness and lust
Dolores Mabry—giving birth to the bitch I married and harboring her
Jeffrey Mabry—betrayal and bearing false witness
Stanford Milo—coveting another man's wife
Dr. Robins—incompetence
Percy Schexneider—for being an asshole

Although Keith suspected more names might be added later, he was content with these—for now. He closed his eyes, reflected on each name, each face, then wiggled his tracing finger over the page and stabbed. Jittery with anticipation, he opened his eyes to see who'd be the first. He snorted his approval. Perfect. Nothing random about this choice at all. He tossed the blood and pus-stained towel onto the bed and headed for the closet.

With clothes being one of his biggest challenges, Keith rummaged through the closet until he found a gray windbreaker. He eased his arms into it, then carefully zipped it over his bare chest. The crusted pajama pants would have to do. So would his bare feet.

Keith limped out of the room and down the hall, taking note that his feet didn't hurt quite as much as they had earlier. Adrenaline. Nature's finest medication. Certainly better than anything that incompetent quack, Dr. Robins, had given him.

It took some time before Keith reached the kitchen. He grabbed his truck keys off the counter. Only a little farther to the garage.

Through the kitchen door, into the utility room—that's when he caught the acrid scent of gasoline. He grinned and crossed the utility room to the garage door. When Keith opened it, he inhaled deeply, sucking in fumes. Against the back wall of the garage, under a paint-stained tarp, sat ten five-gallon cans of gasoline. They would be his coup de main, the denouement of his mission—to destroy the source, the very seed that spawned his misery. Like his list, they too gave him comfort.

Keith went to his truck and peered in the driver's side window to make sure his .30-30 was still cradled in the hunting rack behind the seat. It was, scope and all. He backtracked to a wall switch, hit it, and the wide metal garage door began its ascent with a rumbling clatter. Keith eased his way back to the truck and climbed into the cab. Dusk had already started to settle in, which meant he didn't have much time.

He started the truck, waited until the garage door fully opened, then backed out slowly.

As soon as the nose of the truck cleared the garage's

threshold, he punched the close button on the remote he kept in the cab and waited while the door walked its way downward. He heard laughter nearby and checked his rearview mirror. He saw a group of kids playing tag on the front lawn across the street, a mint green Toyota rolling past his house, and Percy Schexneider pulling up behind him in a Windham patrol car.

"Shit." Keith did a quick scan of the cab. The rifle was standard issue in just about every pickup truck in south Louisiana. That alone wouldn't raise Percy's suspicions, and he didn't see anything else in the cab that would, either. He glanced at his side mirror and saw Percy ambling up to the truck.

"Looks like I caught you just in—sweet Jesus, Lafleur!" Percy said when he reached the driver's window. He took a step back. "What the hell happened to you?"

Keith's fingers itched. Although Percy's name wasn't the first name chosen on the list, he wanted nothing more than to grab the .30-30 behind him and pop a cap into Percy Schexneider's forehead. The man was always nosing around where he had no business.

"Been sick," Keith mumbled, keeping an eye on the windshield. "Going to the doctor."

"Jesus, I would think so," Percy said. "Barbara didn't tell me you were this sick."

Keith felt his blood pressure creeping up. He turned toward Percy, making sure he got a full view of his face. "What *did* my wife tell you exactly?"

Percy's frown deepened, and he stumbled back another step. "Just—uh—said y'all were having some problems out here."

Keith coughed dramatically, then stuck his left arm out the window, knowing the boils on his left hand were no prettier than the ones on his face.

Percy gasped. "Holy shit, Lafleur, man, you need to be in a hospital or something."

Holding back a sneer, Keith said, "Well, if you'd move your fucking car out of my way, I might be able to see about that."

"Oh—yeah . . ." Looking relieved that he'd been given an out, Percy hurried back to his squad car. Before getting in, he called out to Keith, "I'll come back later, when you're . . . uh . . . feeling better."

Keith didn't respond. He watched Percy slide into his car and back out of the driveway.

Five minutes later, when he was sure Schexneider would be far enough away that he wouldn't follow him, Keith took off, heading toward the north side of town.

He took the back roads that ran past sugarcane fields, thinking he might have a better chance of getting to his destination without being noticed. Every bump in the road solicited a groan from him as he bounced in the seat.

Acres and acres of brown, stubbly fields flew past his window, but Keith paid them little mind. When he'd first moved to Windham from Shreveport as a young man, he'd been enamored with its open fields and slower pace. He'd always thought it would be a good place to raise kids, but never had the chance to find out. That was another hope Barbara screwed up with her eggless ovaries.

After taking a right on Russell Road, it didn't take long before Keith spotted the peak of the building he was looking for in the distance. He veered off the road into an open pasture and cried out in pain with the first jolt. Gritting his teeth, Keith nursed the truck forward over ruts and brush. Ahead, about two hundred yards past the field, lay a row of buildings, their backs facing him. The one he wanted sat third from the left. Even without the scope, he could see men working on the roof.

Keith parked the truck behind the trunk of a massive oak and got out. From this distance, he didn't think he'd have any problems getting a clean shot. He slipped the rifle from its cradle and carried it over to the hood of the truck. After easing his elbows onto the hood, he positioned the scope close to his right eye and took aim. As soon as the red crosshairs settled over the familiar face, he pulled the trigger.

With the report of the rifle still ringing in his ears, Keith collected the spent shell from the ground, then got back in his truck and calmly drove out of the field.

One Mabry down, two more to go.

CHAPTER ELEVEN

"I'm tellin' you, it was the devil," Tawana said, pacing in front of the couch, where Moweez sat. A large goose egg had formed over the girl's left eye.

"Stop that," Laura said, nodding slightly toward Seth, who was sitting beside Moweez.

"The devil was here?" Seth's voice cracked with fear.

"No!" Matt and Laura said simultaneously.

"Then y'all tell me what was causin' all that commotion." Tawana hooked a hand on her hip. "All that phone ringin' and door knockin'—it sure as hell wasn't the Easter Bunny."

Laura blew out an exhausted breath and sat on the edge of the coffee table. "I don't know what caused it."

Matt rubbed the back of his neck, feeling as tired as Laura looked. After Moweez had come to and Tawana had determined she didn't need a trip to the emergency room, he'd done a thorough check of the apartment upstairs, then searched every closet and cupboard downstairs. There simply was no explanation for what happened except maybe mass hallucination.

"Son, what did you mean earlier when you said we needed to go home because *they* were here? Who was here?"

Seth shrugged and glanced over at Moweez. She smiled at him and gingerly touched the knot on her head with her fingers.

"Mo said basically the same thing," Laura said.

"Yeah, but hold up." Tawana raised a hand. "Don't be askin' her no more questions. Look what happened the last time we tried to get Mo to talk to us about stuff like that."

"Did you see something or someone in the shop?" Matt asked Seth. The question sounded ridiculous even to him. Had there been someone or something out of the ordinary in the shop, they would have all seen it.

A look of frustration crossed Seth's face, as though he couldn't quite get a memory to flesh out in his mind. "No?"

Matt frowned. "You didn't or you're not sure?"

Seth shrugged again.

"Uh-huh, you see," Tawana said. "I told you it was the—"

"Wana," Laura warned.

Tawana harrumphed.

"Mo hungry." Moweez patted Seth on the shoulder. "—att hungry."

"His name's Seth, Mo," Laura said. She pointed to Matt. "That's Matt."

Moweez cocked her head as if studying Matt, then

looked over at Seth. She turned back to Laura. "Mo hungry."

Laura sighed. "Okay, honey." She got to her feet. "I'll go upstairs and see what I can put together for supper." She turned to Matt. "You and Seth are welcome to stay and eat if you'd like."

"Why don't y'all come over to the café for supper? There's plenty of shrimp sauce piquante left over. The lunch crowd was light today. In fact, if you'd rather not stay here tonight, we can make bunking room in our apartment."

Tawana shook her head. "I don't think Mo should do all that movin' around."

"I can bring the food here then."

"Oh, we can't let you go through all that trouble," Laura said.

Tawana gave her a perturbed look. "Yeah, we can."

"Wana!" Laura's cheeks turned red.

"What? I could use some of that sauce piquante. But we sleepin' here tonight. Ain't no hoogity-boogity gonna chase us out of our own place. We worked too hard to get what we got." With a huff, she turned on her heels, marched over to the reception desk, and slammed the receiver back in its cradle. "Now, let that bastard ring again." She scrounged around on the desk, tossing papers aside. "Laura, where's them car keys?"

"Top drawer of my workstation. Why? Where're you going?"

"St. Paul's, to get me some holy water. I'm gonna spray it all up in here." Tawana headed for the workstation.

"Wana, you're a Baptist."

"God ain't gonna care if I borrow a little water from you Catholics." Tawana jangled the keys when she found them. "I'm not gonna be long, but don't let Mo fall asleep, okay? With that bump on her head, we need to keep her up 'til around ten."

With that, Tawana bounded out of the shop, and within minutes, Matt heard a car engine roar to life.

"I'm sorry about that." Laura's half-smile was shy, a little embarrassed. "Tawana has a tendency to say whatever's on her mind—unedited."

"That's what I like about her." He grinned. "Look, I'll run over to the café and get the shrimp, if that's okay. I know Moweez is hungry, and—"

"I'm hungry, too," Seth piped up. "Can we eat over here?"

"Talk about unedited," Matt said. "He's the champ."

A half hour later, Matt had shrimp sauce piquante heating on the stove in Laura's kitchen and was pouring chocolate cake batter into muffin tins. Moweez and Seth were in the adjoining living room, watching television.

"I wish you'd let me help with that," Laura said from the kitchen table. "I feel like a useless lump over here."

"You can lick the bowl if you'd like."

She chuckled. "If Wana was here, you wouldn't have half the batter you have now. She's addicted to chocolate. You'll have a friend for life with those cupcakes."

"What about you?"

"Both. I love chocolate, and you certainly have another friend here, but not because of the cake. I really appreciate all you've done for us."

"Well, you're very welcome, but I haven't done all that much."

Laura gave him a smile that said she knew better.

"How long have you known Tawana and Moweez?" he asked, wanting to redirect the subject.

"I've known Wana about six years or so. We were in beauty school together, then worked at the same salon for three years. I met Moweez about the same time, but didn't really get to know her until this past year."

Matt held up the chocolate-covered stirring spoon and bowl. "Last chance."

She shook her head. "I'll wait for the finished product."

He grinned and put the bowl and spoon into a sink already filled with warm, soapy water. "So did you always want to be a beautician?"

"Hairstylist."

"Oops, sorry."

She laughed. "That's okay. I went to U.L. for two years right out of high school, but never seemed to quite fit into anything there. When I still hadn't chosen a major by the end of my second year, I knew it was time to do something. So I went to beauty school. I always had this knack for doing hair. I got a lot of flack from my dad about the switch, but I'm glad I did it."

"Your mom was okay with the change?"

"She died a week after my high school graduation. Cancer. What about you? Always wanted to be a chef?"

"No, I sort of fell into it." Matt peeked into the living room to check on Seth and Moweez. They were sitting side by side on the couch, engrossed in an old *I Love Lucy* rerun. He turned back to Laura. "I was in civil engineering for a couple of years after college, but after surveying in the swamps with the mosquitoes and alligators, I knew that wasn't how I wanted to make my living. A friend of mine owned a restaurant in Opelousas and wanted to open a second one in Lafayette. He asked me if I'd run it." Matt shrugged. "I took the job. That's how I got into the food business. Wound up opening my own place on the south side of Windham about five years ago, then moved it here almost a month ago." He glanced at the simmering sauce. "Hey, soup's on."

Laura got up from the table. "Smells delicious. I'll get Mo and Seth."

"Shouldn't we wait for Tawana?"

"Oh, yeah, you should," Tawana called from the living room. She appeared in the kitchen a moment later, carrying a large spray bottle filled with water. "I had to go to three stores to find a bottle like this. Then, when I get to the church, some old fart starts pitchin' a fit 'cause I'm takin' so much holy water."

"Where'd you take the water from?" Laura asked.

"Some birdbath lookin' thing in the back of the church."

Laura groaned. "That's the baptismal font!"

"A who?"

"Where they baptize the babies," Matt said.

"Well, how in the hell was I supposed to know that?

You Catholics got that all backwards anyway. You gotta dunk to be baptized, brother, dunk."

Matt laughed. "Okay, I'll dunk these cupcakes in the oven, then we can eat. How's that?"

Tawana's eyebrows shot up. "Cupcakes?"

He nodded. "Chocolate."

"Oh, yeah!" Tawana did a hip roll. "All right, I'm gonna hurry up and spray some of this up here, so I don't have to worry about it later. I already took care of downstairs. Y'all gonna wait for me?"

"Go on, girl," Laura said, grinning. She headed for the cabinets near the refrigerator. "I'll set the table."

Tawana gave the kitchen a spritz or three, then took off for the living room.

Matt heard Seth ask if he could spray something.

"That devil's pretty quiet, considering all the holy water she's got in there." Laura gathered a handful of plates from the cabinet.

"Guess he got scared and left when he saw her coming," Matt said.

"You blame him?"

Laughing, Matt grabbed the muffin tin and went to the oven, which he'd already preheated. When he opened the oven door, it was as cold inside as when he'd first turned it on. "Oven's down," he said, placing the muffin tin on the counter.

"Oh, no." Laura put the plates on the table and went over to him. She turned the control knob on the oven all the way up to five-fifty, then leaned over and stuck her hand in the oven. "I hate electric stoves," she said, turning her hand first one way then another.

"You can't see the fire come on in the oven like you can with a gas."

"Dad?" Although Seth's voice sounded more quizzical than anything, it still raised the hair on the back of Matt's neck. He hurried into the living room.

Seth and Moweez were sitting in the same spot on the couch, but now the television screen was blank.

"It just went off," Seth said, still staring at the screen.

Moweez glanced up at Matt. "Mo hungry."

Just then, Tawana stepped into the living room from the hallway. "What's the matter?"

"Looks like your television's out." Matt went over to the set and turned the power switch off and on. The screen remained black.

"No, wait!" Tawana's cry sent Matt wheeling about. He saw Seth doubled over and gagging.

Matt rushed to grab the first container he could find, an empty candy dish on an end table. He hurried over to Seth and held the dish under his mouth. "Where's your bathroom?" he asked Tawana.

She pointed to the hall. "Second door on the right."

"Come on, buddy." Matt helped Seth to his feet.

Seth whimpered as Matt led him down the hall. As soon as they turned into the bathroom, he bolted for the toilet and barely got the lid up before vomiting. Matt snatched a washcloth from a rod near the shower stall and wet it in the sink. After wringing it out, he carried it back to Seth and placed it on the back of his neck.

"Can I help?" Laura called from the hallway.

"We've got it," Matt said. "Upset stomach, I think."

Seth shuttered after a hard dry heave, then started whimpering again.

"I probably should take him home," Matt said. When Laura didn't answer, he removed the washcloth from the back of Seth's neck and pressed it to his cheek. "Here you go, champ. Wipe your mouth, then we'll head home."

"I don't wanna go home," Seth whined. "I wanna stay here."

"We'll visit another time," Matt said, leading him out of the bathroom.

"Nooo," Seth whined again.

When they reached the living room, Laura and Tawana were waiting for them. Moweez jumped up when she saw Seth and hurried over to him.

"—att sick," Moweez said, petting Seth's left arm. "All broken."

"I'd better get him home," Matt said to Laura and Tawana. "He probably picked up a bug at school. Sorry about the muffins."

"It's not your fault the oven didn't work," Laura said, dismissing his apology with a wave. "Go on and bring Seth home, and I'll make sure to get your containers back to you in the morning."

"No rush," Matt said.

Seth doubled over and groaned.

"Okay, Pepto here we come." Matt put an arm around Seth's shoulders. "Let's get you to bed."

Laura escorted them down the stairs and through the salon, with Moweez trailing behind, holding onto Seth's hand the entire way. When they reached the front door, Seth began to balk.

"I wanna stay," Seth cried. "You go home. I don't wanna go!"

"That's enough, son," Matt warned. "We're going home."

"No!" Seth let go of Moweez's hand and stomped a foot.

The surly tone shocked Matt. Seth had never spoken to him that way before.

"Yes." Matt scooped Seth into his arms and carried him out.

"I don't wanna go!" Seth yelled.

"Sorry," Matt called back to Laura. "I'll call tomorrow."

She gave a little wave and nodded, and Matt could only imagine what she must have been thinking as she watched Seth screech like a banshee.

Hurrying across the lawns, Matt held tight as Seth kicked and punched to get out of his arms.

"Let me go!" Seth cried. "I don't wanna go!"

When Matt made it into the café, he kept hold of Seth until he had him upstairs and in the kitchen.

"What is wrong with you?" Matt put Seth down and took hold of his arm.

Breathing heavily, Seth glared at him. "I don't want to stay here! I can't breathe in here! I can't!" He pulled out of Matt's grasp.

"What the hell are you talking about?" Matt said.

Seth whirled around and stomped toward the hall, his hands clenched into fists at his side. "You don't care. You never cared."

"Seth Michael!"

Seth stopped short midway down the hall and

turned to him. "You don't care about me, just like you didn't care about mom!"

"What—"

"You left me with her. You knew what she was doing but you left us with her anyway!" Seth screamed. He kicked the wall, then spun around and marched to his bedroom door.

"You get back here, young man," Matt demanded.

Seth looked back at Matt. "It was you that did it, not her. You! You killed us all!" With that, he crossed the threshold of his bedroom and slammed the door shut.

Openmouthed, Matt stared into the empty hallway, wondering if Tawana's devil might not have been a joke after all.

CHAPTER TWELVE

"What'd ya do, pull a looper last night?" Lerna Mae asked as she flipped a burger on the grill.

Matt finished his yawn. "Just didn't sleep well." He wasn't about to tell Lerna Mae about the incident with Seth last night, or she *really* would have thought he'd gone on a bender.

"It's full moon, that's why," Lerna Mae said. "I knew it was fixing to come around when my bursitis started acting up this week. That and my legs start twitching when there's a full moon. You know, when I'm trying to go to sleep. Ever hear of anything crazier than that?"

Oh, yeah, Matt thought. After Seth had blasted him last night with all those bizarre accusations, he'd wanted to barge into his son's bedroom and yank him up by the collar. It was as if the boy had suddenly developed a split personality, and the ugly half, the half Matt had never witnessed before, had taken over.

But he hadn't barged in. Instead, he waited, giving his son time to cool off and considered the possibility that Seth wasn't thinking clearly because he was sick. He'd let ten minutes or more go by before going in to check on him, and he'd found him already tucked under his comforter, asleep. This morning, Seth still didn't seem to be himself; uncooperative, grouchy, and about as communicative as the Frosted Flakes he'd had for breakfast. Although Matt offered to keep him out of school for the day, Seth refused without explanation. He hadn't even waved good-bye like he normally did just before getting on the bus.

"You lost your hearing along with your sleep?"

Jerked out of his reverie by Lerna Mae's question, Matt looked up. "Huh?"

"I was saying—oh, never mind 'cause you're not gonna hear me again anyhow." Lerna Mae slapped the grilled burger onto a bun with a spatula and handed the sandwich to Matt. "Here, go do something useful."

Matt took the plate from her and glanced over the service window to the man who'd ordered the burger. Besides him, there were two other people in the café. The last time the Tin Cup had seen a lunch crowd this light was over five years ago, when he'd first opened the café across town. "I don't understand why there aren't more people in here," he said. "Especially with everyone setting up for the street parties tonight."

"I was wondering the same thing." Lerna Mae shook her head. "If you had trouble sleeping last night, you're sure gonna have a fit trying to sleep tonight. The last band's supposed to finish up at midnight, but you know how that goes."

"We'll be lucky if they shut it down by two."

"Yep, and don't forget about tomorrow."

Matt groaned. Tomorrow was the Courir, the running of the Mardi Gras, which meant Windham would be in a festive uproar until midnight once again.

He was about to set the burger on the service window when he remembered Sam wasn't there to wait tables. First time in three years the boy calls in sick, and it had to be today.

With burger in hand, Matt pushed through the swinging doors that led to the café's seating area and spotted Percy Schexneider trudging toward a booth. His face was drawn and haggard, his uniform rumpled. He slid into a booth, stuck his elbows on the table and rubbed his face with both hands. The man looked like he needed a good belt of bourbon instead of a meal.

After dropping the sandwich off to its owner, Matt went over to meet him. "All ready for the Courir, Capitaine?"

Percy peered over his fingers, then slowly folded his arms on the table. "Don't know if I'm gonna make the run this year. In fact, I'd like to cancel the whole damn event."

Matt sat on the bench seat across from him. "What's wrong?"

"Jeff Mabry's been shot."

Matt sat back, stunned. "What? Wait, isn't that the

guy who works for Lafleur, the one you said was his brother-in-law?"

"Yeah. Was shot late yesterday afternoon, while doing some roofing work at the Baptist church. Right in the face."

"Jesus."

"The bullet went in through his right cheek. He was alive when the ambulance picked him up, but barely. I stayed with his family at the hospital all night." Percy let out a heavy sigh. "We lost him this morning."

"Man."

The *squeak-clomp-squeak* of leather shoes preceded Lerna Mae's appearance at the end of the booth. "What'll it be today, Chief? We got chicken and sausage gumbo for the special."

"Just coffee, Lerna Mae."

"Nothing to eat?"

Percy shook his head. "Ain't hungry."

Frowning, Lerna Mae folded her arms across her chest and looked from Percy to Matt. "What's with the long faces?"

"Jeff Mabry got shot yesterday," Percy said. "Died this morning."

Lerna Mae's face went slack with disbelief. "No."

Percy nodded, filling her in with the same sketchy details he'd given Matt.

"Any idea who did it?" Matt asked.

"Not yet. Ben Theriot and Russell Provost were with him on the roof. They said they heard a loud pop but thought a car had backfired."

"Well, yeah," Lerna Mae said. "Who's gonna think somebody's out there shooting people on a church roof?"

"But then they saw Jeff. Ben claims they were so freaked out by all the blood and trying to help Jeff, they didn't think of looking around for a gunman. Russell's the one who got off the roof to call nine-one-one, but he says he didn't see anything unusual around the church."

"Whoever did it had to have been at a distance to get him on the roof," Matt said.

"I figured that, too," Percy said. "So did the state police. They had quite a few units spread out over the neighborhood and in the fields out back. A couple of their detectives have been good about updating me, but so far, nothing."

Lerna Mae's eyes narrowed. "So we got a killer running around Windham right now?"

Percy gave her an exhausted look. "I don't know what the hell we've got right now, Lerna Mae. All I can tell you is to keep your eyes open."

"For what? What am I supposed to be looking for?"

"To be honest, I don't have a damn clue. The only thing I know for sure is Jeff Mabry's dead."

"That poor, poor boy." Lerna Mae pressed a hand to her chest. "When's the funeral?"

"He'll be laid out tonight at Delatross Funeral Home. I think the viewing starts at six. The funeral won't be until day after tomorrow, though, because of the Courir. There's no way they'd be able to get a procession through to St. Paul's if they did it tomorrow. Not with all those horses and riders."

"So cancel the run," Lerna Mae said.

"I can't. Way too many people involved, too many registered. It would be like trying to stop a freight train already blowing at full speed."

"Did Jeff have kids, a wife?" Matt asked. "Is there anything we can do for them?"

"He didn't have either. But his sister and mom are pretty tore up."

"What about Lafleur?"

Percy grimaced and swiped a hand over his mouth like he'd tasted something nasty. "I didn't see him at the hospital last night, but I'm not surprised. Saw him late yesterday afternoon at his house. The man's sick bad. Skin's all broken out with these big sores and stuff. It scared me just to be in the same yard with him. Afraid I was gonna catch whatever he had."

Lerna Mae let out a little snort. "Probably's got one of them verineal diseases, the way he tom cats around."

"I don't know what it is," Percy said. "I just know I don't want it." He pointed his chin toward the lunch counter. "Think I can get that coffee now?"

"Oh—sorry."

When Lerna Mae left to fetch the coffee, Percy slouched in his seat. "I'll tell ya, Matt, if I didn't know better, I'd swear somebody put a mojo on this town. Too many weird things happening lately. Stuff we never had to deal with in Windham before. The Miller girl getting stabbed over at the Dairy Freezo, those dead birds, Mabry getting shot. I'm wondering what the hell might be coming next. You know what I'm saying?"

"Yeah." The answer was as close to noncommittal as Matt could get. He thought of Moweez's drawings, the woman who'd been trapped in the bathroom, Seth sleepwalking and his outburst last night, the chaos they'd gone through in the beauty salon yesterday. When he put all that together with the occurrences Percy mentioned, he could see where a curse might not appear so outlandish.

Lerna Mae made it back to the booth with a mug of coffee and a slice of apple pie. "Sorry it took a little while. Had to ring up a couple customers." She handed the pie and coffee to Percy. "The pie's on me. At least try to eat a little."

Percy's smile was weary but grateful. "Thanks."

She nodded. "Now, what'd I miss?"

"We were just talking about the weird stuff happening around here lately." Percy said, and took a sip of coffee.

"Ain't that the truth? Ever since Lafleur moved this building here, come to think about it."

One of Percy's eyebrows arched. "You know, you're right. It really got started at the beginning of February, though, when they opened the salon next door."

"What's this building or the salon got to do with anything?" Matt asked.

Lerna Mae tapped a finger against her lips. "Maybe nothing, maybe something. Either of you know where this building came from?"

Percy lifted a finger while he took another sip of coffee and swallowed. "Crowley. It used to be an old house in Crowley. From what I understand, a drugstore bought a piece of property out there, and the house was on it. They wanted the house moved so they could build a new store, and Lafleur took it off their hands. Didn't cost him a dime except the labor to have it cut in half and moved. Other than that, I don't know much else about the house."

"What if it was haunted?" Lerna Mae asked.

Matt groaned. "For heaven's sake. I don't think—"

"No, wait, listen." Lerna Mae spread her arms out wide, indicating the whole of the building. "What if an ax murderer chopped up a family in this very room or in the building next door, and their ghosts—"

"Lerna—"

"Hold up, Matt. Maybe the house used to sit on an old Indian burial ground, and when they moved the house, the spirits got all mad and decided to come with it."

Matt dropped his head in his hands. "Good lord."

"Or there could have been a curse on Crowley, and when they moved the house, part of that curse got sent—"

The ringing of the phone made Matt sit up abruptly. It reminded him of yesterday at the salon. With his heart racing much too fast, he signaled for Lerna Mae to answer the portable phone on the lunch counter.

Appearing disappointed that her idea was cut short, Lerna Mae stomped over to the counter and grabbed the phone.

"Tin Cup." Lerna Mae sandwiched the phone between her shoulder and ear and reached for an order pad and pen.

Suddenly, she jerked upright, taking hold of the

phone again. "Is he sick? Yeah, yeah, I'm like his aunt."

Figuring Seth's upset stomach had returned, Matt looked back at her and mouthed, "Seth?"

Lerna Mae didn't look at him. She stared at a nearby chair, as if concentrating on the wood grain. "He did what?" She looked over at Matt, her voice shooting up two octaves. "You sure?"

Matt scrambled out of the booth.

"Someone'll be right over." Lerna Mae hung up before Matt reached her.

"What?" he asked.

"That was Miss Peredon, Seth's teacher."

"And?"

Lerna Mae stared at him, her eyes filled with incredulity.

"Lerna Mae, what?"

"Somebody's got to go pick up Seth," she said haltingly.

"He's sick?"

"I don't—she didn't say he was sick. She—uh—she—"

"Lerna Mae, spill it!"

She eyed Matt solemnly. "She said Seth stabbed another kid with a pencil."

CHAPTER THIRTEEN

Moweez and Tawana each tapped a foot to the accordion razz of Rockin' Dopsie Jr. and the Zydeco Twisters, who played on a flatbed trailer two blocks down from the Beauty Box. Small groups of people wrapped in jackets and rain ponchos strolled along First Street, some swinging their hips to the *thunk-thunk-thunk* of the bass drum, others doing the Zydeco stomp with a Budweiser in one hand and Mardi Gras beads in the other. All day, food and drink vendors had scrambled to set up their booths along First in preparation for tonight's street parties and the Courir de Mardi Gras, which would begin the following morning. The weather hadn't been very cooperative with its cold and drizzle, and the forecasters called for storms around midnight, which was only four hours away.

With a perfect observation spot on the porch of the salon, Laura had hoped her mood would lighten once the parties and bands started. But it didn't. Like the weather, it only grew darker and heavier with each passing hour.

They'd only had two customers all day, and both were eight-dollar trims. Even worse, the rent on the building was due next week, and she'd received word this morning that their bank account held little more than dust mites. Somehow, over the last two weeks, she'd forgotten to deduct a couple of ATM withdrawals from the company checkbook. That memory snafu caused checks to bounce and overdraft charges to accumulate. If business didn't pick up, they'd be lucky to afford toilet paper next week.

"Hey," Tawana said, nodding toward three women who were laughing and singing their way to a beer vendor half a block away from the shop. "You saw what them hussies just did?"

Laura shook her head. She hadn't seen much of anything in the last hour or so. She'd been too focused on their lack of funds and business.

Tawana pointed to the sidewalk in front of the shop. "They was walkin' on this side of the road, and when they got close to the Box, they just up and crossed the street, like we had some kind of disease or somethin'. Everybody's been doin' that tonight, crossin' the street, crossin' the street—I'm tellin' you, I'm startin' to get a complex about it."

"They *have* to cross the street to get to the beer truck."

"Even the ones not drinkin' beer?"

Laura shrugged. "Maybe they're selling something other than beer on that truck, like hotdogs or po'boys."

Tawana tsked. "Girl, get real. You see any weenie pictures on that sign? No, it's got Budweiser all up on that truck. Oh, hey, since we talkin' about weenies, I seen Matt's sauce pot still in the kitchen. How come you didn't bring it back to him today like you said?"

"I got tied up with the bank, and why did talking about weenies make you think of Matt?"

Tawana smirked. "Must've been those jeans he was wearin' last night. For a white man, he's sure got a cute butt, and the way I figure it, if it's cookin' in the back, it's gotta be hot in the front."

Laura grinned and shook her head. "You're too much."

"Yeah, I know."

Laura's insides grew warm with the thought of Matt. There was no question he was good-looking, a small town version of Kevin Costner, only with darker hair and a more pronounced cleft in his chin. He'd impressed her when they'd first met, and had scored even more brownie points last night. Easy to talk to: fifty points. Sense of humor: another fifty. Caring father: a thousand. She didn't think he was married, since he wore no ring and had never once mentioned, "my wife," but Seth was proof there was, or had been, a woman in Matt's life. Laura suddenly felt a twinge of guilt. She should have at least called to see how Seth was feeling today.

Moweez pointed toward the café. "—att sick. Light come fast."

Laura glanced back to where she indicated. She didn't see Seth or Matt, but in the distance, way beyond the roof of the café, she saw lightning crackle through the black palette of night.

"Looks like the storm's fixin' to roll in," Tawana said.

"Didn't hear thunder, though, so it must still be a decent distance—"

"Hey, how y'all doing?" Waving gloved hands, Maude Romero and Sadie Babineaux stood in the glow of a security lamp across the street from the shop. They resembled twin flappers in their bright purple shift dresses, complete with large hip bows and gold, green, and purple glittered and striped cloche hats.

"They look like decorated toilet paper tubes," Tawana muttered.

"Be nice." Laura returned the wave and motioned the women over. Their smiles faltered.

"Nice? They the ones who ain't been nice," Tawana said. "All that big talk about comin' back to the shop to get their hair done before the balls, and neither one of 'em showed up."

"Something might have come up."

"Yeah, right, like it did for everybody else who didn't show?"

"Shh."

Maude and Sadie made their way over to the shop's sidewalk, hand in hand. They appeared nervous, as if they were approaching a lion's den instead of a beauty shop. They made it only as far as the barren azalea bushes near the porch.

"Good—good to see y'all again." Maude's smile was as fake as her two-inch eyelashes.

158

"Love the costumes," Tawana said, an edge of sarcasm in her voice.

Laura gave her a stern look before addressing the flapper twins. "Same here, Miss Maude. Good to see both of you out enjoying yourselves."

"How come you girls aren't walking around and having a bit of fun?" Sadie asked.

"Moweez hasn't been feeling well, so we thought it best to keep her out of this weather," Laura said.

"Oh, I don't blame you with it being so wet and cold. We didn't get out here 'til a half hour or so ago, when it finally quit drizzling. Doesn't look like the rain's going to hold out much longer, though." Sadie stood on tiptoe, peering past Laura. "Hope you feel better soon, Moweez."

Maude followed suit, sending Moweez a one finger wave. She looked over at Tawana, frowning. "What happened to her forehead?"

"She fell," Tawana said tersely. "Hit it on a piece of furniture."

Maude cocked her head, giving her a quizzical look. "You sound upset, Tawana. Are you sick, too?"

Laura winced. She knew that was too big an opening for Tawana to miss.

"Yeah, I'm sick." Tawana sat taller in her chair. "I'm sick of people treatin' us like we got lice or somethin'. What's wrong with everybody? Look—see what I'm sayin'? Look how you all jumpy right now."

Maude threw Sadie a worried glance. "We—we're not jumpy."

"And we *never* thought y'all had lice," Sadie said.

"Then how come y'all didn't come back this week like you said?"

Maude fidgeted with the cuff on one of her gloves. "Well—uh, we had to go to Lafayette to do some shopping and decided to get our hair done while we were there. You know, kill two birds with—oh, I'm—I'm sorry—I didn't mean to bring up dead birds. You—"

"Miss Maude, there's no need to apologize," Laura said. "And you certainly don't need to explain why you had your hair done somewhere else."

Sadie nudged Maude. "We should tell them."

"You tell them."

"Tell us what?" Tawana asked.

Sadie sighed. "It's not y'all, that's not why people aren't coming. It's this place. And the café. It's like—"

"Light come fast!" Moweez scooted to the edge of her seat and pointed toward the café again. She looked worried "—att sick. Come-together broken. Mo say, light come fast. Come-together come fast."

Maude inched closer to Sadie. "What's she talking about?"

Laura got out of her chair and went over to the edge of the porch, where she could get a better look at the sky. "The lightning—over there." Jagged streaks of brilliant white ripped through the darkness. A few seconds later, a low rumble of thunder.

"Oh, we'd better get back to the car now before we get stuck in a downpour," Sadie said, already turning away.

"Wait," Tawana said, "you didn't finish telling us—"

A deafening blast of thunder shook the floorboards beneath Laura's feet. Shrieks of surprise rang out along First Street, and people started to scatter back to their vehicles.

Tawana gasped and scrambled to her feet. "Mercy, that sounded close."

Moweez stood as well, folding her arms across her chest. She began to rock in place. "—att sick, —att sick! Come-together come fast."

"Come on!" Maude tugged on Sadie's arm, and the two hurried off with Maude calling over her shoulder, "We'll call, girls, we'll call!"

Lightning ignited the sky; another blast of thunder, even louder than before. Street vendors yelled out to one another as they hustled to close the side flaps or windows of their service trailers. Fat raindrops began to ping against their awnings.

"It's going to get ugly," Laura said. "We'd better dig up some candles or a flashlight in case we lose power."

Tawana put an arm around Moweez's shoulder and steered her toward the shop door. "We got a couple of them red dinner candles left over from last Christmas. I'll get 'em."

Laura followed them into the shop, and the instant the storm door closed behind her, a torrent broke from the heavens. A dozen lightning bolts seemed to vie for dominance, one tumbling over the other, each progressively brighter and closer; no time lag between each boom of thunder.

As Tawana and Moweez went off in search of candles, Laura closed the main door and locked it. She turned off the lights, then went over to one of the front windows and parted the blinds with two fingers so she could peer out. Not even the streetlights were visible through the driving sheets of rain. She wondered if Maude and Sadie had made it to their car in time. No sooner had she finished that thought than a bolt of lightning struck the walkway that led to the shop. Night became day in that single flash, and Laura squinted against the harsh light, braced for the blast of thunder. It came with a vengeance, and the building trembled from its power.

"Lord Jesus of Mercy!" Tawana yelled from upstairs. "Laura, I can't find them goddamn candles!"

"Try the kitchen," Laura shouted over her shoulder. "In the drawer next to the dish towels." She turned back and was about to release the Venetian blinds when she realized a dark-haired woman was staring at her from outside the window—sad, penetrating eyes circled with weariness. Although Laura's gasp came a half second later, it came too late. The woman vanished before she fully sucked in the breath. Now Laura could hardly breathe. There had been no movement from the woman, no quick dash across the porch or leap onto the lawn. She'd just disappeared, like someone had clicked off a slide projector and killed her image.

Laura jerked her hands away from the blinds.

"Hey," Tawana yelled. "I can't see shit up here! Go check in the kitchenette and see if those friggin' candles are down there. They ain't up here."

Wetting her lips, Laura tried to settle her heart back to a natural rhythm. Just an illusion, she thought, created by glass and lightning and rain.

"You still down there?" Tawana called.

"Y-yeah. I'll go see if I can find them." She flipped the light switch. Nothing happened. The power was out.

Holding an arm out in from of her, Laura took a tentative step in the dark, then another. Her only source of light came from the strobes of lightning that snuck past the cracks in the blinds. When it allowed her to see, she was able to quicken her pace. In the dark, images of the woman in the window came unbidden, and fear made it nearly impossible for her to move.

Another strobe of light.

Laura lengthened her stride. Halfway across the shop now.

Darkness, nearly tangible against her outstretched fingers. Something tickled the back of Laura's neck, and she came to an abrupt halt, frantically brushing a hand over the spot. She thought of the woman who'd been bitten by the spider in the café, and it was all her imagination needed to conjure up images of daddy longlegs creeping up the knit of her sweater. Only sheer will kept Laura from ripping the garment off her body. When too much time had passed without a hint of light, she forced herself to take a step, then another. A breeze suddenly caressed her face, as though someone had hurried past her. Laura froze, her heart pounding in her ears.

"Wana?" she whispered. "Mo?"

No one answered.

She inched forward, afraid to let her fingers reach into the blackness that pressed around her.

A low rumble of thunder. A twinkling of milky light.

Grateful for the slight illumination, Laura ran for the kitchenette and managed to make it inside before her path went dark again.

The smaller room was easier to navigate, and it didn't take her long to feel a drawer handle beneath her fingers. She opened it and carefully ran a hand through the contents. Plastic fork, straws, cotton balls, a small, uncapped bottle, papers—no candles.

Laura closed the drawer and was about to feel for the next drawer handle when a pale strobe of light filtered in through the window above the sink to her left. She quickly scanned the countertops for a flashlight, matches, anything that might change black to light, but saw nothing that gave her hope. She spotted movement near the dinette table and her breath caught. A shadow upon a shadow. The meager offering of light from the storm quickly dissipated, however, and she was left with only dark speculation. Had she seen movement over there?

"Hey, I found 'em!"

Laura jumped and cried out involuntarily at the sound of Tawana's booming voice.

"What's the matter? You okay?" A narrow stream of erratic yellow light suddenly leaked down the stairwell into the kitchenette.

While trying to swallow her heart so she could speak, Laura heard the *thump-slap-thump* of Tawana's house slippers as she made her way down the stairs.

"Laura, you there?" Tawana's voice sounded closer and like a choir of angels to Laura's ears.

"Here. I'm over here."

The light stream grew wider, steadier.

"Girl, keep talkin' 'til I get there. It's spooky as shit walkin' around with this dumb-ass candle."

"You should try walking around without one."

Huge shadows danced on the wall adjacent to the staircase.

"I already did that upstairs. It wasn't pretty."

More light; different shadows.

"Where's Mo?"

Thump-slap-thump. "In her bed, already sleepin', I think." *Slap-thump.*

Laura breathed a heavy sigh of relief when the last *thump* produced Tawana at the bottom of the steps.

"I'm drippin'." Tawana held the candle way out in front of her. The new angle of the candle sent light cascading over the dinette table and across the threshold that led into the salon. Melting wax plopped to the floor.

Laura turned toward the cabinets to rummage for a candleholder and froze.

A thin little boy, dressed in blue plaid pajamas, stood between the dryer and the backdoor with his head bowed. And in the same split second it took for Laura to see him, he was gone.

CHAPTER FOURTEEN

Keith Lafleur hadn't counted on the storm. And he hadn't figured on so many people attending the viewing. What was it with people, anyway? Put a dead person in a casket, stick them in a room with flowers and sappy music, and damn near everyone in town showed up like they were on an attendance grading scale. It was all for show. It was always for show. Who had the best dress or suit, who cried the most, who made the biggest spectacle of themselves at the casket . . . it was downright pathetic. Sacrilegious really. In fact, he'd probably be doing heaven a huge favor if he torched the place with everyone in it. But he didn't want to waste the gasoline. It was earmarked for a much bigger event.

Yesterday, after he'd taken care of Jeff Mabry, Keith had driven to Lewisburg, a little town twenty miles west of Windham. All the way there, he sang along with the radio, which he'd cranked up to full volume.

Victory needed its reward. Once in Lewisburg, he'd pulled into an off-road truck stop and bought a ten-gallon plastic gasoline container and a hooded jacket two sizes too big for him. Truckers and store personnel made a point of backing away when he approached the counter to pay. Their revulsion hadn't bothered him. Those people were insignificant. Only background noise. After spraying those closest to him with an exaggerated, openmouthed cough, he'd gone outside to the gasoline pumps and filled the container with fuel. Later, when he'd returned home, he'd stored the container with the others, under the tarp in the garage. The hooded jacket he'd kept for today.

Now, wearing the jacket, he tugged the hood down lower so it shielded both sides of his face. The only way anyone would recognize him was if they stood front and center, and he'd make sure that didn't happen. Tonight, he had much to take care of—three to be exact, and he couldn't afford any slipups.

He'd been standing in the dark under the side portico of Delatross Funeral Home for over an hour, and he shivered from the cold. His body ached all over. Even his hair hurt. The pajama pants he'd put on two days ago were glued to his legs. He'd tried changing out of them this morning, but the layers of dried pus and blood from the boils on his legs wouldn't allow it. He was stuck to clothes that smelled worse than bloated road kill.

Keith rubbed his eyes with a thumb and forefinger. Sties had recently formed along the margin of his right eye, and they pricked and scratched his eyeball constantly. He worried about his vision. Eyesight was crucial in war.

"Well, at least the rain's slacked off," a woman said. Her voice sounded close, like she might have been standing under the colonnade around the corner.

"Jeff liked storms."

His ears pricked when he heard the second woman's voice. It was Barbara.

"I still can't believe he's gone," the first woman said. A choking sob. "Why—why did this happen? I don't understand—I can't understand. Jeff never hurt anybody. Everyone loved him. Why—why would somebody just shoot him like an animal?"

Because he was a lying, conniving bastard, that's why, Keith thought. *And you're not any better. Worse in fact. A lying, conniving whore.*

"Why don't you go on to your mama's home and get some rest," the first woman said. "Viewing hours are almost over anyway."

More snuffling. "I will, but Mom and I want to be the last to leave the funeral home. There's only Uncle Phil, Aunt Darla, and that guy from the lumberyard left inside. It shouldn't be much longer."

Keith couldn't hear what either of them said next because of the blood pounding in his ears. That guy from the lumberyard could only be Stanford Milo. The nerve of that bastard! It wasn't enough the sonofabitch had crippled his business and defiled his wife by turning her into his whore. Oh, no, certainly not enough. He had to rub it in—was probably in there right now, strutting around Mabry's casket, shuffling his ass feathers like a proud peacock in front of Barbara's aunt and uncle.

"Congratulations, dick wad," Keith said under his breath. "You just moved to the head of the line."

Keith forced himself to listen for the women's voices. When he didn't hear either of them, he took off for his truck, which was parked across the street next to the cemetery. Having stood in one place for too long, his feet screamed in pain with each step. The parking lot felt layered with razors and nails, searing coals and glass shards. His pain and weariness had reached a level meant only for martyrs. But revenge kept him moving. Revenge and the sight of Milo's truck parked close to Barbara's sedan in the funeral home's parking lot.

Having reached his pickup, Keith opened the cab and took out the weapon he'd brought with him. Then he went to Milo's truck and with great effort climbed into the bed of the vehicle. Luckily the only sources of light in the parking lot were from a street lamp a block away and two coned-shaped fixtures on either side of the funeral home's front door. Even combined, they produced only haze, which would allow him the freedom to move about without fearing detection.

Keith made his way to the back of the cab and saw that the window had a sliding glass panel in the center that could be opened about a foot. It was already open, which didn't surprise him. The only thing worth stealing in Stanford Milo's truck was the tin of Skoal sitting on the stained bench seat.

Even harder for Keith than climbing into the bed of the truck was trying to find a tolerable position that would allow him to stay hidden until it was time. Even though it was dark, he'd be spotted in a moment if he remained standing. Lying across the corrugated floor was out of the question. The ridges and furrows would kill him for sure. Squatting didn't seem to be an option, either. The boils behind his knees were the size of walnuts.

"Uhhmazeeeing grace, how sweet the sound . . ."

Stanford Milo's off-key version of "Amazing Grace" signaled the end of Keith's deliberations. He quickly squatted and had to grab hold of a side-mounted tool chest to keep from falling over. The pain in his thighs and calves was so horrendous it blurred his vision. He tasted blood from having bit his tongue to hold back a scream.

Keith heard the cab door open, then felt the weight of the fat slob settle into the truck. From the sound of his labored breathing, one might have thought Milo had run a marathon instead of walked across a parking lot. Seconds later, the cab door closed with a solid *clunk*. Keith waited.

The jangle of keys—Keith held his weapon at the ready.

Springs squeaking beneath the seat—he made certain the safety was off.

The sputter and ping of an abused engine coming to life—he pivoted slightly.

Keith saw the fear in Stanford Milo's eyes only seconds after he shoved the CO_2 nail gun through the opening in the back window. Before the pig could squeal, Keith slammed the gun against Milo's right temple and pulled the trigger. With a loud *thwack!* the three and a quarter-inch long framing nail drove into the man's head, leaving him wide-eyed and dead. It also left him sitting upright and visible.

Adrenaline muted Keith's pain as he scrambled out of the truck and went over to the driver's door. He opened it, intending to have a little target practice with Milo's groin, but there was too much stomach flab in the way for him to reach it. Enraged, Keith shot Milo through the left temple twice, then with a grunt, shoved his body sideways on the seat.

"How's this for amazing grace, asshole?" Keith drove a nail into Milo's ass for good measure. He killed the truck engine, closed the cab door, then hobbled over to Barbara's sedan, which sat three parking spots away.

Keith tested the back passenger door and found it unlocked. "Dumb bitch," he muttered, and opened the door.

A small overnight bag and two Nora Roberts novels sat on the backseat. Keith pushed them aside and climbed in. He rammed the head of the nail gun against the plastic overhead light shield. It splintered, and the light blinked out. He closed the door, taking care to make as little noise as possible.

Keith sat in the darkness, panting from exertion. His skin burned, and the pain roiling through his body made him want to cry. To keep himself from tumbling into a well of self-pity, he thought of Barbara and Milo together—his wife on her knees, that pig grunting his pleasure. They deserved each other—

the pig and the whore. Barbara never realized how good she had it at home. Hadn't he given her everything she wanted? Love, attention, money? It was about time someone taught her a lesson in gratitude.

He saw the front door to the funeral home open and Barbara and her mother, Dolores, step outside. Following right behind them were Barbara's aunt and uncle. Hissing through his teeth from pain, Keith eased himself into a crouch behind the front seat.

A decade seemed to go by before he heard a vehicle start, then drive off the lot; even longer before he heard Barbara and her mother close in on the car.

The clack of heels on concrete.

"I hate to leave him."

"Me, too, Mom. But it'll only be for a few hours. We'll come back first thing in the morning."

The driver's door opened.

"Barb, honey, isn't that Keith's truck?"

"No—his truck's newer and a different model. I think it's Mr. Milo's."

Keith frowned. Barbara's voice had sounded deadpan when she'd mentioned his truck, but the moment Milo's name came out of her mouth, there'd been a change of tone. A definite change, like she was happy. He gripped the nail gun tighter.

"You're talking about that nice man who left just a little while ago? The one who offered to go get us some food?" Dolores asked.

"Yeah."

"Wonder why his truck is still here?"

"He might have gotten a ride with someone else."

"Why would he leave his truck here, though?"

"Mom, it's late. Let's—"

"Maybe we should go tell Mr. Delatross. I mean it's just sitting there. Somebody could steal it."

"Nobody's going to steal that old truck. Come on and get in the car, okay? It's chilly and damp out here, and we don't need you getting sick."

The passenger door opened, and the front seat pressed a little closer to him as they got inside. The doors closed within seconds of each other.

"God, what's that awful smell?"

The sound of keys rattling against the ignition; the engine chugging to a start; a window powering down.

"Smells like raw sewage."

"More like something rotten." Jerky movements from the driver's side of the seat. "The smell's stronger in the back."

Keith's pulse raced. From the sound of Barbara's voice, he knew she was looking over the seat. It wouldn't take long before her eyes adjusted to the dark. It was now or never. He pushed himself upright, and their collective gasps seemed to anesthetize his pain. He slammed the nail gun into his mother-in-law's face and before she fell unconscious against the passenger door, he had it aimed at Barbara's forehead.

"I swear if you scream or do anything but go where I tell you, I'll drive a nail through your brain," he said. "You got that?"

The horror on Barbara's face as she stared at him was worth every ounce of pain he'd suffered so far. Her hands shook violently as she turned and grasped the steering wheel. She held onto it as though expecting the car to take off on its own.

"Drive!" he demanded through clenched teeth. He stuck the nose of the nail gun against the back of her head.

Barbara jumped, then whimpered as she struggled to put the car in gear. The car jerked forward and he tapped the gun against her head to remind her of the person in charge.

"Take a right outta the lot."

She did as she was told. The car soon picked up speed, and as soon as they passed his pickup, he tapped her head again.

"Slow this sonofabitch down."

She whimpered again and the car immediately slowed.

"Turn left—there, the road past the cemetery gate."

The car came to a complete stop.

"I said turn!"

With a sob, she shook her head and put the car in park. "I'm not—Keith—there's nothing down—nothing down there."

He cocked his head to make sure she saw him. "You're not going? Is that what you're saying?"

Her whole body shook now. "There's—I—don't—Keith, please!"

"Barbara, Barbara," he said in a singsong voice, "you always were a terrible listener, you know that?" He turned the nail gun on his mother-in-law and shot her behind the left ear. Her body jerked as the nail countersunk in her head.

Barbara's scream was loud enough to worry him. They weren't far enough away from the funeral home. Someone might hear her. To make matters worse, her hands flailed everywhere, like she wanted out but couldn't remember where the car door was. He knew she'd eventually find it.

So Keith shot his wife.

The first nail went through her right eye. The second plowed through the center of her forehead. The third and fourth on either side of the second.

Only then did the bitch stop screaming.

CHAPTER FIFTEEN

By the light of a single candle, Matt searched the face of the stranger sitting across from him. The boy looked like Seth: same light brown eyes, same unruly cowlick, the same tiny scar on his left cheek from the time he'd fallen off his bike two years ago. He even ate a sandwich like Seth, biting off the crust, then eating around the sandwich until the bread looked like a shrinking pinwheel. But the boy didn't act like Seth. It was as if his son had been snatched away and replaced with a defective clone.

Matt had found him in the principal's office when he arrived at school that afternoon. He appeared confused, barely capable of stringing two sentences together to complete a thought. According to Seth's teacher, he'd gotten into an argument with Cody Benoit, a friend of his since kindergarten. The squabble escalated so quickly, she didn't have a chance to intervene before Cody slapped Seth on the side of the head. When Cody hauled back to hit him again, Seth grabbed a pencil off the nearest desk and stabbed him in the forearm. Fortunately, the wound was only as deep as the point of the pencil, but it was enough to have Seth suspended for two weeks. Cody got three weeks.

Before taking him home, Matt stopped in to have Dr. Robins, their family physician, look Seth over. Since they didn't have an appointment, they'd had to wait two hours to see him, but it had been worth it just to hear Robins declare Seth healthy and "growing like a weed."

On the ride home, Seth wouldn't answer any of Matt's questions. He just gazed out the window as though they were traveling through a town he'd never seen before. When they pulled into the driveway of the café, Seth staunchly refused to get out of the car. He looked frightened, claiming he couldn't breathe in their apartment, that he didn't want to hear the boys talking and crying in his closet, and that he didn't want to live here anymore. It took a while for Matt to coax him out of the car, and by the time he managed to get him into the apartment, Seth looked exhausted and resigned. He went straight into the living room, laid on the couch, and quickly fell asleep. Matt left him alone, hoping a nap would help, but when thunder woke Seth hours later, he was still sullen and withdrawn.

Now, in this straw-colored light, his son appeared fragile and lost. The dark circles under his eyes made him look as if he hadn't slept in days. Matt thought about taking Seth to a hospital. But what would they be able to do for him? According to Robins, there didn't appear to be anything physically wrong with Seth. The problem seemed to be in his head. That frightened Matt. A cut he knew how to bandage, but what was he supposed to do with this?

"Hey, how about another sandwich?" Matt asked, hoping to coax his son into a conversation.

Seth stared at his empty plate and shook his head slowly. "Not hungry for another sandwich."

"Afraid that's all we've got until the power comes back on."

Silence fell between them, and after a moment or two Matt found it deafening.

"Wanna talk about what happened between you and Cody today?"

More silence.

"Son?"

The eyes that peered up at Matt belonged to someone much older, someone who had carried too much heartache.

"He called me a liar," Seth finally said.

Matt took his time responding. He didn't want to say anything that might cause Seth to shut down again. "I'd have probably gotten upset, too, if someone called me a liar."

Seth stared down at his plate again.

"What did he think you lied about?"

"The boys in my closet."

Matt felt a chill run across the back of his neck. "You told Cody about that?"

Seth nodded.

"Any particular reason why you told him?"

" 'Cause he's my best friend, and best friends are

supposed to tell each other stuff. But he didn't believe me like she did."

"She?"

He nodded again. "She helped me build a bridge on the coffee table, then hurt her head."

Matt frowned. "You're talking about Moweez from the beauty shop?"

"She's my only best friend now because she didn't call me a liar."

A barrage of questions wanted to burst from Matt's mouth, but he kept them in check. Seth might offer more if he didn't push him.

"Do you think I'm a liar?" Seth asked.

"No."

"Then you believe me about the boys? The ones in my closet?"

Matt searched his son's face for a hint on how he should convey his answer. He saw only quizzical expectation, the first sign of the old Seth he'd seen all day.

"If you say you hear boys talking in your closet," Matt said carefully, "then I believe you. But don't you think maybe you might be dreaming when you hear them?"

"No."

Seth's abrupt answer made Matt feel like he'd slipped back on tenuous ground. He didn't push the dream possibility any further. "So what did Moweez say about the boys when you told her?"

"She hears them, too."

"In her closet?"

"In mine."

Matt folded his arms and rested them on top of the table. "So Moweez has been in your room?"

Seth frowned, as though he'd had the answer to that question only a second ago but lost it. After a moment, something flickered in his eyes, but it died quickly. To Matt, that something looked like hope.

"I wanna go to bed," Seth said quietly. "Can you bring the candle and come stay with me 'til I fall asleep?"

Matt wanted to ask how he could possibly be sleepy after having slept seven straight hours, but he locked that question away, too. He thought it best to placate Seth until he either figured out a better way to handle this himself or found someone who could. "Sure."

Seth got up from the table, picked up his plate, and carried it over to the sink. With that chore done, he turned back to Matt. "I'm ready."

The resignation in those two words made Seth sound like he was heading to his execution instead of to bed. It made Matt's heart ache.

He stood, took the candle from the table, then walked over to Seth and held out his free hand. Seth hesitated before taking the offer. Matt let him lead the way down the hall to his bedroom, all the while so very aware of just how small his son's hand felt within his own.

"Don't be afraid," Seth murmured as he opened his bedroom door. At first, Matt thought he was talking to himself, but then Seth glanced over his shoulder at him. "Don't be afraid. It doesn't really hurt."

The hair on Matt's arms stood at attention. "What doesn't hurt?"

Instead of answering, Seth led him into the bedroom. Once inside, he let go of Matt's hand and headed for his bed.

"Don't you want to change out of your school clothes?" Matt asked when he climbed into bed fully dressed.

Seth lay on his bed, turned on his left side so he faced the wall, then curled his body into a ball.

Rubbing the back of his neck wearily, Matt turned to place the candle on the dresser. It was then he spotted the valve lever on top of the dresser next to a pair of Seth's socks. Just the sight of it sent bile racing up Matt's throat. He backed away, his body beginning to tremble. The flame from the candle threw a flurry of shadows across the room. It made no sense that such an innocent object could affect him so drastically. All he knew was he didn't want anything to do with it.

Keeping one eye on the lever, Matt made his way to Seth's toy chest. He closed the lid, then placed the candle on top of it. When he was sure it wouldn't topple over, he turned back to tuck Seth into bed. But his son was already asleep, the comforter pulled up to his chin. Tears stung Matt's eyes. The simple act of tucking himself in seemed to qualify the emptiness Matt had seen in Seth's eyes earlier. Like the boy had no one in the world to turn to, no one but himself to count on.

Matt sat on the toy chest beside the candle. As right as the world seemed only a month ago, it was now utterly wrong. What was happening to Seth? *Why* was it happening to him? And more importantly, how was he supposed to make it stop?

He glanced over at the window, remembering Moweez's drawing. The girl knew something; he felt that as sure as he felt the sneakers on his feet. It was in the way she'd taken to Seth so quickly, clung to him. Somehow Moweez not only understood what was happening to Seth, she understood why it was happening. Trying to get those answers from her, though, bordered on impossible. But he had to keep trying.

Closing his eyes, Matt worked to clear his mind; then, one by one, he gathered the pieces of the strange puzzle together to see if a plausible picture emerged. Somewhere between the dead birds and the sound of stomping feet in the salon, a thought occurred to Matt. All the strange occurrences, even with Seth, began when Laura, Tawana, and Moweez moved in next door. Percy and Lerna Mae had even commented on that very thing today. And they were right—before the salon opened, it had been business as usual for him—better than usual in fact. So what was the tie-in? Why would three women moving into the building serve as a catalyst for all these strange events? Matt played around a little with Lerna Mae's notion that the building might be haunted, but quickly dismissed it. Not that he was close-minded to the possibility; it just didn't feel like the right answer. Still, no matter how many ways he looked at it, the café and the salon did seem to play a part. But exactly what parts were they playing and why?

Left with more questions than he started with, Matt opened his eyes and picked up the candle. He got up from the toy chest, went over to look in the closet as an afterthought, then walked over to Seth, his heart unbearably heavy. Maybe the Mardi Gras festivities tomorrow might cheer Seth up, help him snap back to normal. With that small thread of hope, Matt kissed his son, then left the room, leaving the door open in case he called out for him.

He wandered into the living room, but it felt too empty and lonely without lights or television, so he made his way back into the kitchen. Wishing they had a gas stove, Matt went over to the counter near the fridge and pulled out one of the recipe books he kept on a rack there. Preparing meals had always been cathartic for him. For a month after his wife left, he'd broiled, boiled, baked, roasted, and sautéed damn near everything in sight. The same cooking urge came over him now, but the best he'd be able to do was read about it.

Matt brought the cookbook over to the table and sat, placing the candle close by so he'd have enough light to read. No sooner did he open the book than he heard Seth's voice.

"If y'all don't stop making all that noise, she'll hear you. You're not supposed to be here. . . ."

Matt got to his feet, listening. Was Seth talking in his sleep? He took a step toward the hall.

"Wake up . . . why won't you wake up? No, I don't want to go with you . . . stay away . . . leave me alone!"

The bloodcurdling scream that followed sent Matt flying. He snatched the candle from the table and raced down the hall. The flame flickered wildly as he ran, then winked out before he reached Seth's bedroom. "Sonofabitch!" Matt dropped the candle and frantically felt his way through the inky black.

"I don't want to go—stop! Daddy!"

"I'm coming!" Matt's fingers tripped over a door-jamb, and he used it for leverage to hurl himself into the room. He flung his arms out wide, searching for his son. "Seth!"

"Don't let 'em take me, Daddy, please!"

Matt heard the rustle of sheets, creaking from the headboard, muffled struggling noises like Seth was wrestling with someone on his bed. He hurried toward the sounds.

"Stop pulling me!"

His shins found Seth's bed first, ramming against the metal frame that held the mattress. Matt fell forward and immediately felt Seth beneath him. He flung out an arm but felt no one else on the bed. The boy began to writhe and buck like his life depended on it.

"Get off! Leave me alone!" Seth pummeled Matt's shoulders with his fists.

"It's me, Seth, it's Dad!"

Seth's fists came down again, a little softer this time.

"It's me, son, it's me."

Seth began to cry, loud, racking sobs that shook them both. Matt gathered him in his arms and quickly carried him out of the room.

Estimating where he'd dropped the candle, Matt held Seth close to his chest and worked off each of his sneakers with the opposite foot. With just his socks on, he was able to feel the candle between his feet after only a few steps. Hanging on tightly to Seth, he leaned over, picked up the candle, and carried it into the kitchen.

With Seth sobbing in his ear and clutching his arms and shoulders like he was afraid he would fall at any moment, it took a while for Matt to locate the matches.

He was shaking so hard that the first match went out before he reached the wick. The second burned his finger after he struck it against the matchbox, but at least the flame held out long enough to be transferred to the candle.

Matt set the burning candle on the table, then pulled out a chair and sat with his son on his lap. Still sobbing, Seth buried his face in Matt's shoulder.

"They almost took me!" he cried. "Why didn't you come? Why did you let them almost take me?"

"I did come, and nobody took you." Matt held him close, rocking gently.

"But they almost did! They pulled and pulled and almost did!"

Matt stopped rocking and sat farther back in the chair. "Son, look at me."

"They almost did!"

"Seth," Matt kept his voice quiet and soft. "Look at me for a minute, okay?"

Seth rubbed his nose against Matt's shirt, then slowly sat back. His face was soaked with tears, his nose still running and red. He shook his head as though he faced the unbelievable. "Why didn't you come?"

"I did."

Seth's eyes flicked past Matt's shoulder to the hallway. "But they almost got me." His voice was a choked whisper.

"You were dreaming. There was no one in the room but—"

"I wasn't dreaming, I wasn't! They grabbed my feet and tried to pull me out of bed. They hurt me." Seth pointed to both his ankles, which were covered with white tube socks. His eyes pleaded. "You have to believe me, Daddy, you have to!"

Matt pulled him close. "*Shh,* all right, son, all right."

Seth curled up against Matt's chest, his breath whistling through a stuffy nose.

"You can sleep with me tonight, okay?"

Seth nodded.

Matt got to his feet, picked up the candle, and once again carried Seth down the hall. Seth's legs and arms tightened around him when he stopped in his room for pajamas.

"I don't want to be in here," Seth whispered.

"If you're afraid, hold tight to me and keep your eyes closed. I just want to get your pajamas."

When Seth's grip tightened even more, Matt held the candle out in front of him and quickly surveyed the room. Seth's bed was in shambles; even the mattress hung askew. He went over to the bureau, held his breath when he saw the lever, then yanked open the top drawer and hurriedly pulled out a pair of blue flannel pajamas and a clean pair of socks. Matt left the drawer open and, for his own peace of mind, went over to Seth's closet and checked inside. As he'd suspected, nothing but clothes and toys. Kissing the top of his son's head, Matt left Seth's bedroom and walked across the hall to his own.

Just as he sat Seth down on the bed, the lamp beside his bed flickered to life. The central heater kicked on, and a high-pitched beep from the microwave in the kitchen informed him it was now back in business.

Matt let out a huge sigh of relief. "We've got power, champ."

Seth only nodded.

He sat beside Seth and helped him out of his school shirt and pants and into his pajamas. When the last button was in place, Matt motioned for Seth to put his feet on his lap. Seth grimaced and did as he was told.

Wanting to keep the mood as light as possible, Matt tweaked Seth's toes as he pulled off his socks. "Hey, at least we'll be warm tonight with the heater—" Matt's eyes zeroed in on Seth's exposed ankles.

"I told you," Seth said quietly.

With his heart slamming against his rib cage, Matt gently ran a finger over the bruises circling Seth's ankles.

CHAPTER SIXTEEN

Mardi Gras was Laura's favorite time of year. It was the apotheosis of all south Louisiana festivals, a time when Cajuns, Creoles, and everyone in between let their hair down, hiked their skirts up, and didn't give a damn who noticed. Each town had its own way of celebrating Fat Tuesday. New Orleans brought in serious money and earnest partiers with its grand floats and extravagant balls. Bourbon Street, St. Charles, and Royal turned into clogged arteries as a million people jammed the streets to celebrate the last day before Lent. Lafayette and Carencro catered to a more family-oriented crowd, where costumed children were able to stand in the back of pickup trucks along the side of the road and yell, "Throw me somethin', Mister!" to passing floats without the fear of being trampled. Rural towns like Mamou, Church Point, Eunice, and Windham maintained a more traditional Courir de Mardi Gras, where revelers sang, danced, and drank either on horseback, flatbed trailers, or on foot. Just about everyone in the community participated in one way or another, which created a sense of family much larger than one's own.

With her parents long dead and her brothers building lives of their own in Texas and Missouri, Laura normally drank heartily from this kindred font. Today, however, despite the sapphire blue skies and light jacket weather, the music and crowds rankled her nerves.

Last night's storm might have cleared a path for the day's perfect weather, but it also left a nightmare she couldn't shake. Laura hadn't told Tawana about their phantom visitor. They'd had enough turmoil lately, and she saw no need to add more to her friend's plate. For hours after they'd gone to bed, Laura struggled to convince herself that the boy had been an optical illusion. She turned the event over and over in her mind, revisiting the angle of the light, the shadows near the dryer, but a logical explanation refused to jell. Even more troubling than not being able to explain the boy's sudden appearance and disappearance was the feeling she'd seen him before. She still couldn't figure out from where, though, and that ate at her.

"Where's your head at, girl?" Tawana shouted as they zigzagged through a crowd dancing in Teeman's Grocery's parking lot. Steve Riley and the Mamou Playboys had their speakers cranked up and the accordion at full stretch as they played "La Danse de Mardi Gras" atop a low-boy trailer in front of the store.

"I'm good," Laura shouted back. She checked on Moweez, who'd fallen back a few steps. The girl was snapping her fingers and shuffling her feet to the beat of the music. The knot on her forehead had shrunk in size and faded to a dull yellowish-green. Compared to the color and costumes swirling around them, it wasn't even noticeable. The three of them had been walking Windham since early morning, not long after the Courir began their run, but Moweez looked as fresh as when they'd started. When she spotted Laura looking at her, she smiled broadly. Laura quickly returned the smile. It had been a long time since she'd seen Moweez this happy.

"Mo, come on up here so I don't lose you," Tawana said, signaling to her. She yanked on Laura's sleeve. "Hey, let's go get some boudin over there."

"You've already had three links."

"So."

Laura grinned. "Okay, it's your butt."

She followed Tawana and Moweez to a food trailer across the street, where at least twenty people already waited in line. Some were dancing, Mardi Gras beads jangling around their necks. Almost all of them carried a beer. Near the front of the line, Laura spotted Valentine Nestler, the owner of the little sewing shop that sat between the beauty salon and café. She looked like a lemon drop in her bright yellow moo-moo. Her thick white hair had been teased into a stiff bouffant that bounced each time she moved.

As they brought up the rear of the line, Tawana leaned in close to Laura and said, "Get a load of Mr. Nose Hair up there."

A couple feet ahead stood Thomas Sterner, Windham's postmaster—the old guy Sadie Babineaux thought should be Krewe King. He wore a purple and gold capuchon with the tunic and loose-fitting pants to match. She noticed he carried a handmade wire screen mask that had a phallic-shaped nose attached to it. As ridiculous as it looked, the mask might have served him better if he wore it. His own nose had almost an inch of hair sprouting from the nostrils. The only thing that kept Laura from staring was the snippet of conversation she overheard as he talked to a potbellied man with no teeth.

". . . all three dead, shot with a nail gun for God's sake. Found 'em this morning. One in Delatross's parking lot, the other two over by the cemetery. That makes four this week."

"I bet it was them terrorists who did it," the potbellied man said.

"What terrorists?"

"You know, just terrorists. They everywhere."

Thomas shook his head. "I think Lafleur killed all of them."

"The one who owns the construction company? How you figure?"

Sterner held up a hand and started ticking off fingers. "Brother-in-law, wife, mother-in-law, and Milo sold him lumber. They're all tied to him."

"Percy think that, too?"

A group of whooping teenagers ran between her and Sterner, drowning out his answer. By the time they moved on, Sterner was facing forward, and Laura couldn't hear anything he was saying.

She grabbed Tawana by the arm and pulled her close. "Did you hear that?"

"Hell yeah, I did. And if they think I'm gonna pay eight dollars for that sorry-ass boudin—"

"No, no, about those dead people and Lafleur—the guy we rent the shop from."

Tawana's eyes widened. "Dead people?"

"Three—no, four—four dead this week. And they think Lafleur killed them."

"Get the fuck out!"

"Shhh!"

Tawana leaned in closer. "You shittin' me, right?"

"That's what Sterner was just talking about."

"Who's Sterner?"

"Nose hair."

Tawana looked up, her eyes flitting about nervously.

"Remember when I told you Percy came by the shop the other day and told us something was wrong with Lafleur?"

"Yeah."

"Maybe he was right."

"So the man's in jail, right?"

"I don't know."

Tawana's nostrils flared like they often did when she was either angry or scared, and she reached for Moweez's hand. "Suppose the man's so whacked out he plans on killin' everybody he knows—like us?"

Laura chewed her bottom lip, not wanting to admit she'd thought the same thing.

"Okay, look, I ain't hungry no more. Let's just go on back to the house."

"Mo say stay," Moweez said, pulling away from Tawana. "Dance. Mo dance."

"We leavin', and you comin'," Tawana said firmly. "Now that's it."

Moweez's frown deepened.

"You can dance at home, Mo," Laura offered. "The parade will have lots of music, and it's going to pass right in front of the shop in a few minutes. We can watch it from the porch."

Tawana didn't wait for her cousin's approval. Clutching Moweez's hand, she took off for First Street, which was five blocks away.

By the time they reached the Beauty Box, Tawana was nearly running. She let go of Moweez's hand when she reached the steps, then cleared the porch in two strides. The storm door banged shut behind her when she raced inside.

Moweez looked over at Laura. Her eyebrows were arched in quizzical peaks. "Wana scared?"

Laura smiled and patted her arm. "Nervous, I think. Come on, let's sit and wait for the parade."

As they made their way over to the chairs at the end of the porch, Laura heard someone call her name. She glanced back and saw Matt and Seth walking toward the shop. Both looked sullen and exhausted, and Seth was limping.

Moweez spun around when she heard Matt's voice. She pointed toward them. "—att sick. Mo say—att sick." With that, she hurried off the porch, then ran over to Seth. His face lit up with a smile when he saw her.

"Got a minute?" Matt asked as they approached.

"Of course, come on up," Laura said. The worry lines creasing his brow concerned her. Was he bringing bad news? "We were just settling in for the parade. You two can hang out here with us if you'd like."

His smile was weary. "Thanks."

"Close the café early today?"

"Never opened it."

Laura looked at him quizzically, but he didn't offer an explanation.

Seth gave Laura a little wave as he followed Moweez over to the porch chairs.

"Hey, what happened to your foot?" Laura asked.

The boy shot Matt a nervous look, mumbled something Laura couldn't understand, then quickly took a seat by Moweez.

"Okay!" Tawana suddenly burst onto the porch with one hand rolled into a fist, the other clutching a five-pound, electric blue dumbbell. She shook the dumbbell at no one in particular. "Mr. Crazy can come all he wants now, 'cause Tawana Batiste is packin'."

"Who's Mr. Crazy?" Matt asked.

Laura motioned Matt and Tawana to the other side of the porch so Moweez and Seth wouldn't hear.

"Keith Lafleur," Laura said, keeping her voice low.

"Yeah, the asshole killed his whole family," Tawana said, nostrils flaring.

"We don't really know that for sure," Laura said.

"And he's probably gonna do us next," Tawana said.

Matt shook his head and held up a hand. "Hold on, hold on. Start from the beginning."

Laura told him everything she'd overheard from Thomas Sterner's conversation. When she finished, Matt looked shell-shocked.

"A nail gun . . ." Matt said the words as if his mind couldn't wrap around the concept.

"Don't you think Sterner makes a good point about them all being connected?" Laura asked.

"Percy told me about Lafleur's brother-in-law yesterday when he came to the Cup. Said the guy was shot while working on the roof of the Baptist church. He didn't say anything about suspecting Lafleur, though. In fact, he said Keith had been real sick."

"Sick in the head, yeah," Tawana said.

A police siren went off nearby, and all three of them started. Verneese Credeur crept past the salon in a Windham squad car and waved. "Y'all get ready," she shouted. "Them crazy bastards are not far behind me." She steered the car toward the center of the road and tapped the siren again to clear the pedestrians off the street.

"Since when does Verneese drive Percy's car?" Laura asked.

"Percy was supposed to be capitaine this year," Matt said, "but he told me yesterday he wouldn't be making the run because of the Mabry shooting. If three more people were killed yesterday, I'd bet he's up to his neck in problems right now. Probably got Verneese to help out here with crowd control."

"Mabry's the guy on the roof?" Tawana asked.

Matt nodded. "Jeff Mabry."

Laura heard the steady clop of horse hooves in the distance. "I think we should talk to Percy about Lafleur, find out what's really going on." She eyed Matt. "I don't know about you, but if Lafleur's even a suspect, I don't feel all that safe being in one of his buildings."

"I don't know that I care to be in the building even if he's not a suspect," Matt said, then glanced away as though embarrassed by what he'd just said.

"How come?" Tawana asked.

"We, uh . . ."

"What?" Laura asked.

He raked a hand through his hair. "Guess there's no other way for me to say it but straight out." He shoved his hands in his jean pockets. "There's something in my apartment—and it's trying to hurt Seth."

Tawana grew bug-eyed. "What do you mean, 'it'? Like the other day in the shop when we had all that crazy shit going on? That kinda 'it'?"

"My phone wasn't ringing or any of that other stuff, but something grabbed Seth last night."

Laura listened in astonishment as he told them about the strange things Seth had been saying and doing, about him wanting to sleep all the time, about the bruises on his ankles. But what sent ice sliding down Laura's spine was when Matt told them that Seth heard boys talking in the closet.

"Lord sanctified, gimme strength." Tawana began to pace. Short, quick steps, like she had to go to the bathroom. "You see, I told y'all, I told y'all it was the devil."

Laura saw more in Matt's eyes. He hadn't revealed everything he'd intended to say. "What else?" she asked.

He looked at her intently. "I think there's a connection between the three of you moving in here and the stuff happening in both places."

"You tryin' to say we brought a conja' on this place?" Tawana asked.

"No, not a curse. More like a catalyst, like you were a key to an engine. Before you came it wouldn't run. After you moved in . . ."

The sound of hooves and Cajun music began to push its way down First Street. The riders were much closer. Soon they wouldn't be able to hear one another without shouting

"Has Seth ever mentioned *seeing* any boys in the closet?" Laura asked.

"Not to me."

"Now see, that's good," Tawana said, nodding earnestly. "The boy's not seeing no ghost. I like that. I can't take no ghost. Uh-uh, put a ghost in front of Tawana Batiste, and poof, she dead. Heart attack for—"

"I saw a boy in the kitchenette last night," Laura blurted.

Tawana's face went slack. "Huh?"

"When you came downstairs with the candle, and I went to look for a candleholder in the cabinets. He was standing by the dryer. But he disappeared so fast I thought I'd imagined him."

"He *disappeared*?" Tawana flopped against a porch column like all the strength had been sucked out of her. "Why didn't you tell me?"

"I didn't want to worry you."

"Then why the hell you worryin' me now?"

"Because Matt might be right about this stuff tying together somehow. I couldn't not say anything, Wana, especially after he told us about Seth hearing boys in his closet."

"I think we need to find out more about this building," Matt said. "What it was used for, who lived in it, things like that. That might give us some answers."

"And I think we just need to move the fuck out," Tawana said. "To hell with answers."

"Move out and go where?" Laura asked. "With what money? We put every cent we had into this place, Wana. And what happened to all that big talk you had going on the other night? Spraying holy water everywhere, saying no hoogity boogity was going to chase you out of here?"

"That was before the ghost. I don't do ghost."

"Laisser les bon temps rouler!" Less than a block away, the Courir's capitaine sat astride a chestnut gelding, waving a white flag. His command to "let the good times roll!" detonated a maelstrom of drunken whoops from the hundreds of riders behind him. Horses sauntered; revelers in bright colored tunics and capuchons sang and danced in their saddles, a Budweiser in each hand. Thousands of Mardi Gras beads in every shape and color sparkled in the afternoon sun as they were tossed to the onlookers lining both sides of the street.

Moweez suddenly jumped up from her seat and faced the oncoming riders, waving her arms. "No, no! All broken! Come-together broken!"

Her words were quickly lost to the neighing and whinnying of horses. Paints and Thoroughbreds, Quarters, and mules began to prance restlessly. The capitaine, now directly in front of the shop, struggled to keep his horse in check. The animal's ears were pinned straight back, and it reared twice, refusing to go forward. In that moment, a hundred yards back, the front line horses took off in full gallop as though a starting gun had been fired, and within seconds a stampede ensued. Riders who had been standing on their horses fell over into a tangle of stomping, piercing hooves. Men still sitting in their saddles jerked uselessly on reins, shouting and cursing for their horses to stop. Manes flying, nostrils flared, the four-legged mammals stormed down First Street. Bystanders fled in every direction, a few escaping, many not. Horses fanned out into yards and collided with fences and parked cars, but most of the herd was heading for the capitaine, whose horse seemed mired in mud in front of the café.

Laura and Matt reached Seth and Moweez at the same time and pulled them away from the edge of the porch.

"Here!" Tawana held the shop's storm door open.

Everyone rushed inside, and Laura made it to a window in time to see a wall of horses slam into the capitaine. The animals reared, their huge eyes wild, their mouths open and straining against bits as if they were trapped and could go no farther than the café. Hooves jabbed at the air, pummeled riders, slashed other horses. Screams and cries, shrieks and neighing merged into a horrific symphony as half-ton bodies tumbled over one another, crushing any man who'd managed to stay astride. Brightly colored tunics no longer served as uniforms for vivacious revelers— they were now blood-soaked shrouds for the dead.

CHAPTER SEVENTEEN

A black wreath hung on the front door of Nestler's Sewing Cottage, but there was no one on First Street to see it. The road had been cordoned off since last night, when police and rescue workers from two parishes took over Windham.

Thirty-four people dead. Sixty-one injured. Twenty-one lifeless horses lifted by front-end loaders into hay wagons that carted them away for incineration. Blood still stained the street despite the cleaning efforts of three sanitation crews.

From her bedroom window, Laura watched two calico cats meander around a broken fence across the road. She knew the fence would eventually be repaired, but part of Windham would remain broken forever. No town survived the kind of trauma they'd witnessed yesterday without bearing scars.

She traced the edge of the windowsill with a finger, her mind and body still numb from lack of sleep.

She'd had so many hopes when they moved in here. This was to be her new beginning, the start of a simple, independent life that would prove once and for all that her father had been wrong. She'd disappointed him from the day she was born by being the wrong gender. As she grew older, their relationship became tenuous at best. When she dropped out of college, he didn't talk to her for a month, and once his reign of silence ended, he'd badgered her incessantly until the day he died. His daughter, the blunder of an impaired spermatozoon, would never amount to anything more than a minimum wage hairdresser.

Now her hopes were dying, just like the riders and horses, right before her eyes, one by one. Gossip about the building bringing bad luck to Windham had already taken business away from them. With last night's tragedy happening right in front of the shop and café, they'd be lucky if a mob didn't show up to torch the place. And she probably wouldn't blame them. Had they been able to leave the shop last night to search for hotel rooms, they would have. The turmoil in the streets had them trapped, however, and they were forced to stay. They'd compensated by staying together, with Matt and Seth bunking in the living room.

Spotting a car turn onto First Street from a nearby crossroad, Laura pressed her forehead against the pane to get a better look. Chief Schexneider's cruiser crept along the center of the road until it reached the parking lot of the salon. He turned in.

"Want coffee?" Tawana stood in the bedroom doorway, still dressed in her street clothes from yesterday. A lime green do-rag covered her hair.

Laura tapped lightly on the window. "We've got company. Chief Schexneider."

Tawana groaned. "I ain't even had one cup of coffee yet."

"You go on and get the coffee ready. I'll see what he wants."

"Matt's already got the coffee ready. I just gotta go drink some."

As Tawana trudged off, Laura hurried over to her closet and pulled out a clean pair of jeans and a sweater. She closed her bedroom door, then quickly stripped out of the jogging pants and sweatshirt she'd slept in and threw on the jeans and sweater. After pulling her hair back into a ponytail, she headed downstairs to meet the Chief.

Halfway down the stairs, Laura heard Matt behind her.

"Everything okay?"

She glanced back, suddenly aware of how horrible she probably looked with so little sleep. Matt, on the other hand, looked freshly scrubbed, like he'd recently had a shower. "Chief Schexneider's here," she said.

"Tawana told me. Want me to go down with you?"

A loud knock echoed up the stairwell.

"That's okay. I'll bring him up," she said, and hustled down to the salon.

When she opened the front door, Percy Schexneider had a fist raised, ready to knock once more. His uniform was disheveled, and the circles under his eyes were so dark they looked like charcoal smudges.

She opened the glass storm door to let him in. "Chief." It was all she could say. Asking him how he was doing would have been an insult.

"Laura." He glanced toward the back of the shop. "Matt here?"

"Upstairs. Would you like some coffee? We just made a pot."

He nodded, looking too weary to talk.

She led him upstairs. His leather boots landed heavily on each step, as though he carried someone twice his weight on his back.

When they reached the apartment, Moweez and Seth were sitting together on the couch watching cartoons. Tawana and Matt stood in the kitchen doorway, sipping coffee and waiting.

Laura motioned Percy into the kitchen. "Come on in and have a seat, Chief. I'll get you that coffee."

"Percy," Matt said, pulling a chair out for him.

Percy sat and took the mug of coffee Laura handed him. "Thanks. Sorry to bust in on y'all so early."

"We were already up," Laura said. She took the seat beside Percy. "I don't think any of us got much sleep last night."

"Same here." He took two quick sips of coffee, then idly scratched the stubble on his chin. "Y'all were here yesterday?"

"Oh, yeah," Tawana said wearily. "We was all here."

"So you saw what happened?"

Matt nodded. "We were out on the porch."

"A damn nightmare, I swear to Jesus of Nazareth," Tawana said.

Percy slumped back in his seat. "That's no lie. I've

been riding Courirs for twenty years, and I've never known anything like this to happen. Something had to gig those horses. Any of y'all see anything unusual, something that might've spooked them?"

Laura shook her head. "Nothing. The capitaine rode ahead of the Mardi Gras like usual, but when he got in front of the shop, his horse got real jittery, like he couldn't control—"

"Then them other horses just came runnin' and crashin' into him and each other," Tawana said, then slapped her hands together. "Just like that."

"See, that's what doesn't make sense to me," Percy said. "If a herd's gonna stampede, they're gonna run until they get themselves blocked in somewhere or they tucker out. There was nothing blocking the road past the café, was there?"

"Not that I saw," Matt said.

"I didn't see anything either," Laura added.

Percy frowned. "Everybody I talk to says the same thing, but *something* made those horses pile up like that. And it was something here, this section of First Street." He clinked a fingernail against his mug. "Seems like that's all I'm getting lately, a whole lot of questions with no answers. I was sure hoping one of y'all might've been able to shed a little light on the situation."

"Wish we could, too," Laura said.

"Guess it was a good thing you wasn't ridin' yesterday, huh?" Tawana said.

"You're not kidding." Percy shook his head pensively. "If I hadn't been tied up with those other cases,

I'd be one of those poor folks in Delatross's freezer right now."

Seeing a lead-in that might get some of her questions answered, Laura said, "I heard Delatross had problems at his funeral home the other night."

Percy harrumphed. "More than problems. Barbara Mabry and her mother were killed in his parking lot. Stanford Milo, too. All three shot with a nail gun. Can you believe it? A damn nail gun. I've been telling Delatross for years to put pole lights in that parking lot, but the cheapskate wouldn't do it. Said the streetlights a block down gave the lot enough light. Bet the idiot's gonna put 'em in now, though."

"Any idea who did it?" Matt asked.

"Oh, I've got a theory or two. Waiting on answers from the crime lab in Lafayette, and we're still questioning a few of their relatives."

"Like Keith Lafleur?" Laura asked.

Percy cocked his head toward her. "Why? You hear anything on Lafleur?"

"Just speculation, people talking."

He let out an exasperated breath. "Yeah, well people around here do a lot of that."

"So is Lafleur a suspect?" Matt asked.

"Let's just say he's a person of interest," Percy said. "And I'm sure interested in where the hell he went."

"You can't find him?" Laura asked.

Percy shook his head and got to his feet. "Ain't nobody seen him since the day Jeff Mabry got shot." He carried his mug over to the kitchen sink and drained it before placing it inside. Then he stared straight ahead, out the window, as if caught in a daydream. "I swear it's like this town's been cursed," he muttered. "All those people dead. So many dead."

A heavy silence settled over the room, and it remained until Percy released a deep sigh. He started to move away from the window, then did a double take and whistled in astonishment.

"What?" Laura got up and went over to him. Matt and Tawana followed.

Percy pointed at something in the backyard. "Biggest web I've ever seen."

Laura stood on tiptoe and peered past him. Behind the building, silver threads stretched across a five-foot span between two catalpa trees. The huge swirls and dashes reminded her of the web in Moweez's drawing. Her pulse quickened. She looked back at Tawana and Matt. They must have been thinking the same thing because they both stared at her earnestly. None of them dared say anything in front of Percy.

"You should take a picture of it," Percy said. "It's kinda pretty." He gave them a half-smile that quickly faded. "Gotta run. Give me a call if y'all remember anything about yesterday that you think I should know about, all right?"

"Will do," Matt said.

"I'll walk you out," Laura said.

"No need. I know the way." Tossing a wave over his shoulder, Percy left the kitchen, and it wasn't long before Laura heard his boots clomping down the stairs.

"Where's the key to the back door in the kitchenette?" she asked Tawana.

"First drawer by the dryer," Tawana said, already heading out of the kitchen. Laura trailed behind her and Matt quickly fell into step.

"We're going downstairs for a few minutes," Matt told Seth and Moweez as they crossed the living room. "Be right back."

Seth and Moweez nodded, but neither took their eyes off the television.

When they got downstairs, Tawana went to the utility drawers to look for the key, while Laura peeked into the salon to make sure Percy was gone. He was, and the main door was shut.

"Here!" Tawana said, holding up a silver key.

"Open it," Laura said.

"You crazy? I ain't openin' that door! You open it."

"I'll do it," Matt said, and took the key from Tawana.

Laura chewed her bottom lip as he went to the back door and slipped the key into the lock.

He turned the key and the dead bolt clicked open. Putting one hand on the doorknob, Matt looked back at them. "Ready?"

Laura nodded.

Tawana covered her eyes with her hands.

Matt opened the door wide and their gasps came in unison.

"What?" Tawana said. "It's bad?" She peeked through her fingers. "Oh, sweet Jesus."

The spider web they'd seen from the window upstairs was apparently only an offshoot of a much bigger orb. The main web hung ten feet away from the door. Laura inched forward cautiously until she was able to see outside. The glistening silver threads stretched from an oak tree that stood west of the salon all the way to the middle of the building, where it ended on a guide wire. The span was nearly fifteen feet.

"What kind of spider spins a web this big?" Matt said, his voice tempered with awe.

"I don't know, and I don't want to know," Tawana said, coming up behind them. "Now close that damn door before whatever's out there comes in here!"

"Where's Moweez's sketch pad?" Laura asked.

"Over there on the table. You gonna close that door or do I have to get loud?"

Laura stepped away from the door and motioned for Matt to close it as she went over to the table. "I want to see if the web looks the same in the drawing."

"It's across the front of the building in the drawing," Matt said. "We don't even see the back."

"That's what worries me. The way Mo drew the birds was exactly the way we saw it. Why is this one different? Why wouldn't she draw the back of the shop covered with webs if that's what was going to happen?" Laura found the sketch pad under two hair-styling magazines. As she flipped open the cover, Tawana and Matt came closer for a better look.

"See?" Laura ran a finger across the scatter of dead birds shown in the first picture. "It's not like she drew one or two. They cover the yard, just like we found them." She flipped through a couple more pages at random. "It's like she—" Laura blinked, unable to process what she was seeing. She stretched the pad open and smoothed a hand over a brand new sketch.

"Oh, uh-uh." Tawana took a step back, holding up both hands. "I got enough of this crazy shit."

This new drawing showed in vivid detail the muddle of horses and horror they'd witnessed yesterday. Even the blood-soaked costumes weren't spared. The view was from the other side of First Street, directly across from Nestler's. The east end of the salon had been drawn at a slight angle so the upstairs windows were clearly visible, the same for the café, except it revealed its west end. Just above the gabled roof of the salon sat an hourglass, only a hair away from empty. Silver threads ran through this sketch as well, connecting the café and salon as they had in the second sketch. Seth's face appeared in the upstairs window of the café as it had before, but this time he looked petrified—and he wasn't alone. A slim, dark-haired woman stood behind him, one hand on the windowpane, the other on his shoulder. And the salon wasn't alone either . . . in the upstairs window, where Tawana and Moweez's bedroom would have been, stood a young boy in pale blue pajamas. Both of his fists were against the windowpane, as though he were beating against it. He looked panicked and afraid—and exactly like the boy Laura had seen standing by the dryer.

Laura's mouth went bone-dry. She licked her lips, pointed to the boy, but still couldn't form the words.

"When did she draw this one?" Matt asked. His face was pinched, his eyes angry. He looked over at Tawana. "When?"

"How'm I supposed to know?" Tawana said, holding a hand to her forehead.

"It's him," Laura said, her voice hoarse. "The boy from the other night. The one I saw in here."

Tawana shook her head. "Oh, no, okay, we leavin', you understand? We gettin' outa this place."

"When did Moweez draw this?" Matt pressed.

"I don't know! Why don't you ask—"

"Come-together broken." Moweez stood at the foot of the stairs, watching them.

Laura quickly turned the drawing around so it faced her. "Mo, you drew this?"

Moweez nodded and held out her hands, palms up. "All broken." She placed the top of one hand into the palm of the other. "Mama fix. Mo say mama fix."

Pointing to the boy in the blue pajamas, Laura asked, "Do you know who this is, Mo?"

Moweez tilted her head and eyed the drawing. "—att sick."

"Mo, Wana can't take this no more, honey." Tawana shook her head. She sounded on the verge of tears. "You gotta tell us who all's in that picture? What you tryin' to tell us?"

"—att sick."

"Where's Seth?" Matt asked suddenly. He looked ready to sprint for the stairwell when Seth stumbled up alongside Moweez from behind. His hair was tousled and his eyes looked heavy with the need for sleep.

Matt turned to Laura. "We need to get to Crowley."

"What?"

"Crowley. Percy told me that's where the original house came from. I think that's the only place we're going to find answers about what's going on here."

"Uh-uh," Tawana said with a snap of her head. "I ain't goin' to no Crowley. You wanna go diggin' around and stirrin' up some hoogity boogity shit, that's all you."

"So you're just going to give up?" Matt held his arms out at his side. "Just let everything you worked so hard for crumble down around you?"

Tawana folded her arms across her chest. "Yep."

"Even if we do find out more about the house, how's that going to help us here?" Laura asked. She turned the sketch pad back around, gathered the rest of the pages beneath a thumb, then let them fall one by one, checking for more sketches.

"I don't know," Matt said. "Maybe it won't help at all, but we won't know unless we try."

"Unless *you* try," Tawana corrected.

Matt sighed. "Tawana, if I have to go alone, I will. But we're tied together in this somehow. We—"

"We—we're going," Laura said, barely getting her voice above a whisper.

"No, girl, you ain't hearin' me. I said—"

"We're going." Laura turned the pad around so they could see the sketch that was not yet finished.

Only two things in the drawing had been given detail so far: First Street—and Seth lying across it, dead.

CHAPTER EIGHTEEN

It was nearly noon before Matt reached the first Crowley exit off Interstate 10. Although it had only been an hour's drive, it had taken him a good part of the morning to locate Lerna Mae so he could ask her to watch Moweez and Seth at her house for the day. Both were too exhausted to chance dragging around to places unknown. Fortunately, Lerna Mae had agreed and even had a hot brunch waiting for Mo and Seth when Matt dropped them off.

By the time they'd reached the interstate for the longest haul of the trip, Tawana was already snoring softly in the backseat. Through the traffic congestion in Lafayette and the open fields of Mire and Church Point, Matt and Laura discussed possible strategies to find the property where the house once sat, then what they would do once they found it. He'd been impressed by her quick thinking and taken aback by the intensity in her eyes. And in the last few miles, when she'd dozed off, he stole glimpses at the delicate beauty of her face.

The car jostled her awake when he veered onto the exit ramp and hit a small bump in the road.

"We're here?" Laura sat upright and rubbed her eyes.

He nodded and came to a stop at the end of the ramp, which intersected Highway 1111. "There's another Crowley exit past this one, but I figured we might as well see what's down this way first."

"Only rice fields, looks like," Laura said, gazing out her window.

Matt took a left and nursed his Camry across the overpass and down Highway 1111. Open rice fields seemed to stretch across forever on either side of the road. Some had short grassy levees circling their perimeter, and inside their shallow bowls sparkled ponds of golden water, each dotted with small orange buoys. The buoys marked the crawfish traps hiding beneath the water. Even with the windows rolled up, the fecund odor of those ponds wafted in through the air vents. It was a rich, wet, earthy scent that reminded Matt of the times he'd fished for brim with his dad on the banks of Bayou Courtableau.

The road soon merged with U.S. 90, which led them to Crowley's south side. Two doglegs later, they came to a main intersection. A railroad track lay to their left, and beyond it, Mill Street, appropriately named judging from the steel rice-milling plants that stood on either side of the street like sleek, silver giants. To their right was Highway 13, the main thoroughfare through town. When he turned onto the highway, Matt had a sudden flash of déjà vu, and his stomach balled into a nervous knot.

They drove past a hodgepodge of old and new storefronts and bank buildings, the Rice Theater, and Parkerson Avenue Baptist Church. Nothing looked familiar to him, but everything *felt* familiar.

"You okay?" Laura asked, startling him.

He glanced over at her. "Feels like I've been here before."

"You haven't?"

"Not unless my dad took me here as a kid, and if he did, I don't remember."

A dark, well-manicured hand plopped onto the top of the front seat between them. "Where we at?" Tawana asked, peering over the seat.

"Crowley," Matt said.

"We're looking for a drugstore," Laura added.

"Why, you sick?"

"Percy said a pharmacy outfit bought the property where the house was," Matt said, stopping for a red light. He looked back at Tawana. "Lafleur moved the house sometime back in October, so the drugstore we're looking for is going to be new. Probably one of the chains."

"Like that one?" Tawana pointed ahead and to the right.

A new brick building stood at the corner of Parkerson and East Northern Avenue with a bright red COSTLESS DRUGS sign perched over the entrance. Matt glanced over at Laura just as an impatient driver blasted them with his horn. The light had already turned green.

"This has to be it," he said, turning right onto East Northern. Directly across from the drugstore sprawled a large neighborhood, its composition a fusion of old and new, clapboard and brick, single and two-story homes. Matt drove slowly past the drugstore, then took a left on a narrow road that ran parallel to the side of the building. Across the road sat another neighborhood, this one smaller, the homes newer and more consistent in design.

"What we supposed to do now?" Tawana asked when he pulled into the side parking lot of the drugstore.

"I guess we should make sure we've got the right store first," Laura said.

"Just how many big-ass drugstores like this you think they gonna have in this town?"

Matt pointed toward the back of the building. "They still have scaffolding stacked back there. This has to be the one."

Laura opened her door. "I'll go in there and ask so we're sure."

"We might as well go with you," Matt said.

"Y'all make me tired," Tawana said, opening her door. "Y'all can go ask all the questions you want. Me, I'm gonna get some Cheese Doodles. A store this big's gotta have Cheese Doodles."

Inside, the store looked twice as big as it did from the outside. Multiple aisles ran the length of the store, each with overhead signs that identified the stock. Tawana headed for the chip aisle, while Matt and Laura went over to one of the registers to talk to a cashier.

Matt took a pack of gum from a display rack and handed it to the young girl standing behind the counter. She wore a red bib apron over street clothes and looked no older than twenty.

The girl scanned the gum and smiled at Matt. "Will that be all for you today?"

Matt returned the smile and pulled his wallet out of his back pocket. "A friend's getting some chips. She should be here any second."

"Oh, sure, no problem." The girl straightened a small stack of coupons near the register while waiting.

Laura stepped up beside Matt. "New store?" she asked the girl.

"Real new. We've only been open about a month."

"Looks like you're the only game in town," Matt said.

The girl gave him a quizzical look.

"The only drugstore," he said.

"Oh, yeah." The girl giggled. "No, there's Carmichael's down the road, but they've been here forever, and they're small. Other than them, though, we're it."

Tawana showed up with two bags of Cheese Doodles, a six-pack of Orange Fizz, and a bag of Double-Stuff Oreos. Matt motioned for her to put the groceries on the counter.

"Do you know who lived in the house that was here before they built the drugstore?" Laura asked the girl while she scanned the additional items.

"That old place? Nobody lived in it as long as I can remember. It was just kinda always there."

"Know anybody who would know?" Matt asked.

"Mr. Courtier might. He works here part-time. He's like eighty or something, and he's always lived here." She pressed a button on the register. "That'll be nine seventy-eight."

Matt handed her a ten. "Is he working today?"

"I think so. He restocks the shelves most of the time, so take a look down the aisles; you'll probably find him working around one of them. Old guy, bald head, wearing an apron like me."

"Thanks." Matt picked up the sack of groceries.

"Oh, if you're going back there, you'll have to leave the bag with me," the girl said. "You can pick it up on your way out."

Tawana snatched the bag from Matt. "No, no, we're pickin' it up now. I'll go sit in the car and have me a little snack while y'all do what y'all got to do."

Matt handed her the car keys. "We won't be long."

"I ain't rushin' you," Tawana said, already digging into a bag of Cheese Doodles. She had a bounce to her step as she headed out of the store.

Matt and Laura began searching aisles, and it didn't take long before Matt spotted an elderly bald man wearing a red bib apron. He stood on a small stepladder, straightening shampoo bottles on a shelf.

Not wanting to startle the man, Matt called to him while they were still a distance away. "Mr. Courtier?"

The old man turned toward Matt, peering over brown framed reading glasses. "Yeah?"

Matt smiled and walked up to him. "The girl at the register suggested we talk to you."

The lines on Mr. Courtier's forehead deepened as he studied Matt. "I know you?"

"No, sir, I don't think so. My name's Matt Daigle, and this is Laura Toups. We wanted to ask if you knew who lived in the house that was on this property before they built the store."

Mr. Courtier slowly stepped off the ladder, then turned to Matt and adjusted his glasses. "Who's your daddy?"

Matt frowned. "Sir?"

"Who's your daddy? What's his name?"

"Paul Daigle."

The old man pinched his chin between a thumb and finger. "Paul Daigle, Paul Daigle. The name don't sound familiar."

"No, sir. We weren't from here. I grew up a little north of Windham."

"Who's your mama?"

Matt held back a sigh of frustration. "Marie Daigle, but both my parents have been dead for years."

"Marie Daigle, Marie Daigle, hmm. Nope, that name don't ring no bell, either."

"Mr. Courtier, do you know who lived in the house that used to be here?" Laura asked.

The old man pursed his lips as though pondering the question. After a long moment, he shook his head. "I don't remember the name. It was a long time ago, and I'm old, you know, hard to keep things in my head. It was a family, I know that much. The man either had a rice farm or owned one of the mills, but I'm not sure."

"Do you know anybody around here who would know?" Matt asked.

"Oh, now *that* I know," the old man said, shaking a finger enthusiastically. "Thelma Sonnier, she'd know, Pierre Naquin, too. Oh, and Mercedes Theriot and Doraleese Babin—no, no, wait, not Doraleese. God rest her, she passed on five or six months ago. The rest been around a long time, like me, but their memory's better."

Wishing he had something to write on, Matt asked, "Do you know where we might find these people?"

"Yeah. They all live across the road over there." Mr. Courtier pointed toward the front of the store. "Thelma lives in a blue house on Passe Noire. You can't miss it if you look for the garden in her front yard. It's got one of those ceramic cats in it. She says it keeps the birds out of her garden. I don't know if that's true, though. Mercedes, she lives up the street, half a block over to the left on Simone. Her name's on the mailbox that looks like a little red schoolhouse. You can't miss that one, neither. Then Pierre, he lives on Blanc Teche. That's about two, three, maybe four blocks on the other side of Mercedes. Look for an old white house with a green porch swing. That's him."

Matt glanced over at Laura, worried that he'd already forgotten half of what he'd been told.

"Thelma, blue house, Passe Noire—Pierre, porch swing, Blanc Teche—Mercedes, mailbox, Simone," Laura said, and winked.

He grinned.

After thanking Mr. Courtier, they left the store and went back to Matt's car. They found Tawana wrist deep in Cheese Doodles. The bag of Oreos sat on the seat beside her, empty.

Tawana held out the chip bag. "Y'all want some?"

"No thanks," Matt said.

Laura shook her head while digging through her purse. She pulled out a pen and a rumpled envelope, then scribbled down the information Mr. Courtier had given them. She handed the envelope to Matt. "Should we split up and do them all at once or do them one at a time?"

"Split up and do what?" Tawana asked.

"Talk to some people about the house," Laura said. "Find out if they know anything."

"I ain't gonna talk to none of 'em by myself."

"Why not?"

"Girl, in case you ain't noticed, they got a lot of white people livin' up in here. For all I know, they see a big black woman walkin' up the driveway, they gonna come runnin' out their house burnin' crosses and shit."

Laura rolled her eyes. "Oh, please."

Tawana harrumphed and shoved another Cheese Doodle into her mouth.

"We do it together then." Matt started the car and headed back to East Northern Avenue.

The first street that led into the neighborhood was St. Martin. Matt turned in and let the car creep forward. "There're quite a few cross streets. I'll keep an eye for the street signs on the left. Y'all watch the right."

"What names we lookin' for?" Tawana asked.

Matt double-checked the names on the envelope and recited them to her.

They rode down St. Martin in silence, each straining to see the next street sign. They were nearly at the end of the road when Laura tapped her window with a finger.

"Blanc Teche!"

Matt made a quick right.

"Pierre Naquin," Laura said. "White house with a green—there!"

He brought the car to a stop in front of a dented mailbox. Beyond it was a white shotgun house with a narrow porch and sagging roofline. A gaunt old man watched them from a green two-seater porch swing. The scowl on his face suggested he might not be up for company.

"Y'all wait here," Matt said, putting the car in park. "Mr. Happy doesn't look like he could handle all three of us right now."

"You're not kidding," Laura said.

Matt got out of the car but left his door ajar. "Mr. Naquin?" he called to the man on the porch.

"Whatchu want?" a gravelly voice shot back.

"Mr. Courtier over at Costless said we should come talk to you. Said you'd probably know something about the house that used to be on that property."

"Cedric Courtier?"

"I don't know his first name. He's an older gentleman, bald, kind of short. He works at Costless."

"Yeah, that's him," Naquin said, and settled back on the swing.

Matt waited a minute or two, but the old man said nothing more. He stared straight ahead, working the swing back and forth with a slippered foot.

"Do you know who lived in that house, Mr. Naquin?" Matt asked.

"Yeah, I know." The swing moved a little faster.

"Mind if I come talk to you about it?"

"Got nothing to say about that house."

Matt started to walk around the car toward him, but Naquin held up a gnarled finger.

"I said I got nothing to say. No use you come over here. Just go on about your business."

"But, sir—"

"I said no!" The swing came to a stop. "Nothing but bad happened in that house, and when you talk bad about the dead like that, they can make all that bad come back on you. But not me, no, uh-uh, it's not going to happen. So just get in your little wagon there and go on about your business like I said."

They stared at each other for a while, but Matt saw no chink in the old man's mulish armor. He turned away and got back in the car.

As he drove away from Pierre Naquin's house, he said, "You heard?"

"How could we not?" Laura said. "Most of Crowley probably heard him."

Tawana scooted closer to the front seat. "Nana used to tell us the same thing."

Laura turned to her. "About what?"

"That you not supposed to talk bad about the dead or it flips back on you."

"How do you know that wasn't just an old wives' tale?" Matt asked.

Tawana shrugged. "Guess nobody wanted to cross that bridge to find out."

Matt drove another block, bringing them onto Beau Basin, a street that ran parallel to St. Martin. They were nearly back to East Northern Avenue before he spotted Passe Noire. He took a right and steered the car into a dogleg turn that had him heading north again.

"There's a garden with a cat in it," Laura said, pointing left. "Blue house."

Turning into the driveway, Matt noticed that the side of Thelma Sonnier's house and her garden faced the drugstore. A three-foot wide drainage ditch bordered by a hurricane fence kept anyone from accessing East Northern Avenue from this direction.

"Think she's home?" Laura asked when he stopped the car.

The front door of the single story clapboard was shut tight, the shades drawn over all the windows. An old white pickup sat near the front of the drive, but it was dusty, like it hadn't been driven in a while.

Matt killed the engine and opened his door. "Only one way to find out."

Laura looked back at Tawana. "You coming?"

"You crazy? After what happened with that old jackleg back there? Uh-uh."

"Maybe you should wait here, too," Matt said to Laura.

"I'm coming with you." Laura opened her door and got out of the car.

Circular stepping-stones led the way from the driveway to Thelma Sonnier's front door. Matt took two at a time, trying to catch up with Laura. She reached the door first and jabbed the doorbell button near the jamb. When the bell sounded inside, they glanced at each other, then stared at the door, waiting. Laura was about to ring the bell again when Matt saw the doorknob turn. He caught her hand and signaled to the knob.

The woman who greeted them wore a faded print housedress and white tennis shoes that had a small hole over the big toe of her left foot. She looked close to ninety, with wispy strands of white hair and a tanned, heavily wrinkled face. Her nose was thick and long with a prominent hook at the end. It made Matt think of Seth, and the night he'd walked in his sleep and talked about seeing a witch.

"Ma'am, we're looking for a Mrs. Thelma Sonnier," Laura said.

Squinting, the old woman opened the door wider. "Who y'all?" She placed a hand over her eyes like a visor.

"My name's Laura Toups, and this is Matt Daigle. We're—"

The old woman stepped out of the house, pushing Laura aside. The hand that had been shielding her eyes from the sun dropped to her mouth. She walked haltingly over to Matt.

Puzzled, Matt wasn't sure what to say. The old woman looked dumbstruck, her eyes roaming over every inch of his face. When she stood no farther than a foot away from him, she slowly removed the hand from her mouth and reached out to touch his cheek.

"I knew it," the old woman said, her voice trembling. "I knew dat you'd come back here one day."

No sooner were the words out of her mouth than Matt's legs buckled out from under him.

CHAPTER NINETEEN

"Whoa!" Laura caught Matt before he hit the ground. They stumbled forward, then sideways until she was able to brace herself against the house.

A car door slammed and Tawana came barreling up the sidewalk. "What happened? Why he fell like that? He sick?"

Matt's face looked gray and it was dripping with sweat. His eyes rolled up to meet Laura's. "Can't—can't breathe."

"Bring dat boy in de house," the old woman said, motioning Laura to the front door.

"We need to get him to a hospital," Laura said.

Tawana spun about. "Yeah, okay, the hospital—I'll go start the car."

The old woman slapped her hands together. "Listen to what I say. You got no time for de hospital. Bring him in dis house."

The surety in her voice frightened Laura. It was as

if the old woman knew something about Matt's condition that they didn't, and that something was deadly.

"Help me," Laura said to Tawana, as she struggled to keep Matt upright.

Matt groaned as they crossed the threshold and his complexion went from gray to green.

"Are you Thelma Sonnier," Laura asked as the old woman led them to a brown Naugahyde couch in her living room.

"Yeah, dat's me." She pointed to the couch. "Put him dere. I'm gonna get a washrag." With that, she shuffled out of the room.

Laura and Tawana sat Matt on the couch and his head flopped back. His breathing sounded raspy and labored. His eyes were open, but unfocused.

"He sounds like Mo when she's having one of her attacks," Tawana said.

"I know."

The squeak of tennis shoes on the hardwood floor announced Thelma's return to the living room. She carried a yellow washcloth and a small glass container that looked like a baby food jar. Clear liquid sloshed in the jar as she walked.

Thelma handed Laura the washcloth. "Put dis 'round his neck." Then she turned and handed Tawana the jar. "Can you open dis for me? My hands don't work too good no more."

Doubting the washcloth would do any good, Laura placed it around Matt's neck. Whatever Thelma had planned, Laura figured she had five minutes to do it. If Matt looked no better by then, she was calling 911.

Thelma took the open jar from Tawana and sat beside Matt.

"What is that?" Laura asked.

"Dat's a special oil." Thelma dunked her right thumb into the jar. "My ol' mama taught me how to make dat." She marked a cross on Matt's forehead with her thumb, then placed the jar on a narrow end table beside the couch before making a sign of the cross.

With her lips moving silently, Thelma placed her hands on either side of Matt's head, then moved them down slowly until they reached the washcloth. Once there, she wiped her oily thumb on the rag, then placed both of her hands on Matt's chest. He gasped loudly, and his eyes seemed to focus on her face. Thelma nodded, her lips still moving, and she crossed herself again. Matt's breathing didn't sound as labored.

Thelma looked over at Laura and Tawana, her body rocking gently. "Y'all just as soon sit. I got to do two more treatment, but I got to wait a few minutes before I do de next one."

Laura sat in a worn recliner, Tawana on a pale orange ottoman.

"You're a treateur?" Laura asked. As a child, whenever she came down with a minor ailment, she was brought to a neighborhood healer. She recognized the ritual.

"Somethin' like dat."

"That's conja you doin', huh?" Tawana said.

"Non, dis is not conja. I don't mess wit' de devil,

me." Thelma crossed herself again, then dipped her thumb in the oil and brushed another cross on Matt's forehead. Her hands followed the same path as before, pressing against the sides of his head, then moving down to the washcloth, where she wiped the oil from her thumb. This time, instead of Matt gasping when she placed her hands on his chest, he yawned loudly. Thelma crossed herself once more and resumed her rocking.

"How do you know him?" Laura asked.

"I have to tell dat to him first, not you."

Laura frowned. "Are you family?"

"Hush while I do de last treatment."

Laura looked over at Tawana, who shrugged. With Matt's breathing nearly normal now and Thelma going through her rituals, Laura took a moment to examine the room. The dark paneling on the walls made the room appear even smaller than it was. The only other pieces of furniture besides the ones they occupied were an antique upright piano that sat in a far corner, and across from it, a metal card table that held a small television set. Beside the set was an unlit votive candle with a picture of Padre Pio plastered across the front. Pictures hung on the wall behind the couch. Some were of smiling, gap-toothed children, which Laura figured to be Thelma's grandchildren or great-grandchildren, judging from the slight resemblance. Considering the age of the house and its contents, Laura was surprised to find it didn't smell old. A hint of fresh cooked bacon and cinnamon clung to the air. It made her stomach growl.

"Now," Thelma said, patting Matt's knee. "Look how you all better."

Matt rubbed a hand briskly over his face, then looked from Tawana to Laura. "I don't know what happened. One minute I'm fine, the next minute . . . I don't know."

"Oh, I know," Tawana said with a snap of her head. "You damn near scared me white, that's what happened."

He gave her a lopsided grin.

"So you're feeling okay?" Laura asked.

"Fine, thanks to . . ." He looked over at Thelma. "I'm sorry, I don't even know your name for sure. We came looking for Mrs. Thelma Sonnier, but—"

"I already tol' her dat's me." She smiled, revealing a toothless mouth, and patted his knee again. "Now tell me what you lookin' for over here."

"Do you mind if I ask you something first?"

"Go 'head."

"What did you do—I mean, what were you doing a while ago with your hands?"

"Givin' you de treatment."

"For what? Like asthma or something? That stuff you put on my head smelled like mint."

"Non, you didn't have de asthma."

"What was it?"

"You was afraid."

Matt frowned.

"Afraid of what?" Laura asked.

"Dat all de bad was gonna come back."

Tawana cocked her head. "You *sure* you not doin' conja?"

Thelma gave Tawana a look that made her turn sheepishly away.

"I don't understand," Matt said.

"Tell me first what you lookin' for over here," Thelma said.

Matt leaned over and placed his forearms on his knees. "We're looking for someone who can tell us something about the house that used to be where Costless Drugs is now. A man at the drugstore, Mr. Courtier, said you might be able to help us."

Thelma cackled softly. "It's a wonder y'all didn't wind up in Butte LaRose. Poor Cedric, he don't know how to remember his own name sometime. How he remembered where I live, I don't know." She shook her head, clearly amused. "Now how come you wanna know about dat house? Dey moved it over three, four mont's ago."

"I know," Matt said. "We live in it."

Thelma's eyebrows shot up. "You live in de house? All you three?"

"The man who moved the house had it cut in half and remodeled. Now each half has a business downstairs and an apartment upstairs. I have a café in one of the buildings and live with my son upstairs. Laura and Tawana have a beauty shop in the other building, and they live with Tawana's cousin in that apartment."

"And you come here because trouble's in dat house, huh?"

"How you knew that?" Tawana asked.

Thelma looked from Tawana to Laura to Matt. "De troubles bad?"

Matt told her about the Courir disaster, and Laura and Tawana detailed the events before it, all the way back to the dead black birds. The only things they left out were Moweez's drawings.

When they'd finished giving her a full account, Thelma crossed herself. *"Donner pitié, bon Dieu."* She rose slowly to her feet, like she'd just aged another ten years.

"Before we came here," Matt said, "we went to see Pierre Naquin. He said he knew about the house, but he wouldn't tell us anything. Said he didn't want to talk bad about the dead."

Thelma nodded.

"What happened in that house, Mrs. Sonnier?" Matt asked.

Thelma looked at him for a long moment. Such sadness in her eyes. "You already know what happened."

"What do you mean?"

She sighed deeply and stuck her hands in the pockets of her housedress. "I pray all de time dat dis day never come, but de good Lord let it come anyway." She turned and headed in the same direction she'd gone in earlier for the washcloth. "Stay where you at. I'm gonna show you what I mean."

When she was no longer in sight, Tawana whispered, "Okay, straight up, that old lady's freakin' me out."

"You?" Matt said. "You should try being on this end."

"You sure you never met her before?" Laura asked.

Matt shook his head. "If I did, I don't remember."

"Seems like she sure knows you." Tawana said.

"I know."

"What happened to you outside, anyway?" Laura

asked. "Thelma touches you and boom, you're going down on your face."

Matt tapped his chest with a hand. "It's like all the air got knocked out of me from here, and I couldn't suck any back in. What was she doing to me with that oil?"

"Workin' a conja," Tawana said.

"She was not," Laura said in a loud whisper. She looked at Matt. "All she did was put some oil on your forehead and move her hands around your head and chest, like a treateur. I think she was praying while she did it, but I can't say for sure because we couldn't hear her."

"Shh, she's comin'," Tawana warned.

When Thelma came back into the living room she had a photo album clutched to her chest. She went over to the couch and sat beside Matt.

"Okay," Thelma said, motioning Laura and Tawana over. "Come sit close if you wanna see."

Tawana pulled the ottoman up to the couch, and Laura went over and sat on the other side of Thelma.

Still holding the album close, Thelma closed her eyes. "Long time ago, dey had a big rice farmer here in Crowley by de name Joseph Devillier. De man not only had fields all over de place, he worked two mills, too. One here, another one in Kaplan. It was like everyt'ing he touched turn to money. De man was so smart, he even figure out a way to put dis special mix together wit' de rice seed dat would keep de black-birds away when it was time to plant." Thelma opened her eyes and looked at Matt. "Dere's nothing gonna destroy a rice field faster den a flock of blackbirds. Dey eat all de seed, and de farmer don't have nothing left but dirt and poor." She opened the photo album to a newspaper clipping taken from the Crowley Post. The headline read: LOUISIANA RICE NO LONGER FOR THE BIRDS. Beneath the article was the picture of a tall, dark-haired man, dressed in sharply creased pants and a white button-down shirt. He stood beside a harvesting combine, smiling, his sleeves rolled up to his forearms, one fist propped on a hip, his other hand flat against one of the machine's tires.

Unable to read the small print in the article from where she sat, Laura said, "That's Joseph Devillier?"

Thelma nodded.

"What does he have to do with the house?" Matt asked. "Did he own it?"

"He built it. De same year dey took dis picture—de same year he married dat woman."

Tawana wiggled closer. "Okay, now we gettin' juicy."

Thelma flipped through a few pages of the album and settled on another newspaper clipping, this one a photo of Joseph Devillier in a dark suit, narrow tie, his arm around a petite woman who wore a white organza gown and a chapel length veil. Both looked ecstatic.

Matt leaned into Thelma and read the text beneath the picture. "Morgan Theresa Boustany and Joseph Paul Devillier, both of Crowley, became husband and wife during a two P.M. February First ceremony in St. Agnes Catholic Church. The Reverend Martin Lavister officiated at the ceremony."

Laying a crooked finger over the image of the woman, Thelma said, "Joseph was smart wit' everyt'ing but her. Everybody in town knew somet'ing was not right wit' her, but Joseph didn't want to hear dat. He married de woman anyway."

"What was wrong with her," Matt asked, his eyes glued to the picture.

Thelma tapped her temple with a finger. "Somet'ing messed up in here. She was mostly sad all de time. But when she was happy, she was crazy happy, spending money all over de place, dressing up big and fancy just to go to de grocery store. It got to where Joseph couldn't make his money fast enough, and all his business started to go down de drain."

Tawana tsked. "Damn gold digger."

"It got more bad after she had de first baby. She couldn't do all like she did before, not wit' a baby to take care of. And you would t'ink wit' Joseph being smart like dat, he would know better and stop wit' just one baby." Thelma shook her head sadly. "But non, dey had four boys. And she got worse and worse wit' each boy." She looked over at her front door and stared as though seeing something past it. "Even from dis far away, we could hear dose babies crying most de time. Dat woman didn't care if dey cried, not one bit." A tear slipped down Thelma's cheek. "I would go dere sometime, bring a cake, a pie, just so I could check on dem boys. Dey always look hungry and skinny. More den one time I see bruises on dey arms or face." She looked down at the album again. "It was de saddest t'ing I ever saw."

Laura's heart constricted, aching painfully as she pictured the neglect and abuse of four little boys. "What about Joseph? Why didn't he do something?"

"Yeah, like bus' her lip!" Tawana said.

"Just like he didn't listen when people tried to tell him she was no good in de first place, he didn't want to listen den, neither. He started to drink real heavy, and it got to where he didn't come home until late, late every night. He didn't want to see de trut'. Dey fought all de time. She t'ought he was running 'round wit' other women, but I know dat wasn't true."

"How did you know?" Matt asked quietly.

" 'Cause Tee-June, God rest him, used to work at de mill. He saw Joseph dere all de time, working hard, working late."

"Who's Tee-June?" Laura asked.

"My husband. Passed away six years ago come Easter. He worked de rice fields for Alphonse, Joseph's daddy, for years. Den when Alphonse died, he went to work for Joseph at de mill. Dat's when dey got close. Tee-June knew what was de trut' between him and her."

"Is that why you kept these articles and pictures?" Laura asked. "Because your husband was close to Joseph?"

Thelma drew in a deep breath. "Non, everyt'ing close to us dat's big, I keep in here. De before and de after." She stuck a finger between pages in the back of the album and flipped to them. More newspaper clippings. She touched a newspaper photo on the left, then one on the right. "Dis is New Orleans before dat bad hurricane, dis is New Orleans after." Thelma turned to pages in the middle of the album. "Dis is Edwin Edwards when he was de governor and dis one is him when he was de governor and dey brought him to jail."

"What's the after for Joseph and that hussy?" Tawana asked.

Putting a hand to her mouth, Thelma squeezed her eyes shut, as though the memory was no longer a memory, but a reality she faced once more. When she lowered her hand, her lips were trembling, and it took a moment for her to speak. "She got pregnant one more time, and I t'ink dats what broke her. I went to de house wit' some food when she got back from de hospital, but it was like she was dead inside her head already. She didn't want to eat, didn't want to sleep. All she want to do is walk up and down, up and down in dat house." Her hand shook as she swiped a tear from her chin. "Tee-June's de one dat found dem— dead. All de gas heaters in de house had no fire, just de gas comin' out. De fireman said Tee-June was lucky he didn't get blowed up when he went inside."

Laura gasped. "The boys dead?"

"Oh, no she didn't!" Tawana said, pounding fist to palm.

"She was dead, too. Joseph, too. De police said somebody turned all dem heaters off on purpose, but dey could never prove who did it. But we knew it was her. We knew." Thelma flipped through the album again. "After it happened, dey put a picture of de whole family in de newspaper. It was one Tee-June took at de company picnic de summer before."

As though to brace himself, Matt folded his arms across his chest, his face hard, his jaw muscles flexing.

237

Thelma turned the album sideways and held it open on her lap. The black and white photo took up one full page. Joseph and Morgan with a child in her arms, standing side-by-side next to a moss-covered oak, three young boys in front of them. Every face in the picture looked weary, every smile fake, except for the tallest, thinnest boy. He had no smile.

"Oh, God." Laura grabbed the album from Thelma's lap and held the picture close. That face—so thin—those eyes. She stabbed the image of the boy with a finger. "That's him, that's the boy I saw by the dryer. Look!" She turned the album around so Tawana could see.

Tawana scrambled to her feet, backing away fast. "Get outta here with that! I don't wanna see no dead boy!"

"But—"

"Uh-uh." Tawana shook her head rapidly. "The only butt I'm worried about is mine. I don't need no ghost gettin' pissed at me 'cause I was lookin' at his picture!"

Laura looked over at Matt, whose face had grown pale. Without saying anything, he held out a hand for the album. She gave it to him.

Matt put the album on his lap, studying the photo intently, frowning. "I've seen this before," he murmured. "That tree . . ." He turned to Thelma. "I've seen this picture before."

"I know." Thelma pointed to the unsmiling boy. "Dat's because dis boy is you."

CHAPTER TWENTY

Thelma's words didn't sink in. He wouldn't let them. He couldn't let them. If they slipped into his brain, his world wouldn't belong to him anymore. Every memory would be the reflection of a lie.

"Wait, wait, hold up!" Tawana had both hands up, shaking her head.

"That can't possibly be Matt," Laura said, her expression a cross between dumbstruck and fear. She got up from the couch and pointed to the album, still on Matt's lap. "That boy, I saw him, like . . . like a spirit or something."

"Dat boy didn't die," Thelma said calmly.

"But I saw him!" Laura said. "A boy—not Matt, not a man, a boy! And he disappeared right in front of my face!"

"Dat boy didn't die," Thelma repeated, then turned to Matt. "De night it happened I was in my bed, but I couldn't sleep because I had a bad heart-

burn. I got up two, t'ree times, lookin' for some Ro-
laids, Mylanta, anyt'ing to stop de burn, but none was
in de house. It got so bad, I went to wake up Tee-June
so he'd go find me some at de store. I couldn't wake
him up all de way, dough. I guess he was too tired. So
I figure I bes' go myself. I got Tee-June's keys and
when I went outside to get in de truck, dat's when I
saw you in de window upstairs."

Matt tried to swallow, but he had no saliva. He tried
concentrating on the texture of the album in his
hands, but his fingers were so cold he felt no texture.
The déjà vu he'd felt when they'd first arrived in
Crowley didn't feel like an illusion anymore. He *was*
there—in that house—now—seeing Thelma in her
yard looking up at him, her nose, the witch—he was
afraid of the witch.

"Your poor little face . . ." A small sob escaped
Thelma, and she brought a hand to her mouth. "You
was so scared, so small," she said through her fingers.
"You was beating on de glass wit' you hands." With a
shudder, she clasped her hands together and placed
them in her lap. "When I seen you like dat, I knew
somet'ing was bad, bad wrong, so I hurry back in my
house and shake Tee-June hard 'til he sits up in de
bed. I tell him to go over dere and check what's going
on. So he did. I go outside and watch him go inside
de house, right in de front door. Somebody forgot to
lock it I guess, I don't know. But a little bit later, Tee-
June comes out, carryin' you and cryin'. Y'all bot'
cryin'. You coughin' and coughin' and den you t'row
up on Tee-June. He comes runnin' fas' across de
street, gives you to me, then runs in de house here to

call de police. All he kep' sayin' was, 'Dey all dead, dey all dead.' "

Matt's heart stopped. It stopped the moment his mind jumped ahead of Thelma's words and he saw in his mind's eye every step that man took with him in his arms—when the man checked the dead woman lying in a hallway; when he examined the smallest boy for signs of life.

Thelma patted Matt's arm gently. *"Mon pauvre garçon."* Her eyes held his for a long time before she looked away and touched the photo. "You see de small one in your mama's arms? Dat was your little brother, Joseph Junior. The one dat's standing right by you, dat's Peter, and de next one, dat's—"

"Richard." The name came from his lips unbidden.

Thelma nodded and placed a hand on his chest. Matt felt something crack inside him. Instinctively he knew if it shattered, so would he.

"Dey called you Clyde." Thelma drew her hand back slowly. "You middle name was Matthew. I guess Paul and Marie wanted to keep one of you real names."

The sound of his parents' names seemed to slap Matt awake. He blinked rapidly. "You knew my parents?"

"Paul and Marie Daigle was good friends to me and Tee-June. Dey was good, good people, and dey didn't have no chil'ren, so when I heard dere was no family for you to go to, I told Marie about you. They went to talk to de judge before dey put you in one of dem homes. You was seven or eight at dat time, and I t'ink de judge knew it would be hard to get you adopted because everybody wants a little baby. Not Paul and

Marie, dough. Dey fell in love wit' you right away. Dey loved you so much dey even moved from here. Dey didn't want you to grow up wit' all de people talkin' around your back about you real mama and daddy."

Matt handed Thelma the album and got to his feet, flashes of his childhood, his life with Paul and Marie Daigle, vivid in his mind. The special coconut cake Mama made him every birthday; fishing, hunting with Dad; barbeques, holidays, playing Bouree for matches in the kitchen while Mama sang Ernest Tub's "Goodnight Irene" and stirred cush-cush on the stove. He couldn't imagine any parents loving him more. But why hadn't they told him? To protect him? To keep him from eventually hunting for his natural parents only to discover his mother had been a nut-case and his father had lived in denial?

He took a step toward the door, then stopped and turned around. Laura was watching him and crying softly. Tawana stood not far away, wringing her hands. A hound dog couldn't have looked more depressed. They reminded him why he'd come here. His world might have just been knocked off its axis, but it didn't change what all of them were living through now or what might be coming to them soon. He had to find a way to step back from this latest discovery and look at things objectively, analytically. All of it would still be there for him to emotionally process and investigate later. Right now, he had a son, three friends, and a future to take care of. So he pushed it all back, pushed hard, pushed until it didn't mean so much.

Matt turned and faced Thelma. "If I survived—if

I'm that boy, then who did Laura see? Why are all these things happening to us?"

Thelma smoothed her housecoat over her knobby knees and glanced around Laura to the Padre Pio votive candle on the end table. Then she sat back and smoothed a wisp of hair away from her forehead. "I don't know who she saw, and I don't know why all dis stuff is happening to you—but I know somebody who can tell you."

"Who?" Laura asked, wiping the tears from her face.

"Before I say, dere's somet'ing else you gotta know," Thelma said to Matt.

He felt his heart plummet to his bowels.

"Lord, not some more," Tawana muttered.

Matt stared at Thelma expectantly and nodded for her to continue.

"You was not de only child to survive."

Tawana threw up a hand. "Okay, here we go."

He continued to stare at her, unable to say anything. He had a living brother?

Laura got to her feet, shaking her head. "Wait a minute, you said everybody else in the house was dead. Are you saying now that isn't true? That one of the other boys is alive?"

"I can't say no more den I already said."

"Why?" Matt barely heard his own question.

"You remember what you said Pierre told you? That he didn't want to talk bad about de dead? It's de same t'ing here. I don't want to talk bad about de dead, neither."

"But you just got through talking about the dead,"

Laura said. "Joseph and Morgan, the fights, the abuse—"

"Dat's not de same. What I told you was de trut', not jus' gossip dat came from somebody else's mout'. But de other child . . . it's not de same. I didn't see wit' my own eyes. But I know somebody who did. And dat's de same person who can tell you what's happening in you house."

"Who is this person?" Matt asked. "Where do I find him . . . her?"

"Dis person is a black man, and you gonna find him at de Crowley shelter."

"We gotta talk to a brother?" Tawana asked.

Thelma gave her a puzzled look. "I don't know if he's got a brother, but him, he lives and works at de shelter now. De shelter's on Senegal Road. If you don't know where dat's at, I can tell you." Thelma shook a finger at Matt. "But now you got to listen to me good. Dis man's been known to mess wit' hoodoo, so y'all gonna have to be careful."

"Oh, no!" Tawana dusted her hands together. "That's all, we done, Tawana's done. We ain't messin' with no hoodoo."

"What's his name?" Matt asked.

"No use you ask what's his name!" Tawana said. "We ain't goin'!"

Laura took a step toward her. "Wana—"

Tawana snapped a hand up, palm out. "You can back up, sistah, 'cause the answer's still no."

"You don't have to come," Matt said.

"And what *you* think you gonna do with a hoodoo man? A *black* hoodoo man? If you go mess with that, it's gonna come back on everybody in your house, on everybody you know. *Everybody*."

Matt glanced at Thelma.

She lifted her hands as though to surrender. "What she say is de trut', but dat's only if you make him mad, if he work a conja on you."

"I don't plan on making him mad."

Thelma shrugged. "All I gotta say is watch youself. Sometimes you can make dem mad and you don't even know what you did."

"See what I'm sayin'?" Tawana said. "Just don't go messin' around with that man."

"What's his name?" Matt asked again, holding out a hand to ward off Tawana's tongue-lashing.

"De man's name is Jerome Batiste. He used to—"

"Hold on, hold up." Tawana took two quick steps closer to Thelma. "*What* you said his name was?"

"Jerome Batiste. He—"

Tawana spun around to face Matt. "That's my uncle's name! Jerome Batiste. We call him Uncle J— Uncle J for Jerome, that's his name."

"It might not be the same man," Laura said. "I'm sure there's more than one Jerome Batiste in south Louisiana."

"Another Jerome Batiste that works hoodoo? Get real, girl."

"You never told me your uncle was into hoodoo. You said he knew things, like he was psychic or something. And this man's from Crowley, you told me your uncle was from New Orleans."

Tawana tsked. "How you think he knows things if he's not into hoodoo? And people move all the time.

Uncle J ain't been around since I was little. He could've moved to Crowley, for all I know." She whirled back around to Thelma. "How you know Jerome Batiste?"

"Batiste used to work for Joseph."

"In the rice fields?"

"No, most de time he did yard work at Joseph's house. Took care of de lawn, de garden, did small fix-ups on de house." Thelma got up from the couch and placed a hand on the small of her back. She shuffled over to Matt and patted his arm. "It don't matter if it's de uncle or no. Just be good to Batiste and he's gonna tell you what you need to know. Understand?"

Matt nodded.

"Bien."

"Mrs. Sonnier?"

Thelma cocked her head quizzically.

Matt placed a hand over hers on his arm. "Paul and Marie . . . they . . . thank you. I just want to say thank you."

She smiled softly, her lips folding into her mouth. "You a good boy."

He squeezed her hand. "Do you think . . . in my house . . . I mean, all that stuff going on—do you think Joseph and Morgan . . ." Matt glanced away, unsure of how to ask without the words sounding ridiculous.

Thelma touched his cheek, her face solemn. "I'm afraid, *mon garçon,* dat sometimes what haunts is not all de time dead."

CHAPTER TWENTY-ONE

The blood wouldn't come off.

And it might never come off.

Because she hadn't been on the list.

Crouching behind boxes of ice-packed shrimp, Keith Lafleur rubbed his hands together once more. His palms were the color of withered beets. It wasn't healthy, couldn't be healthy to carry someone's blood for this long. What if she'd had a disease, and at this very moment a million impregnable microbes were gnawing their way into his bloodstream? Why wouldn't the blood come off? Wasn't he suffering enough? He'd only veered off course once—once! It wasn't fair.

Barbara; her mother, Dolores; Stanford Milo. They'd been his highest priced tickets so far, and Keith knew the cost would only get higher from here. Last night, when he'd returned home and crossed all three names off the list, it dawned on him then that he'd have to leave home and go into hiding. Too much evidence had been left behind. Fingerprints, his own blood, and the weeping lesions left a trail wherever he went. If he didn't leave, they'd find him, cage him, possibly kill him before he finished the list. The finale was most important to him, though. Without it, everything else felt moot. He couldn't let them steal that away from him. He *wouldn't* let that happen. So, after throwing a few items into a bag, he'd left home. He regretted having to leave his recliner behind, one of the few comforts he had left. And he worried about the gasoline containers in the garage. Those had to stay behind as well. It would have been too dangerous having them slosh around in the bed of his truck, fumes alerting everyone to their presence. He had to have faith they'd still be there when he needed them, which would be very, very soon.

Left without home, recliner, or direction, Keith had driven aimlessly for hours, waiting for morning, eager to cross off the second to last name on the list. Before dawn, he'd pulled into a nearly deserted rest area just outside of Lafayette to use the restroom. That's when he saw her. Tight jeans, low cut sweater stretched tight over milky white breasts, two-inch spiked heels, and hair the color of wheat down to her waist. She stumbled and giggled when she walked. Desire surged through him so quickly, so powerfully, he didn't even bother to check if someone waited for her outside. Pulling the hood of his jacket down low so it covered most of his face, Keith followed her into the women's bathroom. Either drunk or stoned, she'd been too slow to react. He came up from behind, grabbed her by the hair, and slapped a hand over her mouth. With one fierce twist, her neck snapped, and he shuddered with the force of his orgasm. When his tremors abated, he'd slammed her head into one of the steel sinks for good measure. He hadn't expected the blood and still didn't know how it wound up on his hands.

Not long after he left the rest area, the boils covering his body began to percolate with heat—so much heat, cooking the purulence within each one, the pressure building, stretching, pushing against his skin until he thought they would explode en masse and obliterate him. The idea to sit in a cooler came to him when he passed a billboard that advertised Pellerin's Seafood Market. He knew the place, right off Route 35. He'd been there a few times to buy crawfish. It wasn't much more than a tin shack with shelves. It would be easy to get into, and with any luck the temperature in the walk-in coolers would reduce the heat in the boils and moderate the pain.

He'd been right on both counts. The padlock on the backdoor jiggled open with minimal effort, and the cooler had given him some relief. But relief time was over now. With or without that bitch's blood on his hands, he had to get back on the road. The window of opportunity for the next person on the list was very small.

Dr. Obadiah Robins followed the same routine every morning. He arrived at his office at seven-thirty, then left again a half hour later and drove thirty-five miles to a nursing home in Opelousas. His reserved parking spot at Magnolia Ridge was near the back of the building, where he entered. Today, Keith would make sure he didn't make it inside.

After collecting a few items he thought might come in handy later, Keith left the market the same way he came in. He didn't bother replacing the padlock. Any moron would be able to tell it had been jimmied.

The drive to Dr. Robins's office took him longer than expected. Too many stops along the way. As soon as his body warmed from the temperatures in the cooler, the heat and pressure from the boils flared up twice as bad as before. At times, the pain got so intense, Keith felt nothing else. The gas pedal beneath his foot would disappear, the steering wheel from his hand, the seat beneath his buttocks. He surfed on an ocean of fire with never-ending waves. God, the finale had to come soon. It had to.

Keith didn't remember slipping in behind the black Lexus. One moment he was gripping the steering wheel, blinded by a spasm of pain, the next he was reading ROBINS-1 on a moving license plate. He wet his lips again and again to stay focused, gearing himself up for thirty-five grueling miles.

The Lexus's brake lights flashed on and off ten miles down Highway 190. The car slowed, and Keith had to brake to keep from pulling up too close. What the hell was the bastard doing? Brake lights flashed again, then without warning from a signal indicator, Robins hooked a left into the parking lot of a run-down convenience store that had burglar bars on the windows. Keith hit his left signal, but cruised up another half block before turning. He turned left again in the parking lot of a Laundromat, then drove over a curb to get back to the store.

Robins had parked on the north end of the building, but he was no longer in his car. A wall of panic rose in Keith's gut, but he soon released it in an explosive exhale when he spotted Robins coming out of the store with a piece of wood in his hand. The man hurried to the side of the building in frantic close-together steps. Bathroom emergency, no doubt.

Keith cruised slowly past the Lexus and saw Robins standing in front of a warped metal door, fumbling with the key that dangled from the piece of wood. A locked door meant a single bathroom unit, not multiple stalls—which also meant Keith wouldn't have to drive another twenty-five miles to finish his task.

He coasted into a parking slot directly ahead, then killed the engine and got out of the truck. Robins had already made it into the bathroom. Keith checked his jacket pockets to make sure he still had the items from the seafood market, then hobbled over to the bathroom. Quietly, he wrapped a hand around the knob, braced his right shoulder against the door and waited.

A muted cough echoed from inside. Silence for a long moment. The flush of a toilet. Rushing water. Slight movement from the knob in his hand.

Sucking in a breath for strength, Keith rammed the door with his shoulder, and in an instant the weight against it from the other side was released. He hustled in sideways, then slammed the door shut. Robins was sprawled on the floor near the toilet, his suit coat twisted and bunched, his black rimmed glasses dangling from one ear.

The pear-shaped man groaned, rolling to his side as though intending to get up. His glasses fell to the floor. "What—"

Keith kicked Robins hard in the face, causing blood to gush from his nose. The man yelled, an underwater sound that quickly gathered volume, and began backpedaling on the concrete floor. Keith yanked a roll of duct tape out of his jacket pocket and made sure the first strip went over Robins's mouth nice and tight.

The doctor's eyes grew huge with disbelief—and recognition. He clawed at the tape.

Keith kicked him again. "Leave the goddamn tape alone," he said, then ripped off another, longer strip of duct tape. "Gimme your hands, stick them out in front—now!" Another kick, this one landing across Robins's nose, breaking it. "I said, now!"

Two trembling hands were presented, wrist to wrist.

"You see, Robins, the problem is you think you're God, that you don't have to answer to anybody. That you can get away with your little charade of playing doctor and nobody will be the wiser. Take a good look at my face, you worthless asshole! Take a good goddamn look! You didn't do shit to help me! Not shit!"

Keith kicked him on the side of the head, and with a muffled cry Robins drew his taped hands up to his face to protect it. Blood bubbles popped over his nostrils as his breath whistled and gurgled through his nose. His legs sawed the concrete beneath him as he pushed himself backward. Keith watched in amusement until Robins's back touched the wall. Keeping his eyes on Robins, Keith pulled up a flap of tape from the roll and walked over to him. The man began to thrash, kicking out with his feet, his arms swinging from side to side like a golfer practicing for a long drive.

"Stop all that goddamn wiggling around!" Keith slammed a foot into Robins's groin, and the man curled into a ball. As soon as Robins's face drew forward, Keith hammered his face again with a foot. The man's head flew back and smacked into the concrete wall behind him. He went limp immediately.

"About fucking time," Keith muttered, breathing hard. He knelt on one knee in front of Robins and pulled out more tape from the roll. After looping around the tape binding Robins's wrists, Keith yanked the man's body down as far as it would go, then taped his ankles together.

With Robins sandwiched in half, hands bound to feet, Keith removed the box cutter from his pocket, yanked the man's head up by the hair, and sliced open his jugular. The spray was immediate and voluminous, spattering the walls, the floor. Obadiah Robins's eyes flew open, and Keith made sure the man saw his face up close before letting go of his hair. He watched him a moment, the room ripening with the stench of urine and copper.

Keith stood and went over to the sink. He turned on the faucet and rinsed the blood off the box cutter. When it was sufficiently clean, he turned off the faucet, shook the excessive water off the cutter, and glanced over at Robins. The man's eyes were still open, but his movements were mostly spasms, and blood pulsed instead of sprayed from the wound in his neck.

Smiling, Keith turned back to the sink and stared in the mirror. Once again, adrenaline had been his anesthetic during his struggle, but it wouldn't be long before the fire and pressure would start up again. He'd lose his fucking mind when that happened, and he couldn't afford to lose it now. Not with him being so close.

He held the box cutter up to the light, eyeing the blade for signs of blood. Satisfied it was clean, Keith leaned over the sink, tilted his head to the left, and punctured the largest boil on his right cheek with the point of the blade. It felt like a corkscrew driving into his face. Thick yellow-green fluid gushed from the wound and a rancid odor impaled Keith's nostrils. He gagged, waited for his stomach to stop convulsing, then punctured another boil, a large one just below his left ear. Thick lava ran down his neck, so hot he expected to see smoke. Another on his neck, one over his right eye, four on his left cheek. The image in the mirror became one of a melting mask.

Keith unzipped his jacket and punctured the first boil on his chest—that's when he heard the laughter—children laughing—boys laughing.

He closed his eyes, concentrating on the sound. "His iniquity will visit the children unto the third and fourth generation," Keith murmured, then opened his eyes and smiled. The end was closer than he thought.

Another boil vomited beneath the tip of the blade, and that's when he saw it—the brilliance of its light drawing his eye to the mirror—an explosion, a fire, roaring up and up, tongues stretching, licking, unfurling thick black clouds into heaven. Keith nodded. "Just like that," he said. "I want it to be just like that."

Going back to the task at hand, Keith cut through two more boils, then suddenly wondered what Barbara was cooking for supper. It had better be one of his favorite dishes if she wanted back in his good graces. The woman was an airhead. She'd forgotten to lay out his clothes this morning, which pissed him off. If she did something equally stupid for dinner, like cook meat loaf, he'd have to teach her a lesson, one she'd remember for a long time.

"Barbara, Barbara, Barbara," he sing-songed, while zipping his jacket back up. "When will you ever learn? Why won't you just listen to me? Nobody listens anymore." He sighed and peered up once more to make sure the fire still blazed.

Still there—so tremendous and wild, a magnificent accompaniment to the laughter of children—fire to death, laughter to tears. Soon everyone would listen to him. Oh, yes—very, very soon.

CHAPTER TWENTY-TWO

The shelter looked more like an abandoned warehouse than a haven for the destitute. It sat on two-foot piers between Our Lady of Perpetual Mercy Catholic Church and the American Legion Hall, a hulking clapboard in desperate need of repair and paint.

Matt turned into the lot and parked beside an old school bus with curtained windows. He killed the engine and wiped a sweaty palm on his pant leg. Today his world had detoured onto Surreal Lane, and he couldn't steer it back toward normal. Meeting Jerome Batiste wouldn't amend that. If anything, it could send him careening so far off course he'd never find his way to normal again. But it was too late for him to turn back. He knew too little about too much, and if he ever expected to pull his life together, he had to have more answers.

From the passenger seat, Laura reached over and

put a hand on his arm. "You all right?" Her voice was as gentle as her touch.

He turned to her, saw the worry in her eyes. "Confused." It was the most honest answer he could muster.

The backseat groaned as Tawana scooted across it to get out of the car. "Yeah, well we about to go get unconfused." She opened her door. "Y'all gonna just sit in here or what?"

There was no foyer or reception area to ease them into the heart of the shelter. It greeted them as soon as they walked through the front doors. At least thirty long folding tables were set up cafeteria style in the middle of a forty by forty foot room. Each table had ten plastic chairs of various colors assigned to it, as well as two lazy susans filled with condiments. Beyond the main seating area was a serving counter with warming lights, and past it, swinging doors that Matt assumed led to the kitchen. The floors were worn but clean, and the place smelled of pine cleaner, cherry blend tobacco, and fried chicken.

"Anybody here?" Tawana yelled.

One of the swinging doors bounced open and an elderly woman appeared, carrying an empty aluminum tray and a dishrag. She wore a white bib apron over a lavender flowered dress and a hairnet covered her thick gray hair.

The woman smiled broadly. "Sorry, but we don't start serving 'til five. Y'all are welcome to set claim on cots in the other room, though, if you want." Her accent carried a slight twang and noticeable drawl. Definitely not Cajun. More north Louisiana, maybe Mississippi.

"No thanks," Matt said. "We're looking for Jerome Batiste. We were told he works here."

"Y'all friends of Jerome's?" She looked at Tawana. "Family?"

"If he's the right Jerome, then, yeah, we related," Tawana said. "He works here?"

"Sure does. Him and a couple of the other guys are out back taking a smoke break, but I can go get him if you want."

"We'd appreciate it," Laura said.

The old woman nodded and pushed against the swinging doors with her backside. "Y'all go 'head and have a seat at one of the tables while I round him up. Oh, who do I say's come to visit?"

"Just tell him Nana's oldest grandbaby," Tawana said.

When the woman disappeared behind the swinging doors again, Laura said, "Maybe we should have said we wanted to talk to him about the Devilliers. What if he's not your uncle? He won't know who Nana is and might not come out and talk to us."

Tawana folded her arms across her chest. "Oh, he'll come out. Either way."

"How do you know?"

" 'Cause I'll go get his ass if he don't."

It didn't take long before the swinging doors gave way once more, this time revealing a tall, thin black man with closely cropped white hair. He was long-limbed, square-jawed and carried an old scar over his right eye. Despite his age, which looked to be late sixties or early seventies, he had a confident walk, which became all the more evident as he headed right for Tawana.

Tawana's arms dropped to her sides as though she no longer had the strength to keep them crossed. "This can't be for real."

The recognition in the man's eyes as he stepped up to her was undeniable. His smile was soft and held regret. "It be a long time, huh, Wana?"

Tawana stared at him, unblinking, her mouth settling into a tight, hard line, her chest rising and falling rapidly.

His smile faltered. "It's good to see you." He held a hand out to her.

"Why the hell didn't you come?" Tawana said through clenched teeth.

He drew his hand back.

"Why? She was dyin', and you still didn't come."

"I wanted to."

"What the fuck's that supposed to mean?"

His eyes narrowed. "Don't you be using no trash mouth around me, girl. I'm still family, whether you like it or not."

"Just 'cause you my uncle by blood, don't mean you family." Tawana jabbed a finger at him. "Family don't leave their mama on her deathbed callin' his name. Family don't skip out on their mama's funeral, and family sure as hell don't desert their only daughter!"

"I didn't desert Angelica."

"Didn't desert her? Moweez don't even remember what you look like!"

"You don't understand nothing about what happened back then. I had my reasons—"

"Fuck your reasons, Jerome Batiste!" Tawana

slammed her hands on her hips. "Fuck them and fuck you."

He glared at her, silent, his nostrils flaring, his jaw muscles contracting.

Tawana's blowup took Matt by surprise. He'd expected a possible family reunion, but not a family collision. And he didn't know which was worse, the yelling or this silent standoff, which neither of them appeared interested in breaking. He glanced over at Laura. Her eyes told him she was as clueless as he was about what to do with the situation.

Jerome finally lifted his chin. "You done?"

Tawana harrumphed. "I been done with you."

"Why you here then? Just to rag on me?"

"You can bes' believe if I'd come here to rag on you, I'd still be raggin'."

"Then what you want?"

Tawana turned to Matt and Laura. "Y'all gonna just stand there?"

Frowning as though he just realized someone else was in the room and didn't like the notion, Jerome looked over at Matt. He did a double take.

Matt cleared his throat. "We were told to come talk to you about the—"

The front door creaked open, and the sound echoed through the building. A middle-aged man with scraggly brown hair stuck his head inside. "Dey servin' yet?"

"Not yet, Roscoe," Jerome said. "But go on around back and tell Adel I sent you. She'll fix you a plate of something." The man quickly bowed out, and Jerome turned back to Matt. "I seen you somewhere before."

"I don't remember ever having met you."

Jerome stepped closer, studying Matt with squinted eyes. "Where you from?"

"Windham. We want to talk to you about the Devillier house."

The man's head snapped back in surprise. "Who sent you here?"

Matt hesitated, uncertain if he should mention Thelma's name. She'd made a point of telling them not to upset Jerome, which was moot now thanks to Tawana. But would mentioning Thelma only anger him more? Would he see her as a snitch?

Deciding to play it safe, Matt said, "Someone in town."

Jerome scowled. "Yeah? And what this somebody said I'm supposed to know?"

"A couple of things. You used to work for the Devilliers, right?"

The front door opened again, and two elderly black men came inside. Each carried blue plastic shopping bags and a rancid body odor that wafted in with the breeze. "Anybody take the cots by the window yet, J?" one of them asked.

Jerome shook his head. "They all open, Neevad. You and Bone can go 'head and pick the ones you want. Food'll be out soon."

As the two men scuttled across the room and disappeared down a back hallway, Jerome said to Matt, "The place is gonna fill up soon, and I gotta help Adel set up the supper line, so hurry up and spit out what you gotta say. Yeah, I worked for the Devilliers, what about it?"

"We live in their house now."

Jerome arched a brow.

Matt explained how the house was moved and renovated as two separate buildings, and how the three of them wound up renting both.

"You got a beauty shop?" Jerome asked Tawana.

"The shop's for me and Laura. Why you actin' all surprised and shit? You think I'm too stupid to have a business?"

"You wanna get your drawers out the crack of your butt? I never said you was stupid."

Tawana eyed him suspiciously.

"So, okay, y'all in that house," Jerome said, still addressing her. "What's that got to do wit' me?"

Tawana glanced at Matt as if wanting to confirm it was okay for her to explain. He nodded.

"There's some weird shit goin' on in that house," Tawana blurted, then lowered her voice. "In me and Laura's part, and Matt's, too. And it's like whatever's happenin' is bleedin' into the whole damn town." She gave Jerome the details of each incident, starting with the black birds and ending with the Courir. His face was grim by the time she finished.

Jerome looked at Matt. "When all this started?"

"A few days after they opened the salon, I think."

He pursed his lips and glanced at Laura. "You not messing wit' no Tarot cards or Ouija board or nothing like that, huh?"

Laura frowned. "No. I wouldn't even know what to do with them."

"Why you wanna know that?" Tawana asked.

"'Cause sometimes people play around wit' stuff

they got no business messing wit'. They don't know what they doing, so it makes . . . problems."

"That's not what's happenin' over there. It's different."

"And how you know different from different?"

Tawana eyed him. " 'Cause Moweez been drawin' again."

Jerome's shoulders drooped as if she'd just dumped a one-ton weight on them. "She's seeing?"

Tawana nodded. "Just like with Nana."

"But we don't understand what she's telling us in those drawings until after it happens," Matt said. "And my—my son's in her last picture."

"Dead?" Jerome asked bluntly.

Matt hated to release the answer, fearing it would kick-start some cosmic machine and seal Seth's fate. "Yes."

"That's why we're here," Laura said. "We want to know what's going on and how to stop it."

"We need *you* to see," Tawana said.

Jerome abruptly turned away and went to one of the tables, where he repositioned a ketchup bottle and salt and pepper shakers in a lazy susan. "I don't do that no more. Now y'all gotta go, 'cause I got work to do."

"Oh, uh-uh!" Tawana stormed over to the table and slapped a hand on it. "You listen here, Jerome Batiste! All your life you been runnin' from what you supposed to be takin' care of, but you not going to run from this. That place is all me and Moweez got. That's where we work, where we live. You either tell me what's going on with that house or I'm gonna pluck every damn white hair out of your head until you do, you understand?"

So much for not upsetting the man, Matt thought.

Jerome cocked his head and threw Tawana a smirk. "And you think all that bulldog talk's gonna scare me?"

Tawana stared at him for a long moment, then without warning, she hoisted up one of the chairs beside her and threw it across the room. "That's for Moweez!" The chair crashed onto another table before tumbling to the floor.

"Wana, no!" Laura said, heading for Tawana.

Matt caught her by the arm just as Tawana grabbed another chair and flung it in the opposite direction. It ricocheted off a wall and landed on another table, bowling over a lazy susan and everything on it. A bottle of Tabasco sauce dropped to the floor and shattered.

"And that's for Nana!"

The kitchen doors flew open and a young Vietnamese man and the elderly woman in the lavender dress burst into the dining room. Neevad and Bone came running in from the back hall.

"What's going—"

"—gone nuts!"

"Call the—"

"—the police!"

The scramble of frantic voices didn't seem to bother Tawana. She held her ground, staring at Jerome as if he were a cockroach that needed to be squashed.

"J, man . . . man you need us to go get the cops?" Neevad asked. " 'Cause me and—"

"No!" Jerome's answer was loud and firm, and the nervous chatter ceased immediately. He turned to the woman in lavender. "Adel, you and Richard go on and set up the supper line even though it's a little bit early. I'll take your place servin' when I get back. Right now I've gotta go take care of something."

Adel nodded, a hand to her chest. The man next to her shook a large serving spoon he held in his hand at Tawana and began spouting off in Vietnamese. Matt didn't understand a thing he said, but he seriously doubted the guy was telling her to have a nice day.

With jaw muscles rapidly flexing and nostrils flared, Jerome headed for the front door. When he passed by Tawana, he grabbed her arm and pulled her along. Surprisingly, she didn't resist. She signaled for Matt and Laura to follow, then matched Jerome stride for furious stride out of the shelter.

The old school bus was the last place Matt expected Jerome to lead them. The inside had been gutted, the seats replaced with a green army cot, a card table with two metal chairs, and a mini-fridge with its electrical cord running through a hole in the floor beside it. Along the left side of the bus, four elk-blocks supported a wide plank that held a miniature television, a hot plate, a few dishes, and a desk lamp. Each electrical appliance was plugged into a thick, orange extension cord that ran across the bus, then disappeared into the same hole as the cord for the fridge. The space felt stuffy and smelled of strawberry incense.

Jerome turned on the lamp and pointed to the card table. "Sit," he told Tawana, then motioned Laura and Matt to the cot, which sat directly across from the table.

"You live in here?" Tawana asked as she sat.

Jerome ignored her question and went to the front of the bus. He returned seconds later with a tattered box of Squeezers playing cards. After sitting across the table from Tawana, he dumped the cards out of the box and began to shuffle.

"You best listen close, girl," he said, cards fluttering between his fingers. "If you ever pull something like what you did back there again, I'm gonna bus' your ass, woman or no woman, family or no family, you got that, Tawana Farisa Batiste? You hearing me good?"

Tawana nodded once, a sheepish look in her eye.

"Farisa?" Laura murmured.

"And don't you be thinking I'm doing these cards 'cause of your hissy fit, neither. This is for Nana. Nana and Angelica."

"Moweez," Tawana said quietly.

Jerome shot her a hard look, then stacked the cards into one pile and placed them in the middle of the table. He turned to Matt and Laura. "Sit to the edge, up close so you by the table."

"What are the cards for?" Matt pulled himself to the edge of the cot. Laura did the same, scooting closer to him. The heat emanating from her body made him acutely aware of the soap scent on her skin.

"To see." Jerome tapped the top of the deck with a finger. "Since three live in the house, three cut the deck."

"We got five livin' in it," Tawana said. "Us three, then Moweez and Seth, Matt's son."

"The boy's daddy is gonna count for two, the boy and him. You gonna have to count for you and Ang—Moweez." He looked at Matt. "We gotta cut the cards three times. You cut first. Put what you cut on the side of the deck, face down."

Matt removed a small stack of cards from the top of the deck, then placed them on the table as instructed.

Jerome nodded to Laura. "Now you. Same thing."

Laura glanced at Matt nervously, then leaned over and pulled another stack from the pile of cards.

"You," Jerome said to Tawana, then sat back as she cut the last of the deck.

When they were done, Jerome gathered each stack in the order they were placed on the table, then stacked them again into one pile. Holding the deck in the palm of his right hand, he placed his left hand over the top of the cards and closed his eyes. His lips moved as though in silent prayer, then he squared his shoulders and opened his eyes.

One by one, Jerome dealt the cards face up. He laid six across the top of the table, then placed each subsequent card over one of the six already in position, covering all but the top number or letter and suit. Before long, six neat rows covered the table, each row touching the one beside it.

As Jerome sat back and studied the cards, his brow furrowed. He leaned in closer, touching first one card, then another.

"No," Jerome whispered.

Tawana leaned in closer as well. "What? You see somethin'?"

Jerome threw a hand up, keeping his eyes on the cards. *"Shhhh!"*

Matt felt Laura squirm beside him, then her hand sought his. He gently wrapped his fingers around hers and squeezed reassuringly.

"Why you lied to me?" Jerome asked, suddenly turning toward Matt. His brown eyes were nearly black with fury.

"What the hell are you talking about?" Matt asked, taken aback by the accusation.

"You said you was from Windham, but that's not what the cards say." Jerome snapped a look at Tawana. "Why you wanna trick me wit' him? You know better! You knowed I would see."

"Ain't nobody tryin' to trick nobody!" Tawana shouted back.

Jerome turned back to Matt. "Then you tell me who your daddy is. You tell me his name."

"Paul—"

"The truth!"

Matt glared at him, feeling the answer Jerome wanted rising from somewhere deep inside him, swelling in his throat, burning on his tongue. To speak that name, a name he hardly knew, over the one that belonged to the man who'd nurtured him all his life felt wrong. "My father—the man who raised me is Paul Daigle. The man I'm told is my biological father, a man I don't know, don't remember, is Joseph Devillier."

Jerome slumped in his chair. He studied Matt's

face. "I knowed I seen you before. I knowed it. The same chin, the same nose..." He leaned over, propped his elbows on the table, and scrubbed his face with his hands. "They said you was dead. That you was all dead. I knowed better, though. I knowed." He peered up at Tawana. "You ain't never gonna have peace in that house, girl. None of y'all."

"Why? The Devilliers? They ghosts?"

He sat back wearily. "It's more than that." He tapped four cards in the middle of the spread, each falling one beneath the other, all of them sixes. "See this? Them sixes tell me something wants to come together in that house or somebody wants what's separated to come together."

Laura sat up straight, letting go of Matt's hand. "That's all Moweez talks about lately, that the come together's broken. What does she mean?"

Jerome nodded. "That don't make me surprised she says that. She always could see better'n me. Me, I got to see wit' the cards. Angelica, she feels it inside her, and she's back in that house where all the people in it was broken. See, everybody got two sides, one good, one bad. Sometimes them sides get so blurry with lies, nobody can tell which is the good and which is the bad no more. Not even the person hisself. A body can't stand like that for long, it can't rest. Neither a spirit." A sad, pained look crossed his face. "Y'all know what happened in that place, huh?"

"Yeah," Tawana said. "That whacked out bitch gassed everybody."

He scowled. "Don't you pass no judgment on nobody 'less you know all the trut'. Nobody knows for sure all the story about what happened that night. And nobody is ever gonna know. You understand? What happened back then ain't gonna make no difference to what's happening now, anyway. You see this?" He touched a card on the table. "The queen of spades by that second two means a dark-haired woman is the one wantin' something to come together. Now look here . . ." He pointed to a two, three, and four of clubs that extended to the right of the fifth six. "This here's chil'ren, all the same family 'cept for one. Three on this side, two on the other." He indicated an ace of clubs and a five of hearts that extended to the left of the fifth six. "The chil'ren, they not together. Three chil'ren's in one part of the house, two in the other. And this," he traced a diagonal line starting with the eight of clubs located at the top right corner of the spread and ending with the seven of spades at the bottom left corner. "This is worst of all. Somebody else is gonna die for sure, more than one somebody."

The hair on Matt's arms stood on end. He thought of Moweez's last drawing, the one with Seth lying across First Street. "Who, Jerome? Who's going to die? How do we stop it?"

Jerome touched a jack of clubs. "This could be a man or boy, I can't tell which for sure." He moved his finger to the queen of hearts. "This one, a woman or girl. And you can't stop it. It's like when you yell in a big church and the echo goes all over the place. No matter how much you want, *you* can't make the echo stop. It's gotta stop by itself."

"Wait, wait," Tawana said, shaking her head. "Back

up, 'cause I'm all los'. Why the kids ain't in the same place? And why the cards show five kids, when they had four. Three died, Matt's the fourth, who's the other one? Is the other one dead?"

"That's got to be the other brother," Laura said earnestly. "The one she wouldn't tell us about."

"She?" Jerome said. "Who's that, she?"

"The person who sent us here," Matt said. "Her name's not important."

"Not important to me or to you?"

Tawana waved a hand in Jerome's face, catching his attention. "Why you wanna worry 'bout a stupid name that don't make no difference when we got serious shit to talk about? We gotta know about the other kid. And what you mean when you said Moweez is back in that house. She ain't never been in there before."

Jerome let out a resigned sigh. "Yeah, she was there. Long time ago."

Tawana frowned. "When? You brought her to work with you or somethin' when she was little?"

He shook his head.

"Did Nana bring her there to visit you?" Laura asked.

He shook his head again.

"You stop makin' us play fifty questions and tell us!" Tawana demanded.

"Stop with that big mouth you got," Jerome said. "I promised Nana I would never say nothing."

Tawana leaned back in her chair. "But Nana ain't here no more. Me and Mo is. Which one you think's more important, keepin' a promise to somebody

271

that's dead, God rest her, or bein' straight and helpin' the family you got that's alive?"

Jerome looked down and picked at the corner of a card with his thumb. He stayed that way for so long, Matt thought he was purposely ignoring them. Tawana must have thought so too, because she started to fidget. Just when it looked like one of her corks was going to blow, Jerome placed his hand flat on the table and looked up at her.

"When I first went to work for the Devilliers, I seen right away something's bad wrong. Joseph showed the people in Crowley one face, but I seen two. One that says happy, the other one sad and pulled inside itself like a turtle. I see the same thing wit' Morgan and those chil'ren. They ain't got no peace in that house, in nobody that lives in that house, but they make as if there is. Morgan, she's worried all the time. Somebody told her I read the cards, so she come ask me to read for her. So I read. The cards, they don't have nothing good to say. I don't want to tell her, though, 'cause she's already sad all the time. So I made up a good reading to give her some hope. That was the first mistake. After that, every day when I come to work, she comes meet me in the yard. 'Jerome, read for me,' she'd say all the time. What I'm supposed to do? I don't want to lose my job, so I read."

"And you keep lyin' about what the cards say?" Tawana asked.

"Yeah," he said, looking ashamed. "All this goes on 'bout a month. Then I start to notice she comes meet me only when I'm working in the backyard, and she gets up close to me when I read her cards, all the time touching my hands, my arm. Her clothes get different, too. More open, like she wants me to see all that white skin, touch it. Pretty soon, I los' my head. All that perfume, all her soft words, all her sad. I jus' want to make her hurt go away."

"Oh, uh-uh," Tawana said, wide-eyed. "Don' tell me you and her . . ."

He nodded, a faraway look in his eyes. "After that, we was together almost everyday—'til she got pregnant."

Tawana jerked up straight in her chair. "Say what?"

"She hid her belly for a long time, long as she could, but when she couldn't hide no more, she told Joseph."

"Everything?" Laura asked.

"Just that she was pregnant. She was seven months by that time. But he knew the baby didn't belong to him 'cause they hadn't been together in a long time. When he found out it was me—"

"How he find out?" Tawana asked, leaning in closer.

"Morgan asked me to fix a cabinet door in the kitchen, and when I go fix it, she's all over me. She thinks Joseph's at work, but he walks in while we—"

"What he did?"

"What you think? He went crazy. Bus' a chair on my head. That's where I got this." Jerome pointed to the scar over his eye. "Then before I know what's going on, the police come pick me up, put me in jail for assault. Joseph said I beat him up. I didn't have no money for no good attorney. He had all the money, all the connections. I wound up in jail for two years 'cause of that man. Worse than that, Morgan got so

273

upset when we was fighting, she went into labor. Me in jail, her in the hospital. Joseph never let her see the baby, made sure the doctors told her she had a miscarriage. That wasn't the truth, though. Joseph found Nana, brought the baby to her, and tells that old woman, 'Here's your bastard grandbaby. You raise it.'"

"Oh, no he didn't!" Tawana fumed.

Matt shook his head, not believing the tale that unraveled before him. Who were these people? How could he possibly have come from Joseph Devillier's seed?

"Then he pass word to me in the jail that if I ever go back to Crowley or ever told anybody who the baby's real mama was, he'd make sure me and Nana was dead."

"That no good bastard bes' be glad *he's* dead," Tawana said with a snap of her head. "'Cause I'd go bus' up on some Devillier ass right now if he wasn't!"

Joseph nodded. "I wanted to go kill him myself when I got out the jail, but Nana made me swear not to go back. Made me swear never to tell nobody about what happened, 'cause it would wind up worse for the baby. So I didn't have no choice. All I worried 'bout after that was taking care of my baby. I went to work offshore—made decent money, too. The baby stayed with Nana while I worked. Then, one day I'm working in my yard on my seven off, and the police come pick me up, right in front of Nana. Told me all the Devilliers is dead, and they thinking it was me who killed 'em."

"Why would they think that?" Matt asked, dumb-founded.

"'Cause I'm a black man in the south," Jerome said, his eyes hard and cold. "A black man who used to work for Joseph and was fired. They put me back in jail. I was in there two weeks before they figure out there ain't no evidence to keep me. Jus' long enough for me to lose my job. Now I had nothing no more. Nana's the one told me to go, to leave the baby with her and go start somewhere else where nobody knowed me. That's what I did. Only when I built my life back right again and could've taken my baby wit' me, it would have broke Nana's heart. She needed that baby jus' as much as that baby needed her."

Tawana sat back heavily. "There's only been one baby aside from me Nana raised."

Jerome nodded, then turned to Matt. "You don't have another brother. You got a sister, a half sister. And her name's Angelica Mara Batiste."

CHAPTER TWENTY-THREE

Moweez sat at Lerna Mae's kitchen table, washing down the last of a grilled cheese sandwich with a glass of milk. She'd been nibbling on the sandwich for nearly a half hour, hoping if she ate slow enough Tawana, Laura, and Matt would show up before she finished. They hadn't. And that worried her.

In the next room, Seth played bouree with Lerna Mae. She'd given him real quarters to bet with, and Moweez figured she'd done that to keep him interested in the game. It must have worked because they'd been playing on and off for an hour. When they'd first started, Seth had asked Moweez to join them. Even though she'd said no, she loved him for asking. Nobody ever asked her to play anything.

She'd spent most of her life watching other people enjoy life. When she was younger and Nana would take her to the park, she'd watch the other kids laughing and playing on the swings. She tried joining in a few times, but as soon as the other kids realized she couldn't talk like everybody else, they'd laugh at her, then disappear to other sections of the park, leaving her behind.

Nana had been the only person who'd truly understood her. When they were alone, her grandmother would talk to her like she was a whole, grown-up person, like she expected her to answer in full sentences each time. Sometimes Nana would say, "Just open you mout', little bird, and let dem words out big and strong, like you want 'em to reach all de way to God." And although Moweez couldn't, Nana still managed to understand all she'd meant to say.

Now that Nana was gone, she didn't have anyone to hear her anymore. She loved Tawana, and Laura, too, but it wasn't the same. The way she talked confused them, which frustrated her. Sometimes it felt like all the words were right on the tip of her tongue. All she had to do was open her mouth, and they would flow out like sap from a tree. But they never did. If it wasn't for her drawings, Moweez knew she'd have no other way to really communicate with Tawana and Laura, to warn them about what she saw in her head.

So much had happened over the past year. Nana dying, her moving in with Tawana in the apartment above the beauty shop, now the visions again. Nana had been the first one to recognize that gift in her and had taught her how to draw what she saw on paper. Unfortunately, when the visions came, they usually announced bad news, so Moweez never viewed them as gifts.

The first one she had after Nana died was of the

dead birds, and it happened the day they'd moved into the apartment. It had taken her a while to get the whole vision, though, because too much else about the place felt wrong. The air in the shop and apartment didn't breathe right, like it was too thick, and she had a hard time pulling it into her lungs. That made her afraid. Then the voices came. The first night she'd slept in the apartment, she heard a man and woman yelling at each other, and it sounded like they were right outside her room in the hall. It took her a while to get up the courage to check it out, and when she did, no one was there. After the voices started, the vision of the birds got stronger. All those beautiful birds. She didn't want to see them dead, didn't want to draw them dead, but she had no choice. The vision would haunt her, cripple her until she let it out on paper. As she drew, she'd tell herself she'd show Tawana and Laura the picture in progress, but something would always make her forget. That same something that stole Moweez's words when she wanted so badly to speak.

It wasn't until after the bird vision that she saw the lady. Dark hair, dark eyes, so sad. Almost every night Moweez heard the quiet patter of her footsteps as she paced the hall between her bedroom and Laura's. The first couple of times Moweez saw her, there had only been enough of an outline in the white cloudiness that surrounded the woman to identify her. The outline gained more detail the next night and even more the next. Still, Moweez didn't think the lady could see her—until the night she appeared beside her bed. When the lady had leaned over her just a little and smiled, Moweez caught the scent of vanilla and line-dried sheets. The smell made her homesick for something she didn't understand, so much so she'd wanted to cry.

It was the lady who'd told her to go and meet Matt at the café. Seeing him for the first time had been like seeing home after being away on a long trip. She'd felt the same with Seth. For some reason, though, Moweez often had visions of Matt being sick, but he'd be small like Seth, and she'd see him either struggling to breathe or throwing up.

She worried about Matt, but more about Seth. Something was happening to him that she couldn't figure out. It was as if the café and the beauty shop had sores that leaked pus and infection, and they were leaking into Seth, leaking onto First Street, leaking into town. And she didn't know how to stop it.

Moweez gazed out one of the bay windows on her left and watched the sun settle over the treetops. She wished more than anything Nana was sitting next to her right now. Nana wouldn't be afraid, and she'd know exactly what to do.

"But it's not all de time bad to be afraid, little bird."

Moweez swiveled around in her chair at the sound of the familiar voice, then slapped a hand over her mouth to keep a shriek of joy from bursting out. Sitting in the high-back wooden chair beside her was Nana, wearing the same brown dress she'd worn the day Jesus took her home. Her powder-white hair was captured in a small bun, and her smiling face no longer held the road map of wrinkles Moweez remembered. It looked smooth, worry-free, and so very happy to see her.

Nana put a hand on Moweez's arm, her touch as warm and real as when she was alive. Tears stung Moweez's eyes. There was so much she wanted to say to her grandmother, but already she felt the words getting lost on the tip of her tongue.

"You can keep all de words in you head," Nana said. "'Cause I can hear every one." Her lips didn't move when she spoke, yet her words weren't mumbled. They were clear and strong, as if Nana spoke inside her head.

Moweez's heart fluttered with excitement. The thought of freely expressing any and every word that came to mind was almost overwhelming.

"Oh, Nana, I've missed you so much!"

"It's my old body dat's gone, little bird, dat's all. De rest of me's been watchin' you the whole time."

"How come I haven't seen you before now?"

"'Cause before wasn't de time for you to see me."

Moweez wanted to dive into the pools of Nana's warm, wise eyes and never resurface. She would be safe there. She'd be at home there. Tears slipped down Moweez's cheeks. "The world got too big after you left, Nana, and I'm afraid."

"I know." Nana drew her hand back into her lap.

"You've seen everything? The birds? The horses, all those people?"

"I seen."

"Why is this happening, Nana?"

"You already know dat, my little bird. You jus' afraid to open all you mind so you can see it clear. And what you do see, you don't want to believe."

Moweez dropped her head, knowing she was right.

"She was bad to do what she did." She looked up at Nana. "I didn't want my mama to be bad."

"You mama was sick. When she los' you, her heart broke so bad it broke her mind, too."

"How do you know that?"

Nana smiled softly. "I just know."

"Are people dying because she came back and she's still sick?"

"No, 'cause she didn't come back."

Moweez frowned. "But she *is* back, Nana. I hear her and see her all the time. She cries for her babies like they're lost. She wants them together, to all come together."

"Dat's not you mama. Dat's you, seein' what's in de back instead of what's in de front."

"I don't understand."

"De visions you been havin' since you little shows you what's gonna happen in de front. It ain't come around yet, but it's gonna. Dis time you seein' what's in de back, what already happened."

"But she wants her family all together. They were already together when she was alive, so how can I be seeing what already happened?"

"All de family wasn't together when you mama was alive. You wasn't dere, and de family she already had in de house was broke."

Moweez considered what she said for a moment. "If it's not her, then why are people dying? Why are so many strange things happening?"

Nana tilted her head slightly, the look on her face a mixture of compassion and sorrow. "Dey happen 'cause of de house—and 'cause of you."

The words shocked Moweez's brain mute for a second. She was responsible for the deaths of those people?

"No, no, it's not you dat killed dem people," Nana said. She put a hand on Moweez's arm again. "You remember when you and me used to fix dat ol' feather bed in de mornin'? How it would all de time show where I was sleepin' de night before, like my body was still dere?"

Moweez nodded. "We had to use that broomstick to smooth out the lumps."

"Dat's right. Well, de house is like dat bed. So much bad stuff was goin' on in dat house all de time, it wind up makin' its mark in de floors, in de walls, everywhere. When de family died, dere was nobody lef' to make de lumps go away, so dey stayed."

"And when they moved the house, the lumps came with it?"

Nana nodded. " 'Cept when they cut de house, it was like dey cut open all de bad stuff, too. De power inside, you knew it was you mama's house de minute you move in. But it was only half de house. You power don't understand dat, so it try to pull both de halves together, make dem come together like dey used to be. Dat's what killed dem people, what's makin' some people crazy, all de bad tryin' to come together. You understand?"

"But if I made all the bad in that house come together, then I'm the one responsible, Nana."

Nana took her hand from Moweez's arm and swiped the air with it. "If you pass a magnet by a nail in de wall, and it pulls out de nail, you gonna blame de magnet?"

"No."

"It's de same. You just like dat magnet."

Moweez put her elbows on the table and her head in her hands. She didn't want to be a magnet. She didn't want to see what was in front or behind anymore. All she wanted was normal.

She peered over at her grandmother. "More bad's coming, Nana. I saw it. How do I make it stop?"

"You can't make it stop altoget'er. You can only change what's gonna happen, make it go different— if dat's what you wanna do."

They stared at each other, Moweez thinking of the vision yet to be fulfilled, feeling Nana absorb the information.

After a while, Nana nodded sadly with understanding. "It's up to you, little bird." Her body began to fade in the gloom of dusk now invading the kitchen. "All dat's up to you."

Moweez reached out and touched the back of the empty chair, hoping Nana would return. She didn't.

With quiet resignation, Moweez got up from her chair and went into the living room to get her backpack from the couch, where she'd left it earlier. Inside were her colored pencils and sketch pad, a just-in-case-she-got-dirty shirt, and alligator clips for Seth.

Once she'd retrieved the pack, Moweez carried it into the kitchen and placed it on the table. She sat, scooting her chair up as close to the table as possible, then removed the pad and colored pencils from the pack and arranged them in front of her. Usually when she drew, she felt confident, like a normal person. But her hands shook as she tugged the first pencil out of the box. She didn't feel confident at all. Tawana and Laura and Matt might not make it back in time.

Moweez opened the pad to the drawing she'd already started but dreaded finishing. She had no choice but to complete it now. Time had already run out. This sketch was her responsibility, and she needed to make it perfect. It *had* to be perfect. For she knew it was the last one she'd ever draw.

CHAPTER TWENTY-FOUR

For two straight hours, Keith Lafleur roamed the halls of his one-story home, clutching a bloodstained towel. The blood belonged to the neighbor's dog, the towel to the neighbor who'd died a bloodless death. Both were casualties of fate.

When Keith had snuck home earlier to pick up the gasoline containers from his garage, the damn rat terrier had appeared out of nowhere. She barked and yapped so loudly, he thought for sure people across town would hear her. He didn't want to take that chance, so he'd grabbed the hydraulic jack out of the bed of his truck and beat the Terrier into silence. Permanent silence. Such a bloody mess. Keith had just backed away from the dog when its owner appeared in the garage. Of course, the man pitched a fit, cradling the dog, screaming, crying, threatening to call the police. More yapping, only with words.

While he'd yelled and threatened, Keith went over

to a workbench and collected a few feet of twine and a ball-peen hammer. The dog owner had his face buried in his pet's fur and never realized the hammer was in Keith's hand when he walked over to him. All it took was one good swing to knock the bastard out. Once he collapsed on the concrete floor, Keith yanked away the sweat towel the man had wrapped around his neck and replaced it with twine. He held tight until he quit breathing.

He'd left the man and dog where they lay, cleaned the blood off the jack with the towel, then tossed the jack into the cab of his truck. He was about to start hauling gasoline containers to the back of the pickup when he heard a woman call his name. At first he thought it was Patricia, the woman he'd met in Crowley, but after listening to her call him a couple of times, he noticed the voice didn't carry the same drawl as Patricia's. It was deeper in tone, more sensual.

Still hanging onto the towel, Keith followed the voice into the house. The woman called his name again and again, but no matter what room he searched, he couldn't find her. She was relentless, torturous, with that sexy, lilting voice. Before he realized it, Keith found himself pacing the halls of his home, listening to the sound of her voice, not bothering to search anymore, not caring about the pain in his feet, just listening, for two hours.

It would have gone on longer had he not needed to urinate.

The bathroom floor felt colder than usual, so cold he couldn't get his bladder to release when he stood in front of the toilet. Realizing he still carried the towel, Keith tossed it on the floor and stood on it to warm his feet. After a minute or two, fire trickled from his body. He gasped in pain and gritted his teeth as droplets of urine and blood fell into the bowl. As agonizing as this small task was, Keith relished it. The pain meant he was still alive.

When he could take no more, Keith tucked himself back into his pajama pants, flushed, then went over to the sink. He turned on the faucet to wash his hands, caught his reflection in the mirror, and burst into laughter. His face no longer looked human. It resembled what was left of the dog out in the garage—a thick, lumpy mass of raw flesh and blood. And he was worried about washing his hands?

"Keeeith."

The sound of her voice cut his laughter short. There was something different about it, something he couldn't quite put his finger on. Maybe this time she'd reveal herself.

With the water still running in the sink, Keith went to the bathroom door and peeked around the corner. He didn't see anything.

"Keeeith."

His heart beat faster as he crept into the hall. Her voice had grown softer, more sultry. It was obvious she wanted him. He hobbled toward the master bedroom as fast as he could. She had to be waiting for him there. She had to.

The back side of dusk drifted in from the bedroom window and covered the room in a smoky gray blanket. Light enough, though, for Keith to make out the body writhing on the bed from the doorway.

"Yesss, ohhh, yes!"

The sound of passion, her passion, urged him closer. His hand hesitated over the light switch. He desperately wanted to see her clearly, every inch of her, but if he turned on the lights, she'd see all of him, and that might scare her away. Maybe if he remained cloaked in shadows she wouldn't find him so grotesque.

Long, slender arms reached out in the gloom, beckoning him. "Keeeith."

"I'm here," he whispered, and crept toward the bed.

Her face was obscured by shadows, but he easily saw the need in her body. Arms reaching, back arching, legs spreading, beautiful full breasts waiting for his lips.

"Who are you?" Without thinking, he knelt on the edge of the bed, and the boils on top of and behind his knees screamed in protest. Keith cried out and struggled to get back on his feet.

"Keeeith."

The sound of her voice soothed him, called him back. Boils or no boils he had to have her or die.

Grinding his teeth together, Keith knelt once more on the bed. He squeezed his eyes shut against the pain, waiting for it to subside, waiting for her voice.

"Yesss, Keeeith . . ."

He opened his eyes, feeling nothing but the heat of her passion rolling over him. The room was growing darker, and he wished he had turned on the light. "Come here," he said, reaching into the fly of his pajamas. "Closer."

Her body seemed to glide toward him without effort, as though a wave carried her.

His body, however, wouldn't cooperate. As much as he wanted her, craved her, the only thing that had grown hard was his luck. Growling with frustration, he tried a little manual encouragement. All he got for the effort was additional pain and a slippery palm. More pus from a leaking boil. Anger rushed through him. He wanted to howl, to scream until his vocal chords burst, to rip something apart with his bare hands—to rip her apart.

Keith leaned over and was about to grab her leg when the room suddenly exploded with light. He threw a hand over his eyes.

"Jesus—you sick sonofabitch."

The voice was definitely not hers this time.

Keith turned his head toward the voice and lowered his hand, squinting.

Percy Schexneider stood in the bedroom doorway with a service revolver in his hand. It was aimed at him. "Get away from the bed, Lafleur. Now!"

The anger that had raged through Keith only a moment ago intensified with Percy's command. It wanted to consume him, blind him, and it took Herculean strength for Keith to keep it under control. Percy was the last name on his list. If he made too aggressive a move, a bullet from that revolver would wind up in his head. He couldn't die now. Not before finishing the list. And definitely not before the finale, whose time had finally come. Tonight. Tonight all the pain ended.

Moving slowly so he wouldn't startle Percy, Keith

turned back toward the bed, then froze. Barbara's aunt, whom he'd last seen at the funeral home the night he'd had so much fun with the nail gun, lay sprawled across the bed, naked. Her eyes were motionless saucers, her wrinkled mouth locked open in what must have been her last scream. The bed was soaked in blood. Her blood. She'd been cut from throat to groin, then splayed, like a deer being prepared for the freezer. Even worse was the sight of his limp penis hanging out of his pajama pants. Just thinking about what might have happened had it grown hard made him shudder with revulsion.

Keith stumbled away from the bed. How had she gotten here? Who'd killed . . . then he remembered. Pieces anyway. A knock at the door, at the front of the house—a black faux leather purse flying across his line of sight—screams, lots of screams and lots of blood—screaming his name. She'd been the voice?

Percy stepped wide to the left, holding the revolver out with both hands. He wore street clothes and sneakers that made squishing sounds when he walked. "Stick your scrawny dick back in your pants, Lafleur, and move!" He signaled with the gun for Keith to head out of the room.

Stupid, stupid man, Keith thought as he tucked himself away. No uniform probably meant no handcuffs, which meant no chance for Percy. The man wouldn't make it out of the house alive. Keith took a labored step toward the bedroom door, flinching in pain. He took another step, then another—thinking . . . thinking. The end for Percy needed to be something special. Not like the others. He was the last name on the list, after all. He deserved preferential treatment.

Keith took his time getting out of the bedroom. His feet did hurt, but he played up the pain.

"Funny how them feet of yours didn't seem to be hurting you so bad while you was porkin' that dead woman," Percy said as he trailed behind him with the revolver aimed at his back.

"I didn't touch her." Keith pushed the words through pursed lips.

"Yeah, I saw how much you didn't touch her, all over that bed. The guy in your garage, too. We got you solid, Lafleur. You're gonna be locked tight and punked before supper."

"Shut the fuck up." They were moving too fast, halfway down the hall now. Keith knew he had to make a move soon, but he couldn't concentrate with Percy blabbering behind him.

"I know you did them others, too, Lafleur. Barbara, Jeff, all of 'em. Now that we got our hands on you, it ain't gonna take much to tie up them other loose ends."

The hall ended and Keith took a left toward the kitchen, where he hoped to get his hands on a knife.

"Hold up, hold up, go the other way. The living room."

Seething, Keith turned around and headed for the living room. Not much in there for him to work with except his guns, which were stored away in the glass case. No way he'd be able to get his hands on one with Percy stuck up his ass.

"Stop right there," Percy said when they'd reached the middle of the living room. Keeping the gun aimed at Keith, he walked sideways to the end table next to the recliner. Keith spotted the cordless phone before he picked it up.

Holding the phone in his left hand, Percy glanced down at the number pad, quickly punched in one number with his thumb, then looked back up. "Figure we should have us some company. Maybe give you a little parade over to the jailhouse." He glanced down again, taking a little longer this time to punch in a number. The barrel of the gun wavered slightly to the right. Percy looked up, righted the gun.

Keith felt his nerves coil up tight, readying him for action. He held steady, waiting for Percy to dial again, the autographed baseball inches away on the coffee table. He'd have one good shot. If he missed, he was screwed.

The second Percy glanced down at the phone again, Keith scooped up the ball, and threw it as hard as he could at Percy's face. It missed by a mere inch, but the flying ball so surprised the man, he stumbled back into the end table. When the barrel of the revolver dropped south, Keith aimed north and dove into Percy's midsection. They both crashed to the floor.

A thousand arrows doused in cayenne pierced Keith to the bone as he struggled to gain ground above Percy. The pain blinded him, and he swung out wildly, searching for the gun. He hadn't heard it clatter to the floor. Beneath him, Percy rolled from side to side, like a turtle stuck on its back. Keith caught the glint of silver out of the corner of his eye. The revolver was finding its way back to him quick. He balled a hand into a fist and hammered it into Percy's face. Cartilage crunched, blood squirted, and as Percy howled, Keith managed to plow a knee into his groin.

That's when the gun fell to the floor.

He moved now, effortlessly, oiled with adrenaline and rage. Keith shoved off Percy, grabbed the gun, tripped the safety while he aimed, then pulled the trigger. The first shot caught Percy in the right thigh. His scream was shrill and much too long.

Panting, Keith got to his feet and fired again, blowing a decent sized hole in the man's stomach. "See, you need to learn to keep your fucking nose out of other people's business," he said through Percy's coughs and gurgles. "That's always been your problem, Schexneider, you had to play the big man, the big bad cop. But you're nothing but a pain in the ass." Keith aimed for the man's groin and pulled the trigger again. Percy's body bounced with the impact. "Now look at you. This was supposed to be special, but you fucked that up, too. You've got me making all this goddamn noise with this gun when it could have been so much quieter and cleaner."

Keith leaned over and stuck the gun barrel against Percy's forehead. He waited until he heard a faint groan, then fired. Blood spattered across Keith's face and the front of his jacket. "So much for clean, huh, Perc?" He swiped at the blood with his free hand and wound up with a wide crimson swirl on his jacket. "Fuck it. Don't matter anyway. Gasoline'll take it out. Lots of gasoline."

Keith shoved the revolver into his jacket pocket and headed for the garage. More company would probably be arriving soon, which meant he didn't have much time to load the gasoline containers.

He whistled as he crossed the kitchen.

It was showtime.

CHAPTER TWENTY-FIVE

Laura slouched in the corner of a booth in the café and inhaled deeply. Burgers sizzling on a grill. To her, there wasn't a better smell on earth right now. It wasn't so much the scent of cooking beef that comforted her as it was the normalcy of it.

After their meeting with Jerome, they'd driven home in relative silence, each lost in thought. Matt appeared to be the most lost. The frown lines that had formed on his forehead while they talked with Jerome had followed him home. She couldn't imagine the intensity of what he must be thinking or feeling. Had she been the one to find out she belonged to a different family, most of which died by the hand of a sick woman, they would have had to cart her off in a straitjacket. Considering the situation, Matt had shown remarkable strength, emotionally and psychologically. She admired him for that. Anyone else would have probably gone through a major psyche collapse by now.

"I'm gonna eat me four of them bad boys," Tawana said, her voice a little thick-tongued. She sat opposite Laura in the booth, wearing a royal blue, wrap-around blouse that had worked itself loose and showed too much cleavage. Three Budweiser cans were lined up in front of her on the table, all of them empty.

Laura gave her a tired grin. "Burgers?"

"Yeah, the burgers." Tawana tittered. " 'Less I find me some other kinda bad boys 'fore then. Oh . . ." She sat up straighter and turned in her seat. "Hey, Matt!"

Matt peeked out of the service window behind the lunch counter.

Tawana flapped a hand at him. "Can I have some cheese on them burgers? And some of them . . . uh, um . . . grilled onions . . . yeah, them grilled onions?"

"Sure. Anybody else want cheese or onions?"

"I'm good," Laura said, then looked over at Moweez and Seth, who sat together at the last booth near the front of the café. Seth skated Hot Wheel cars across the top of their table. Moweez sat quietly, watching him intently. She'd been unusually quiet and clingy to Seth since they'd picked them up from Lerna Mae's. "Seth, Mo, cheese or onions on your burgers?"

Moweez shook her head.

"Just cheese," Seth said, then went back to his cars.

Laura looked back at Matt to make sure he'd heard. He confirmed with a nod.

"Fries, too?" Tawana asked, giving him her best smile.

Matt chuckled. "Better fries than more Budweiser, Wana."

"Hey, these are holdin' down real good," Tawana declared proudly. "I'm not like drunk or nothin'. Not even a teensy-itty-bitty-nothin' bit. So if you got some more of 'em back there, bring 'em on."

Matt disappeared behind the window with a grin.

Tawana turned back to Laura and folded her arms on the table. "Too bad we related. I think I'd have to try me some of that white meat if we wasn't. Good-lookin', cooks, what the hell's takin' the two of you so long to hook up?"

"That hasn't exactly been on my mind lately."

"Yeah." Tawana's grin faded. She tilted her head, her eyes shiny from the Bud buzz. "What we gonna do, girl? We can't just leave everything we got."

"We're going to eat, that's what we're going to do."

Matt appeared beside them with two plates, large burgers on each. He set the plates down in front of them. "Just put the grease heating for fries. Sorry they're not coming out with the burgers. Didn't think about the fries 'til you said something, Wana."

Tawana patted the seat beside her. "Don't worry about all that. Come sit."

"Hold on a sec." Matt collected two more plates with burgers from a large tray that sat on a nearby table. He brought them over to Seth and Moweez, talked quietly with both of them for a moment, then returned to Laura and Tawana's booth.

"For the life of me, I can't get used to it," Matt said,

sliding onto the seat beside Tawana. He looked past Laura to the front booth where Moweez and Seth sat. "A half-sister."

"You didn't have no other brothers and sisters with the Daigles?" Tawana asked. She took a big bite of her burger and let out a loud sigh of contentment.

He shook his head. "Only child. Not that I minded much, because they were great parents. Always made time for me."

"And you had no idea you were adopted?" Laura asked.

"None. But you'd think I would have suspected something. They didn't have any baby pictures of me. Nothing younger than seven, eight years old. I just thought of that on the drive back from Crowley."

"Does it make you mad that they didn't tell you?" Tawana asked.

"No. Not after hearing what the Devilliers were like. Mom and Dad probably wanted to protect me from all that drama."

"Are y'all going to talk to Moweez about this?" Laura asked.

Matt looked over at Tawana. "I'd like to at some point if that's okay with you."

Tawana shrugged. "You the brother. I don't think she's gonna understand most of it anyways."

"She might surprise us."

"Might." Tawana wagged her half-eaten burger at him. "Before we worry about all that with Mo, though, we gotta figure out what we gonna do."

Laura stared at her burger, what little appetite she

had earlier now gone. Sitting in that cooped up bus next to Jerome, it was easier to grasp and even accept the bizarre answers he'd given them. But under these bright fluorescent lights, she was brought back to a harsh reality. They not only didn't have the money to move away from this problem, they had no other place to go, period.

"It's going to be really tough for me to pull up stakes again," Matt said with a shake of his head.

"It's going to be impossible for us," Laura said.

Tawana looked from Matt to Laura. "Yeah, but we gonna do somethin', right? Uncle J said we ain't never gonna have no peace here, remember?" She lowered her voice. "And what about that 'somebody's gonna die' shit he said? More than one somebody. We gonna just hang around like J ain't said nothing and wait for some of us to get knocked off?"

"I think we should stick close together until we figure out just what to do," Matt said.

Tawana snapped her head in agreement. "Now you talkin' some sense."

"Jerome said we couldn't stop what was going to happen," Laura said, "but what if we changed the elements that are going to cause it to happen in the first place?"

"Whatchu mean, elements?"

"He said a dark-haired woman wanted something to come together," Matt said, picking up the thread. "Are you saying if we find what needs to come together and help put it together we might change the outcome he saw?"

Laura nodded. "Basically, yeah."

"So elements is whatever's gotta come together?" Tawana asked.

"Yes," Matt said. "From what Jerome said, it's either the house, which would be both our buildings, or her children. It could possibly be both."

"How the hell we gonna put a house back together?"

"We can't literally put it back together," Laura said. "But maybe we could do something metaphorically."

"Huh?"

"There is something literal we could do," Matt said. "A breezeway could be built between the two upstairs apartments, connecting them."

"What about Nestler's roof?" Laura asked.

"I can look down on the top of it from Seth's bedroom window. There'd be plenty of clearance."

"Why all that, though?" Tawana asked. "If all we gotta do is make something touch both the buildings, why we can't tie a rope between 'em?"

Matt shrugged. "Good point."

Laura caught sight of Seth and Moweez walking across the dining area. "Hey, where you two headed?"

"Bathroom." Seth pointed to a door next to the kitchen.

"You have to go, too, Mo?"

"Nah, she just wants to come with me."

Tawana wagged a finger at Moweez. "You wait outside the door, you hear? Don't you be going in that bathroom with him."

Seth tsked loudly and rolled his eyes. "She wasn't gonna." He turned away and headed for the bathroom. Moweez followed close behind.

"Hey," Tawana said, cocking her head toward Matt. "You know what I just figured?"

"What?"

"Mo's his aunt."

"Oh, you're right," Laura said. "Maybe Mo felt that somehow, and that's why they got so close so quick."

Matt grinned. "Considering everything else that's been going on, I'd say that's a pretty good possibility."

Laura returned his smile. "Now what about this rope idea?"

"Okay, yeah, the rope. We got a couple things, though." Tawana held out her right hand, palm up. "Here we got the house. Maybe that's what we gotta put together, maybe not." She held out her left hand. "Now here we got the kids. Maybe that's what we gotta put together, maybe not." She shook her left hand. "If it's the kids, how we gonna do that? The rope's not gonna do us no good. We got some dead, some alive?" She looked at Matt. "You and Mo we can put together, but what about the other kids? We can't just go dig 'em up from the cemetery."

"Dad?"

Seth stood outside the bathroom with Moweez at his side. He pointed to the kitchen doors when they turned to him. "Is there supposed to be smoke in there?"

Matt jumped up from the booth and took off for the kitchen. "I forgot about the grease! Seth, Mo, get away from there. Go on back to your table, hurry!"

Moweez grabbed Seth's hand, then ran back to their seats, dragging him behind her.

Laura bolted to her feet.

301

"Lord Jesus merciful, wait for me!" Tawana scrambled out of the booth. "Not a fire, lord, not a fire."

Laura saw flames dance beyond the service window and knew Tawana's prayer hadn't been heard. They raced for the kitchen, Laura bursting through the swinging doors first.

The kitchen was covered in a haze of gray with a thicker cloud of smoke clinging to the ceiling. Fire roared from a steel bin against the back wall. A metal hood sat over the bin, but the flames licked around it, stretching for the ceiling. Matt was at the far end of the kitchen throwing cabinet doors open.

"The extinguisher's gone!" he yelled. "Check around the freezer!"

Laura ran to a double-door freezer across the room. It sat between a long counter that had multiple cabinets beneath it. She pointed to the cabinets on the left of the freezer and was about to tell Tawana to look in them, but she beat her to it. Laura checked the cabinets on the right, shoving aside pots and pans, flour sifters, and metal bowls.

"Nothing!" She turned to make sure Matt had heard her over the roar of the fire and saw him tearing open boxes of baking soda.

"Me neither, nothing!" Tawana coughed and waved a hand in front of her face.

"Stay over there!" Matt grabbed two open boxes of soda in each hand and hurried over to the fryer. He shook the contents of the first two boxes over the flames, and the roar became a swelling hiss as the powder settled into the grease below. Matt tossed the

302

empty boxes to the floor, then sprinkled over the same area with the remaining two. Flames leaped, then fluttered as though undecided about their fate.

Matt tossed them a look. "Grab more."

Laura took off for the other soda boxes. She snatched up two and handed them to Tawana, who'd come up behind her. Tawana spun around and headed for Matt while Laura scooped up the last box.

The three of them sent a shower of white powder over the bin, and when the last of the baking soda disappeared into the vat of grease, the last of the flames died with it.

They stood, peering into the deep fryer, breathing heavily.

Tawana put an arm around Matt's shoulder. "I think we killed your fryer thing."

"It needed killing for catching fire like that. It's not supposed to."

"Want me to call nine-one-one?" Laura asked. "Might be good to have the fire department come take a look, just to be safe."

Matt shook his head. "I think we're okay. They wouldn't make it out here for a half hour or more anyway. They're volunteer. Takes them a while to respond. I'll keep an eye on it for a couple hours to make sure."

"Got a Bud or two we could split in them couple hours?" Tawana asked. "Firefightin's hard work, you know."

Matt grinned. "It sure as hell is. Help yourself to whatever's in the fridge."

After Tawana collected three Budweisers from the refrigerator and handed them out, they went back into the dining area.

Tawana slid into the same booth they were in before, and Laura was about to join her when she heard Matt ask, "Where's Moweez?"

Laura turned to the front of the café. Seth was sitting in the same booth he and Moweez were in earlier, but he sat alone, hunched over, examining something on the table. Moweez was nowhere in the dining area.

"Maybe she's in the bathroom," Laura said.

Frowning, Tawana got out of the booth. "I'm gonna go check."

"Seth?" Matt called.

Seth spun around in the booth, as if startled. "Huh?"

"Where's Moweez?"

The boy shrugged. He turned around, picked up a sheet of paper from the table, then waved it at Matt. "She gave this to me. Said I had to stay here."

Laura followed Matt to Seth's table. A boulder dropped inside her chest when she saw the drawing on the table. It was the unfinished one she'd seen in Moweez's sketch pad, only now it was complete.

The detail in the sketch was nothing short of perfection. Even the grass depicted on the lawns appeared to have been drawn blade by individual blade. Bold, vibrant colors seemed to leap off the page. Oranges as brilliant as the ripest tangerines, reds more vibrant and shocking than the freshest blood.

"How come she drew me sleeping on the road?"

Seth asked, pointing to the image of him lying across First Street. It was just as Laura remembered from the unfinished version.

Only now, the horror had grown far beyond Seth.

The Beauty Box and Nestler's were engulfed in a monstrous ball of fire. Nestler's appeared empty, but not the salon. Behind an upstairs window nearly obscured by flames, Laura saw her—Moweez, her expression calm, one hand pressed against the pane as though signaling good-bye.

CHAPTER TWENTY-SIX

Laura didn't have time to call Tawana over to see the drawing before the world detonated.

The explosion rocked the building and sent a million shards from the plate glass window flying across the dining area.

"Matt!" Laura covered her head with her arms as Matt threw himself over Seth.

Through the shattered window, she saw the black of night turn into a fiercely roaring orange. She couldn't see the source, but there was no mistaking the reflected brilliance or the sound: fire.

The drawing.

"Angelica!" Tawana was near the bathroom, turning frantically one way, then another, crying. "Moweez!"

Shivering from fear, Laura got to her feet and hurried over to her.

"She ain't here, Laura! Mo's gone! She's gone!"

"The shop," Laura said. "I think she went to the shop. The drawing . . . her drawing—"

"What?" Tawana gripped Laura's arms so tightly she cried out in pain. "Whatchu sayin'? What?"

"She's in the drawing—Mo, upstairs."

"Everybody stay down!" Matt yelled from the booth. "There might be more!" He shoved Seth under the table. "Stay there and don't move."

"Moweez!" Tawana pushed away from Laura and bounded for the front door.

"Wana, no!" Laura took off after her, but Matt reached her first.

He grabbed Tawana by the arm before she could push through the door. She pummeled him with a fist.

"Let me go, you. Goddammit! Let go!"

"Stop! Look at me!" Matt demanded, his face set with determination. "I'm going, you hear? You stay. I'll see what's going on. We don't even know for sure if Moweez went to the—"

"Well I gotta know!" Tawana screamed in his face. She tore out of his grip and rammed a shoulder into the door. It flew open and she ran outside. Matt sprinted after her.

"Y'all stop!" Laura cried. When they didn't turn back, she called out to Seth. "Stay here, I'll be right back!" Then she ran after them.

Laura slid to a halt between the café and Nestler's, paralyzed by the nightmare before her. It was exactly as Moweez had depicted it, but reality had given it teeth. Nestler's looked like hell's furnace with an army of fire demons demanding entry. Flames leaped from the walls to the roof, wagging ugly red tails so bright it hurt Laura's eyes. Heat rolled over her in monstrous waves, each stealing the air around her, in her, until she gasped. Beside Nestler's, six-foot flames danced up the side wall of the Beauty Box. The porch was nearly engulfed; the azalea bushes out front meager torches. She stood hypnotized—the deafening roar of the blaze, the crackle of wood, the screams . . . the screams.

The shrill cry, the frantic begging, snapped Laura to attention. In that instant, she saw Matt lower his head and run for Nestler's front door. The shrill cries from within the little clapboard grew louder and elongated into excruciating, torturous sounds, into the song of the damned. Matt crashed through the door, disappearing into the inferno.

"Matt, no!" Laura screamed.

"Daddy, come back! Come back!"

Out of the corner of her eye, Laura saw Seth jump off the café's porch. In the time it took her to turn toward him, he was already sprinting across the lawn, right for Nestler's.

Laura dashed after him. "Seth!"

Her lungs burned so badly from the smoke and heat, they felt ready to disintegrate in her chest. She pushed harder, faster, until she was close enough to bring Seth down with a flying tackle. They both landed on the ground with a loud *oomph!*

Seth struggled beneath her. "Get off!"

Laura rolled off but quickly grabbed his arm. She scrambled to her feet, pulling him up with her. "You've got to stay with me, buddy, you've gotta."

"Let me go! Daddy!" He yanked and jerked as she hurried him over to the sidewalk.

Just as they reached safer ground, the sound of Tawana's voice froze both of them in their tracks.

"You hearin' me, Mo? Wana's comin'! I'm gonna get you out, I swear to God I'm gonna!" Tawana had already rounded the walkway in front of the salon and was racing toward the blazing porch. There was no doubt where she was headed, for the face in the upstairs window verified it.

Moweez, with a hand pressed against the pane, looked down at them.

Spotting her, Seth let out a deep keening howl and lifted his arms, stretching them toward the window.

Still holding onto Seth, Laura cried out, "Wana, come back! Wana!"

But Tawana didn't come back.

Part of Nestler's roof collapsed with a thunderous crash, and Laura pulled Seth to her. She stood there, watching Nestler's crumble before her eyes, seeing the flames rise and rage against the upstairs window in her apartment, holding Seth as he struggled for freedom. It took a moment for Laura to realize the sobs she heard were her own.

They needed help, somebody's help. Laura turned toward the street, half blinded with tears. She pulled Seth along, wiping her nose with her shirtsleeve, intending to stand in the middle of First if she had to and flag down a car.

By the time they reached the middle of the road, it dawned on Laura that she hadn't seen even one car pass since she'd come outside. Even now, the street was deserted. Not one person stood on the other side of the street gaping. Not one soul on a stoop or step. No one anywhere. It was like she and Seth had been dropped in the middle of an apocalypse and left to fend for themselves. Laura turned back to face the nightmare.

The oak tree at the end of the alley between Nestler's and the café had caught fire. Sparks flew from its crackling branches and flitted toward the café like ominous fireflies.

911, Laura thought. Surely someone had to have called the emergency number by now. But she had to call, had to call to make sure.

She started for the café to find the phone, but Seth dug in his heels and refused to budge.

"I need a phone, Seth," she said, tugging on his arm. "We need help. We've gotta get help."

"But I can't go, they're crying!"

"Seth—"

"The boys are lost. They don't know where to go, and she's crying. We can't leave them. You can't make me go!" He yanked hard and broke free of her grasp. Just as he turned to run, Laura grabbed him around the waist with both arms and lifted him up.

Seth swung his arms out wildly, twisting in her arms, kicking at her legs. It took all her strength to hold him.

"Put the heathen down!"

Seth went motionless at the sound of the booming voice. The ferocious tone of it sent such an icy finger of panic down Laura's spine, she wanted to run in the opposite direction without even seeing who it was.

With Seth hanging limp in her arms, she turned toward the salon, in the direction of the voice.

The man limped as he walked. Slow, determined steps that brought him closer to her little by little. Something was wrong with his face, with his clothes, with him. In the flash of firelight and the wash of street lamps, he looked red and distorted and wet. He carried something in his right hand. A box, a cage, something with a handle.

Laura held Seth tight against her as he drew nearer. Her mouth went dry. The fire that raged beside her seemed small compared to the threat emanating from this man.

"It ends tonight," he declared. He pointed to the salon. "The den of iniquity." His finger traveled to the café. "The brothel of demons. I'm sending all of them back to hell where they belong. My suffering is done! No more! I will suffer no more!"

Seth whimpered and wiggled in Laura's arms as though he wanted to get even closer to her.

Laura took a step back. His voice sounded familiar, but she couldn't place it. "Who are you? What do you want?"

There was nothing humorous in his laughter. "Are you that blind, bitch? Does somebody have to spell it out for you?" He took two quick steps forward, and Laura gasped, stumbling back.

"Hurry, run!" Seth cried.

The man's laughter rang out again, sharp and

loud. It echoed above the roar of the fire. He drew closer still.

Laura spun around and took off for the café, Seth bouncing in her arms.

"Stop or he dies!"

The threat froze Laura immediately. She turned back slowly. He was no more than fifty feet away now, his face a vivid mask of raw meat. She gasped. Seth began to cry.

He came to a halt about thirty feet away from them and set the container on the ground. "Didn't you hear her? The whole time you were in there, wasn't she loud enough?" He fumbled in the pockets of his jacket. "I heard her. Every goddamn day I heard her. The same fucking thing over and over again until I wanted to puke. 'The iniquity of the fathers will visit the children unto the third and fourth generation.' Blah, blah, fucking blah. If she wanted me to torch the goddamn place, all she had to do was say so. I didn't need to hear all that Bible shit." He pulled something small out of one pocket, held it way out in front of him; then a small flame sprang to life. A lighter. His face glowed wetly in the illumination, a mask more hideous than anything Laura could have imagined.

Seth screamed at the sight. "Daddy! Daddy!"

"Shut up!" The man bellowed. The lighter winked out.

Seth trembled violently and went silent in her arms.

"You spoiled-ass brat." He took a step closer, pointing at Seth. "You should have died along with the rest of them, you little fuck."

"You shut the fuck up!" Laura yelled. "Don't you talk to him that way!"

With a howl of anger, he drew his other hand from his pocket, revealing a gun. He waved it at her, aimed it at her, made shooting noises with his mouth. Then he grew quiet and solemn, the gun still pointed at her.

"There was no way they could have made it," he said, shaking his distorted head. "None of them. But I can't leave him behind." He motioned with the gun to Seth. "It just wouldn't be fair, would it? I mean really, look at him. A face full of snot, crying like a pussy. He really shouldn't live. He can't. She already said so. It's all about blood, ain't it, sister? That shit that's running through his veins right now is some of the same poison that infected me. The same shit that killed them. It's in his blood, man, it's in his blood. And all that poison's going to drain into some other kid when he gets older and starts fucking women, you know what I mean? Of course you do. She'll get pregnant, you see, and there you'll have it—another kid with the same poisoned shit that he's got." He waved the gun. "Put him down."

"No."

"Bitch, put him down or I'll fucking shoot him right where he's at."

Laura leaned over and lowered Seth to the ground, keeping an arm around him.

"Let him go. You're going to turn him into a pussy hanging onto him like that."

Seth whimpered again as she slowly moved her arm away. She wanted to charge the bastard and rip his eyes out.

He motioned with the gun for Seth to step away from her. "Move."

Seth shivered and glanced up at Laura.

"I said move!"

With a startled cry, Seth took a step away from Laura.

"Go, go!"

Laura couldn't bear seeing the terror in Seth's eyes. "Leave him alone!"

The man quickly stepped another two paces. "You just don't fucking listen, do you?" He aimed the gun at her head. "Somebody's got to teach you to shut up, to shut the fuck up." His shoulders suddenly drooped. "Hell, only got one bullet left." He cocked his head to one side, then pointed the gun at Seth. "Do I do him," he swung the gun back to her, "or you?" He swung the pistol back to Seth. "Him?" Back to Laura. "Or you?" He paused, as though contemplating the situation. "Aw, fuck it." He cocked the hammer back on the gun, still aiming at her face. "I think . . . I'll choose . . . him!"

Laura gasped as he swung back toward Seth, and without thinking, threw herself between the gun and the boy.

Something punched her hard in the back, and Laura flew forward, landing on Seth, toppling them both to the ground. Fire spread from her back to her belly, fire and pain. Stabbing, grinding, horrific pain.

She heard Seth crying but couldn't see him.

Sounds around her deepened and slowed. Laura lifted her head, tried blinking the wavering world back into focus, but it wouldn't hold still. The flames consuming the shop seemed to move in slow motion. The café, now smothered in orange tongues, leaned slowly to the left. And the man, a blur of arms and legs. The lighter and another spark of light.

Whoosh!

She watched him—dancing, arms lifted high—a man of fire, of dancing fire.

Then the world finally stilled and went black.

CHAPTER TWENTY-SEVEN

The Living Chapel in Delatross Funeral Home over-flowed with potted plants and flowers, mourning wreaths decorated with carnations, roses, juniper, daylilies, baby's breath, and snapdragons. At the front of the chapel hung a four-foot wooden cross back-dropped by a rich blue velvet curtain. Beside it, an old oak lectern and a closed mahogany casket that lay atop a two-foot bier.

The long padded pews that weren't occupied had handbags and bereavement cards placed on the seats as holding placards. Church music, the kind Matt imagined would resound through a cathedral or basilica, drifted down from overhead speakers. A chuckle here, sobs there, a symphony of whispers from hundreds of visitors staking their claim to mourning territory.

Two viewing rooms flanked the chapel, and both were overrun with people. An empty casket sat in one with a memorial table beside it. On the table stood a picture of Valentine Nestler, sitting in front of a lake with her two oldest sons. Her body, or what little had been retrieved from the charred sewing cottage, had already been sent to Reshaud's Crematorium in Lafayette. In the second viewing room, a handsome bronze casket held the body of Percy Schexneider. This casket remained closed as well, for the mortician had been unable to reconstruct Percy's face.

Matt stood between the viewing rooms and chapel, his arms bandaged from wrist to shoulder to protect him from infection. His heart was heavy with regret. As much as he'd wanted to save her, there'd been little he could do for Valentine. He'd gotten there too late. The flames had reached her before he did. Her screams still haunted him, her writhing, burning body still vivid in his mind. He had no memory of how he'd escaped. One moment he was coughing, gasping, blinded by smoke; the next, lying face down on a bed of cool, wet grass behind the cottage. His own burns didn't register until they'd lifted him onto the stretcher.

Someone called his name, and Matt blinked out of his reverie. He saw Maude Romero and Sadie Babineaux wave to him as they made their way into the chapel. Thomas Sterner shuffled along behind them, holding on to Verneese Credeur's arm. Verneese's face was puffy and red from crying. A few feet to her left Matt spotted Jerome Batiste, his lanky body clad in a faded black suit. He looked uneasy and self-conscious in the crowd. Matt wondered if at this moment, Jerome was thinking about the predictions he'd made. The man had been right, so very right. More than one somebody did die.

Keith Lafleur's truck had been found abandoned two blocks north of the Beauty Box, and his charred body discovered in the alley between Nestler's and the café. His remains had been sent to a forensics lab, where they hoped to harvest enough for DNA testing. Detectives had little doubt they'd have a match with Lafleur and the evidence taken from Windham's recent homicides.

What would drive a man to such destruction, such madness? Based on recent events, Matt couldn't help but wonder if Lafleur's role in dividing and transforming the original house had led to the ultimate division and transformation in him. No one would ever know for sure.

There was a lot no one would ever know for sure.

Nearby, the crowd parted, clearing a path to the chapel for a group of teens dressed in red choir robes. Their appearance told Matt it was time. He lowered his head and followed the robes inside.

Lerna Mae had a hand up, signaling her location. Beside her, Seth peered over the pew wide-eyed. Matt inched his way over to them. The chapel had filled up quickly, and he had to squeeze through groups of people who had nowhere to sit.

When he finally sidestepped into the pew, Seth patted the open spaces on either side of him. They'd saved plenty of seats. As soon as Matt sat down, Seth scooted closer to him.

"How come there're so many people, Dad?"

"I guess they came to say good-bye, just like us."

Seth peered up at him. "I wish we didn't have to, say good-bye, I mean."

"Me, too, champ."

Seth leaned his head against Matt's arm. Three days had passed since the fire, and still he showed no signs of emotional trauma from the event. Matt was amazed at Seth's resilience and grateful to have his son back. Not once since the disaster had Seth exhibited any of the strange behavior he had prior to it.

Matt closed his eyes for a moment, resting them. So much had changed in such a short period of time. They no longer had a business or home. The Holiday Inn in Lafayette had become their temporary residence, but he didn't plan on them being displaced for long. The friend who'd started Matt in the food business was interested in selling his restaurant in Opelousas. The place was huge, much more square-footage than he needed—but huge also opened the door to other opportunities. Ones he hoped to explore in the very near future.

Matt felt a tap on his shoulder and turned around to see Sadie and Maude sitting in the pew behind him. Both sat at the edge of the cushioned seat and leaned towards him.

"I'm so sorry for the loss, honey," Sadie said. "I know y'all were close."

"Oh, yes," Maude said. "We're so sorry."

"Thank you." Matt wasn't sure of what else to say. He'd always felt awkward saying thank you when people offered condolences. It just felt . . . off, like he was grateful for them sharing in his sadness. He preferred if they didn't share it. In fact, he preferred they didn't have any sadness at all.

Sadie shook her head sadly. "So much tragedy. Windham's never going to be the same, you know."

Maude agreed. "With Percy gone, especially. It's going to be so hard adjusting to a new police chief." She leaned in farther. "We're thinking about moving to Jennings. It's a nice little town, quiet, like Windham used to be."

"Well, I wish both of you the best, wherever you go," Matt said.

Sadie dabbed her eyes with a tissue. "You're such a sweet boy. We're going to miss you. I know we won't find a soul in Jennings who'll cook étouffée like you do."

Matt smiled. "I hear they make a mean gumbo out there, though."

"Oh, he's here," Maude said, glancing over her shoulder. "Reverend Taylor's here." She gave Matt a departing pat on the shoulder, then sat back in her seat. Sadie did the same.

By now those without seats had found a standing niche at the back of the room, and the center aisle was clear. Reverend Brian Taylor walked from one end of the aisle to the other, shaking hands and offering condolences. He wore a flowing black robe with three gold cords running from each shoulder to the bottom of the garment. Between the cords, in the center of his chest was a gold embroidered cross. His face, a rich chocolate brown, glimmered with sweat.

At the front of the chapel, the choir stood in order of ascending height. Three in the front row, four in the second, and six in the third. A large black woman wearing a white robe with a red collar stood in front of the group, smiling.

Reverend Taylor grew solemn when he reached the front of the chapel. He folded his hands together and lowered his head as he approached the casket. The room fell silent when he laid a hand on the polished mahogany box.

Seth leaned into Matt and whispered. "What's he doing?"

"Praying, probably."

"What's he praying for?"

"I don't know. Maybe he's asking God to let her into heaven."

Seth craned his neck for a better look. "How does he know for sure she's even in the box?"

"I guess he's just trusting that she is."

Seth looked at him. "Did you see her in the box?"

Matt shook his head and glanced away when he felt tears welling up in his eyes. There hadn't been much left of the body for anyone to see. It didn't seem fair that he'd only been given a short amount of time to know her.

"Do you think she's sad that she's dead?" Seth whispered softly. "Do you think she's scared?"

"I don't think so, champ. She's probably watching us right now."

Seth looked up, his eyes scanning the length of the ceiling. He turned toward the back of the chapel and let out a little gasp. "She's here."

A little concerned about the "she" Seth meant, Matt glanced over his shoulder. He smiled when he saw Laura heading slowly toward them. She'd all but threatened death to any physician brave enough to try and keep her from the funeral. She was lucky to be here at all. The bullet they'd removed from her back had lodged in her left scapula.

When Laura stepped into the pew, Lerna Mae slid over to the right and motioned for her to sit next to Matt. She did, giving him a small, sad smile. He wished he could hold her and take away her pain, physical and emotional. The last couple of days he'd worried about her incessantly even though the doctors assured him she'd have a complete, albeit slow, recovery. Seth had been anxious about her, too, which only confirmed for Matt that the direction he was heading in for the future was the right one. He saw the restaurant in Opelousas as a possible new beginning for both of them. If things worked out, and she agreed, he'd have the restaurant redesigned so it would house two businesses. A smaller café for him, a beauty salon for her. He hoped for so much more with Laura. For now, though, he'd settle for her smiles.

Laura leaned closer to him and whispered, "Would you watch for her? She had to go to the bathroom. I told her we'd keep an eye out for her, then signal so she'd know where we were."

He nodded.

"Beloved friends and family," Reverend Taylor began. He stood behind the lectern with his arms outstretched. He looked over the crowd and smiled warmly. "Today we gather here to celebrate the life of our sister and to bring comfort and hope to all who loved her."

Matt glanced over his shoulder, checking. He didn't see her.

"Our hearts grieve, for she's no longer with us," he continued. "But there will come a time, my brothers and sisters, when there will be no more weeping."

A chorus of "Amen, preacher," echoed through the chapel.

"A time when He will wipe away every tear from our eyes."

More people chimed in. "Hallelujah, yes, Lord."

Reverend Taylor clasped his hands together dramatically. "A time when there will be no more death, no more mourning or crying."

"Thank you, Jesus."

"Let us rejoice today, brothers and sisters, for we have a merciful God, who right this minute is leading our sister down the streets of glory!"

Loud applause joined the hallelujahs and amens. Music started playing, a lively tune that soon had people bobbing their heads. The choir clapped in time to the rhythm and their voices lifted in perfect harmony.

"Oh, happy day—oh, happy day—when Jesus washed—when Jesus washed—Jesus washed—when Jesus washed—all my sins away."

Matt glanced over his shoulder as the song picked up tempo, and the choir grew louder. Too many people were standing now for him to get a clear view of the back of the room. Everyone swayed and clapped, singing along with the choir.

"When Jesus washed—when Jesus washed . . ."

Matt turned back around and noticed that even Seth was enjoying himself. He clapped and rocked his head from side to side, his feet swinging freely beneath the pew.

Suddenly, the volume in the chapel dropped by half, as many of the mourners stopped clapping. One by one, three by three, they turned in their seats, looking toward the back of the room.

Matt turned with them, craning his neck to see what had captured the attention of so many.

Moweez walked down the center of the aisle, nodding her head from side to side and clapping. She stared straight ahead, her eyes bright, her steps joyful. She looked stunning in a simple black fitted dress, her long braids flowing about her as she moved.

Matt held up a hand so she'd see him, but Moweez kept walking toward the front.

When she reached the casket, even the choir's volume decreased to a more respectful level. Moweez put her hands on top of the casket, then leaned over until her left cheek touched the wood. Her lips held a smile, and her eyes closed. After a long moment, she opened her eyes, then turned her head and kissed the polished wood. She righted herself, turned to face the crowd, and began to clap again.

The choir, evidently seeing the shift in mood, put their hearts into the chorus once more. They cranked it up louder than ever, swaying in unison—altos, sopranos, basses, tenors all sharing, trading, harmonizing notes that quickly filled the funeral chapel with life. Moweez's smile was immeasurable. She began to dance.

Matt's heart beat faster. He stood, keeping his eyes on Moweez. Something was going to happen. He knew it as sure as he was standing in front of the pew. And he was sure he wasn't the only one who felt it. The room seemed charged with anticipation, with expectation. Almost everyone stood now, their hand claps even more enthusiastic than before. He turned to Laura. She was standing along with everyone else, so was Lerna Mae. Seth scrambled up beside Matt and stood on the seat.

Moweez raised her arms high, fingers outstretched—and sang. . . .

"He taught me how—to watch—to fight and pray—and he taught me how to live rejoicing, yes, He did—each and every day! Oh, happy day!"

Her voice rang out pure and strong, each word and note perfectly clear. She lifted her head, pushing the song from her lungs as though it needed to burst through the gates of heaven—so it would reach Tawana Farisa Batiste.

Every person in every pew stood in awe, captured by the power and purity of her voice.

Tears flowed without hindrance down Matt's cheeks. He looked over at Laura, who had a hand over her open mouth and tears streaming down her face. She looked at him. Their eyes locked with questions that would never be asked. For it didn't matter how Moweez was able to sing now. It only mattered that she did. He thought of the few words she'd spoken over and over when he first came to know her. "Come-together all broken."

Matt smiled, seeing her whole and happy, his sister, his family. His tears flowed all the more. "It's not broken anymore, Mo. Not anymore."

ATTENTION
BOOK LOVERS!

Can't get enough
of your favorite **HORROR**?

Call **1-800-481-9191** to:

— order books —

— receive a **FREE** catalog —

— join our book clubs to **SAVE 30%!** —

Open Mon.-Fri. 10 AM-9 PM EST

Visit
www.dorchesterpub.com
for special offers and inside
information on the authors you love.

 We accept Visa, MasterCard or Discover®.

DEBORAH LeBLANC

Award-winning suspense author Deborah LeBlanc, a Cajun native of Louisiana, has spent time in an insane asylum (as a visitor!), been sealed in a coffin, and helped embalm bodies, all for research. Prior to writing chilling novels, she worked in the oil and transportation industry and started two corporations. She currently lives in Louisiana with her husband and three daughters. You can find out more about Deborah on her website, www.deborahleblanc.com.